Death in the Valley of Shadows

DERYN LAKE

ISIS

LARGE PRINT

Oxford

First published in Great Britain 2003
by
Allison & Busby Limited

Published in Large Print 2007 by ISIS Publishing Ltd.,
7 Centremead, Osney Mead, Oxford OX2 0ES
by arrangement with
Allison & Busby Limited

British Library Cataloguing in Publication Data
Lake, Deryn
    Death in the valley of shadows. – Large print ed.
    1. Fielding, John, Sir, 1721–1780 – Fiction
    2. Rawlings, John (Fictitious character) – Fiction
    3. Pharmacists – England – London – Fiction
    4. London (England) – History –
    18th century – Fiction
    5. Detective and mystery stories
    6. Large type books
    I. Title
    823.9'14 [F]

ISBN 978–0–7531–7896–6 (hb)
ISBN 978–0–7531–7897–3 (pb)

Printed and bound in Great Britain by
T. J. International Ltd., Padstow, Cornwall

For Tony Fennymore — whose true story was the
inspiration for the plot

Acknowledgements

As usual there are several people to thank. First Judy Flower for looking up the history of West Clandon, East Clandon and Stoke d'Abernon for me. I am most grateful to her. Then my editor, David Shelley, who continues to inspire, and my agent, Vanessa Holt, who has such a naughty laugh. Finally, the people who keep me sane: Anoushka Ainsley, Susan Carnaby and John Elnaugh. Where would I be without them?

CHAPTER
ONE

What a morning it had been. First, April had laughed, then she had wept, and the apothecary's shop in Shug Lane, Piccadilly, had emptied and filled accordingly, customers leaving to embrace the first of the spring sunshine or take shelter against the penetrating showers that had followed all too quickly. The bell above the door had constantly pealed, merry as a marriage chime, so that either John Rawlings, Apothecary, or his apprentice, Nicholas Dawkins, had been sent scurrying out of the compounding room, away from their herbs and simples, to serve the passing parade. So it was that when the bell had rung with a particular urgency, just after the hands of the clock had reached noon, they had looked at one another and shrugged.

"Your turn, Master," said Nicholas, still using the term of address beholden on him until his indentures were finally served.

"Damnation," answered John, who was weighing the powdered root of Devil's Bit, a powerful antidote to plague, and had reached a critical stage in his calculations.

"Shall I go?"

"No, fair's fair. It is my shift." And the Apothecary passed the hand-held scales to Nicholas and went into the shop.

A man stood panting in the doorway, his pale, somewhat crab-like eyes rolling in his head.

"Help," was all he said.

"Are you ill?" John asked, hurrying round the counter.

The newcomer shook his head. "Place to hide," he gasped.

The Apothecary stared. "What?"

"I mean it. Help me. I am being pursued." The man took a further step into the shop, his face, florid at the best of times through a liberal consumption of wine, John thought, now purple. "Please," he added despairingly.

The Apothecary did not hesitate. There was something frantic about the man. "The compounding room, quickly," he said, shoving the newcomer towards the back of the shop.

Nicholas, hearing a scuffle, came out hurriedly. "Master, are you all right?"

"Yes. Conceal this man. There's someone in pursuit of him."

"Who?"

"How would I know?"

But even as they pushed the quarry into the dark recesses behind the rows of hanging herbs, the answer came. The door flew open once more, the bell jangled frantically, and a woman with a marked West Country accent demanded, "Has a man just come in here?"

2

She was like last Christmas's spiced orange, John thought: red, round and starting to wizen. She also had the most irritating teeth.

"Well?" she said.

The Apothecary was more than annoyed, not having seen such a display of bad manners in quite a while.

"Well what?" he asked coldly.

The woman simpered, realising that she had not made a good impression. "Forgive me, Sir. I forget myself." The burr in the voice indicated the Bath area, John decided. "I am looking for a friend of mine. I thought I saw him step through your doorway."

The Apothecary hardened his eyes. "No one has come in here, Madam."

She looked to the ground, then up again, clearly not believing him. "Are you certain?"

John felt frankly furious. "Do you doubt my word?"

The woman raised her chins, there were several of them, with an air of challenge. "Yes, Sir, I do. I demand to search your premises."

"What?" said John, exploding with wrath. "You demand what? Out with you, Madam, before I call the watch."

"How dare you! Don't you lay a hand on me or I shall create a scene that will be heard from here to Covent Garden."

"Create away," the Apothecary answered coolly. "I shall declare you mad and that will be an end of it."

Nicholas, looking pale and somewhat sinister, stepped out of the compounding room. "Do you need help, Master?"

"If this woman refuses to move, yes. For I intend to put her bodily into the street."

A pair of snapping dark eyes, the colour of the hard fruit of horse chestnut trees, known by children as conkers, regarded John nastily.

"You haven't heard the last of this. I'll be avenged for this insult, just you wait and see."

"I tremble in my boots. Good day to you, Madam."

She snorted and went out, leaving behind the stale odour of flesh that had remained unwashed for a considerable number of days.

"Harridan!" John called after her retreating back.

She quivered but did not turn, leaving the Master and his apprentice to stare at one another bemusedly.

"What a terrible woman —" Nicholas began, but before he could get another word out there was the sound of a groan from the compounding room.

"Damme, I'd almost forgotten him," John exclaimed, and they hurried into the back to administer.

The man had slumped into a chair and was presently leaning forward on the wooden table, his head buried in his arms, his face, what little could be glimpsed of it, quite dangerously mottled.

"Loosen his neckwear," the Apothecary ordered, and went to pour out a tot of brandy from the bottle which he kept for medicinal purposes alone.

Nicholas duly struggled with shirt and cravat, not an easy task, for their visitor kept moaning testily and moving away, presumably believing that somebody was trying to molest him.

4

"Steady, Sir, steady," the Apothecary said reassuringly. "You are in no danger now. Your wife has gone. At least I presume she was your wife."

One of the crab-like eyes rolled in his direction. "No spouse she," its owner said gustily, then he sighed and sat upright, taking the proffered tot of brandy with trembling hand. Sensing that some interesting saga was about to be revealed, John took the other chair while Nicholas crouched on a low stool, his elbows resting on his bony knees, his chin cupped in his hands.

"So, Sir, are you able to tell me of your predicament?" the Apothecary asked encouragingly.

A hand came out for another brandy and then a third, after which the man sighed again, then said heavily, "That woman was once my mistress."

"But no longer?"

He shuddered. "Heaven forbid." The pale eyes looked at John piercingly. "Are you a man of honour, Sir?"

"I belong to an honourable profession. As to my personal life, I have never cheated or robbed a living soul, though I must admit to telling the odd falsehood."

The newcomer nodded silently, consumed a fourth brandy, then spoke again. "I feel that I can trust you and might safely take you into my confidence. But before I do so, allow me to introduce myself; Aidan Fenchurch, importer of fine wines."

John gave a polite bow of the head. "John Rawlings, Apothecary. And this is my apprentice, Nicholas Dawkins."

The Muscovite, as Dawkins was nicknamed because of his Russian ancestry, heaved himself to his feet and bowed. "Your servant, Sir."

"So, Mr. Fenchurch, you have an angry woman on your trail. I presume you told her that your affair was over?"

Aidan nodded gloomily. "Yes. But let me start at the beginning of it all. I was happily married for several years, indeed had a most accommodating wife who catered for my every whim. But then, alas, a disease of the lungs took her to her rest and I was left alone with three daughters to rear."

"How terrible for you."

"It was a grievous blow. Fortunately I had many good servants and their governess saw to their youthful upbringing until I was able to put the girls into school."

"And your mistress?"

Fenchurch ran his hand over his brow. "A married woman I fear; indeed married to one of my business acquaintances, Montague Bussell. Gentlemen, may I speak freely?"

"Of course."

"She threw herself at me. Begged me to service her. Said that since the birth of her sons she and Monty had had little to do with one another in that regard." He smiled deprecatingly. "I am a man after all, at that time recently robbed of my conjugal pleasures. I accepted her offer."

"Gracious!" exclaimed Nicholas, wide-eyed, then clapped his hand over his mouth for daring to be so presumptuous.

Mr. Fenchurch ignored the interruption. "She was insatiable, even forcing her way into my bedroom when I took a bath and heaving within the water beside me."

6

John, having just met the woman, had a vivid mental picture and fought fiercely to control his mirth. "And you tired of such ruthless pursuit?"

"Truth to tell I met another. A comfortable widow, a Mrs. Trewellan, whom I had a mind to marry. Further, I feared that Bussell might discover the truth. So I told Ariadne that all must end between us."

"And she did not accept this?"

"That, Sir, is to put it at its mildest. I do not believe that I exaggerate when I say that she completely lost her reason."

"What happened?"

"At first she followed me wherever I went. There was not a theatre, assembly or dining party in town at which she did not appear. It was almost as if she employed magic to find out where I was going. I was so disturbed that I retreated to my country place and she turned up there as well, albeit that she must have journeyed some forty or fifty miles from London. She took to driving a horse and trap through the night and appearing at my gates in the morning. On one occasion she gathered together every letter I had ever written to her, tore it into little pieces, and desposited them all over my front doorstep, like snow."

"But what did her husband say to all this? Surely he didn't turn a blind eye."

"Bussell is a merchant whose business necessitated him travelling to Bristol and staying there for some considerable time."

"So while he was away . . ."

"Precisely."

"And she stalks you to this day?"

"Yes, though now the method of it has changed."

"In what way?"

"Bussell became less active in his firm, handing his more onerous tasks to younger members. Suddenly he was at home more often and so, to cover her tracks, Ariadne adopted the guise of friendship."

"She didn't seem very friendly just now."

Fenchurch shook his head sorrowfully. "That is because she didn't know you and therefore allowed her true self to show. But with her husband present so much, she nowadays showers me with invitations and blinds me with great smiles."

Remembering Ariadne's set of alarmingly large teeth, the Apothecary gave the slightest of shudders. Nicholas spoke up.

"Did you marry Mrs. Trewellan, Sir?"

"Alas, no. Her son, a spoilt, precocious youth of unpleasant mien, took a dislike to me and interfered in the match. She and I are still friendly, however."

"And what does she make of your shadow?" John asked.

Fenchurch paused, staring at the Apothecary intently. "What an excellent description. The Shadow. Yes, that is exactly what she is: a huntress, a pursuer, a grinning evil eminence." He relapsed into silence, contemplating the new soubriquet, and John found himself thinking that he did not altogether like Mr. Fenchurch, finding his eyes a little too small and his countenance a little too shifty. His mind roved on to the

8

idea of he and Mrs. Bussell making sexual connection and stopped short, aghast.

Aidan was speaking once more. "I realise I was wrong to dally with a married woman in the first place but, rest assured, I have paid my penance and am still paying; witness today's events."

The Apothecary decided that, little eyes or no, he felt genuinely sorry for the man. "I do not envy you your position, Sir. And as to your affair with Mrs. Bussell, which of us has not been involved in intrigue at some time or other in our lives?"

Fenchurch sighed for the umpteenth time and at that moment the shop doorbell rang again.

He looked sick. "Do you think it is her come back?"

"I doubt it very much but, Nicholas, if it is, just call for me."

"Yes, Sir."

And the apprentice made his way into the front of the shop.

Aidan thrust his head between his hands, slightly dislodging his wig, displaying rather long grey hair beneath. "She'll do for me one day, I'm certain of it."

"What do you mean?" asked John, pouring out the last of the brandy and including a glass for himself.

"Ariadne. I'm sure her cruel nature will not be satisfied until she sees me dead."

"But you are not old, Mr. Fenchurch."

"Past fifty-five, Sir, alas. But that is not exactly what I implied." He leant forward, twirling the brandy glass in his fingers. "No, I believe that if nature does not accomplish her purpose for her, she will do it herself."

"You don't mean . . . ?"

"Murder? Yes, that is precisely what I do mean."

"But surely . . ."

"She is capable of it, believe you me. Though it is her ploy to mask her loathing with grins, she continues to hate me deeply and bitterly."

"Then she is probably still in love with you," the Apothecary said wryly. "Wasn't it Shakespeare who said something about 'the lady doth protest too much'?"

Aidan Fenchurch nodded. "It was indeed. But if that is a form of love, God spare me from it." He drained his brandy, then said, "For no reason that I can think of I have confessed more about myself to you than any other man alive."

"What about Mrs. Trewellan? Do you not confide in her?"

"Most certainly not. She would be upset beyond measure. Remember that I wanted to set up home with her and still nurture hopes. So, Mr. Rawlings, I have made you my confidant. I trust that you do not object."

John smiled crookedly. "Sir, as a man who tends the sick I hear a great many of the world's secrets. Without wishing to sound cynical, I have grown quite accustomed to it."

The shift of Aidan's features changed before the Apothecary's eyes and he suddenly became a sad and bedraggled fox. "Then, Sir, may I entrust you with something further?" he asked, his voice tentative.

Loathing people who answered 'it depends on what it is', John said, "Yes, of course."

Without warning, Mr. Fenchurch's little eyes filled with tears. "As I told you, she'll finish me yet. I swear it."

"Do you mean what you say? Do you truly believe the Shadow wants to kill you?"

"Yes. And to that effect I have left papers — sealed documents revealing the whole sad story — that I wish to entrust to an honest citizen to take to Sir John Fielding of the Public Office in Bow Street in the event of my sudden demise."

"I see," said John, thinking what extraordinary cards fate was capable of dealing out, for how could this man have had any inkling that the Apothecary and Sir John were close friends?

He fingered his chin. "About Mrs. Bussell. If she is pretending friendship with you, trying to deceive her husband and the world on that score, why should she suddenly kill you?"

"Because," said Aidan Fenchurch very simply, "she is quite, quite mad and capable of turning on me for no clear reason. So, Mr. Rawlings, even though we have been acquainted a mere thirty minutes, I would ask if you might be custodian of the papers I intend to leave."

"But wouldn't your family lawyer be a better person?"

"That old fool? No, I would not trust him not to take a peek inside."

"Then Mrs. Trewellan."

"Likewise." Mr. Fenchurch stood up. "But I can see I have presumed too much. We'll say no more of it."

John felt immensely guilty. There could be no doubt that the man was deeply distressed. "I'm sorry, Sir. I was only trying to be sensible. I shall gladly guard your papers for you."

The crab eyes bulged with sudden relief. "Then I shall bring them to the shop tomorrow."

"Better still, come to my house. For that is where I intend to store them, under lock and key with my own personal documents. I live at number two, Nassau Street, Soho. I shall be at home after six o'clock."

"I shall attend you there, bringing some of my choicest wines as a gift."

"How very kind of you," said John, and escorted his visitor through the shop.

Aidan Fenchurch bowed deeply to his host, inclined his head to the apprentice, then having looked closely up and down the street, scuttled off fast in a way most reminiscent of a crustacean heading for the sea.

"It occurs to me," said John, looking at his wife with both a professional and husbandly eye, "that you could well benefit from a few days in the country. You are very pale." And also very enormous, he thought but did not add.

Emilia Rawlings, not a tall girl and at the best of times quite small in physique, now resembled a grape ready for the wine harvest. The child that she was carrying had dropped low, so much so that the Apothecary's wife had taken to waddling rather than walking, an unattractive mode of gait of which she was

12

more than painfully aware, being naturally rather graceful.

"I would love to get away but could your father cope with a woman in my condition?"

"He's seen it all before. My mother was pregnant with his child, remember."

"The one that died?"

"Yes." John could have added, 'As did she,' but held his peace, considering his wife's condition and not believing for a moment in deliberately frightening women who were about to give birth.

"Should we not write and ask his permission?"

"I'll do that tonight and send Irish Tom with the letter first thing tomorrow morning. He is immensely idle at the moment as you are not going out and about."

"He's thoroughly enjoying himself, though."

"That is not what I pay him for," the Apothecary answered primly, only to hear Emilia peal with laughter.

"Don't put that face on. Trying to be respectable simply doesn't become you."

"But I *am* respectable, very respectable indeed. People trust me with their life stories. Which reminds me . . ." And John told her of the extraordinary incident in his shop earlier that day.

Emilia listened, round-eyed. "You mean that this woman, this stalker, this shadow, continues to follow him about?"

"Yes."

"How cheap. What does she look like? Is she handsome?"

"I suppose she was once. But now she relies on a powerful personality, which would be perfectly fine if it were pleasant."

"And what about him? Is he worth all this attention?"

John leant back in his chair and laughed. "Frankly, no. He is small of eye, large of gut, and with a suspicious, florid countenance that can look quite crabby, in every sense of the word."

"A fine couple indeed."

"As you say. Apparently they once mated in the bath."

"Difficult," said Emilia, "given his physical attributes."

The Apothecary laughed again. "You might see him if you leave for Kensington the day after tomorrow."

"I think I will forgo the pleasure. As soon as Sir Gabriel invites me, I shall take my leave of London. Thank God it isn't hot. Oh John, I don't know how a woman could bear to be *enceinte* in the summer."

"How long will you stay away?"

"Only a week. The baby is due in a fortnight remember."

"How could I forget? You have been marking off the days."

"Is it very boring of me?"

"On the contrary, it is very, very exciting."

"Then I'll hurry back. I don't want you to miss anything."

14

"Of course," said the Apothecary, but his mind was not with his words. Much as he loved Emilia and was looking forward to the birth of their first child, his thoughts were going down other paths. He saw again the stricken face of Aidan Fenchurch, the faded mirthlessness of Mrs. Bussell's smile. Was she a potential killer? John wondered, contemplating those he had known who had committed that most heinous of crimes. Without doubt the answer came back with a crystal and unnerving clarity. Ariadne Bussell would be more than capable of taking the life of anyone who in her belief had thwarted her wishes.

At daybreak Irish Tom, John Rawlings's idiosyncratic coachman, left for Kensington, the home village of Sir Gabriel Kent, the Apothecary's adoptive father. Within three hours he was back with an invitation for Emilia to remove herself to the fresh country air and not endanger her child by breathing in stinks.

"I shall be down on Saturday to dine," John said, as he assisted her to clamber awkwardly into the coach.

"I shall miss you and would stay if I didn't feel quite so heavy."

"Make sure you eat and rest well. Labour is hard work."

"I shall be ready for it," Emilia answered with a definite look of panic in her eye.

"You'll sail through," her husband answered reassuringly, and kissed her as she leant her head out of the coach's window, then waved farewell as Irish Tom cracked his whip, called to the animals, and the carriage set off in the direction of Kensington.

Still preoccupied with thoughts of Aidan Fenchurch and the Shadow, half wondering whether the man had exaggerated the position and was only imagining the threat that Mrs. Bussell posed, John set off to visit various patients, particularly enjoying a visit to a young woman much plagued with the illness red-eye. After trying various remedies, the Apothecary had finally decided to use bruised leaves of that most dangerous of plants, hemlock. Well aware of its deadly quality as a poison, John had insisted that his patient had put the substance nowhere near her mouth and now after a week of laying the bruised leaves on her forehead, results could be seen. The redness of the eyes had vanished and the swelling round the woman's lids had gone.

"Well, Apothecary, you have cured me," she said, much pleased.

John shook his head. "Let us be careful. Red-eye has a nasty habit of returning if you stop the treatment too soon. Another week of applying the leaves, I think. I've brought you some fresh and I want you to continue using them until I call again. Not for internal consumption, remember."

"What would happen if I did?"

"You would be very ill and might well die. Hemlock and some of the members of its family are amongst the most deadly poisons known."

"What are the others?"

"That," said John, grinning at her, "would be telling. Now, I shall see you next week and expect to pronounce you recovered."

16

"It will be my pleasure," the young woman answered demurely, and dropped a somewhat flirtatious curtsey as she escorted him to the door.

The Apothecary worked on, carrying his bag himself and leaving Nicholas in charge of the shop, finally stopping and walking back to Nassau Street long after the hour to dine had officially arrived. The house was quiet with Emilia gone and John felt pleased that he had invited Aidan Fenchurch to join him for the evening. Accordingly, he had the library prepared for receiving and went to sit by the fire and read the newspaper until six o'clock came.

Sir Gabriel's longcase clock, which played a tune upon every quarter of an hour, had been removed to Kensington, but his adopted son, missing the sound, had bought another one to replace it. Though not nearly as fine, only chiming the time rather than a melody, the Apothecary listened to it with a small part of his brain while he read, and was quite surprised when it sounded half-past the hour and there was still no sign of his guest. He rang the bell.

"Yes, Sir?" said the footman who answered.

"Nobody has called have they?"

"No, Sir. It's very quiet in the street tonight. Only one carriage has been past all evening."

"Well, I'm expecting a Mr. Fenchurch who is now half an hour late. Can you show him in at once. Don't bother with his card."

"Very good, Mr. Rawlings."

The Apothecary read on, then, tiring of his own company, sent for his apprentice who, by custom, would not join his master unless called upon to do so.

Nicholas appeared in the library doorway. "Yes, Master?"

"Nick, sit down. I'm waiting for Mr. Fenchurch but he hasn't yet appeared so I thought we might play chess."

"Wasn't he due at six?"

"Yes, and he's now an hour late. I'm beginning to get rather concerned."

"You don't think Mrs. Bussell has struck, do you?" asked the Muscovite, laughing.

John regarded him seriously and the atmosphere in the room changed very subtly. "I don't know."

"But surely he was deluded about that. She looked formidable but she did manage to smile at me."

"I think she smiled too much," the Apothecary answered.

"But, Master, she was furious with you. She glared."

"Until the moment when she decided to become winsome."

Nicholas was silent, his amusement gone. "So you think something *has* happened to him?"

"I don't know. He was an odd sort of man but not the type to be late for an appointment I would have thought. Besides, he wanted to entrust papers to me."

"Oh dear, it doesn't bode well, does it?"

"No," John said. He pulled out a small table. "Let's play. There is nothing we can do till the morning."

"But even then what? Do you know his address?"

"No," admitted the Apothecary with a certain reluctance. "In all the hurly-burly I forgot to take it."

"Then," said Nicholas solemnly, "I'm afraid we've lost him."

CHAPTER
TWO

They hadn't lost him at all, of course. As soon as John entered the shop on the following morning, he went straight to an old copy of Pigot's Street Directory and there, listed as an importer of fine wines and spirits, was Aidan Fenchurch. The address given was Elbow Lane in the City of London.

"But I wonder where he lives," said Nicholas, peering over John's shoulder.

The Apothecary handed him the book with a crooked grin. "Look through, my friend, street by street. He's sure to be somewhere."

"But what about my work?"

"I shall take care of that."

It was a slow day with few customers and those that there were demanding very ordinary physicks. The high spot came in a call from a salesman representing a warehouse where sheaths or cundums were manufactured. The name, of course, came from the deviser of this form of birth control, Colonel Cundum of the Guards, though the great Venetian, Casanova, also laid claim to having invented this boon to man — and woman — kind.

"Note the delicacy of the sheep gut and the satin tying ribbons, Apothecary," said the salesman. "These sheaths — which have all been tested by blowing therein — are designed for persons of quality, no less."

"I'll take two dozen," answered John, who was realistic about the need for such things. "And also some of your cheaper variety."

"The linen soaked in brine tied with mere strings?"

"The very same."

"Don't forget to warn the purchaser to wash them thoroughly between uses."

"I always do," John replied solemnly.

"You are a learned man, Apothecary."

The salesman laid the goods upon the counter and John settled the account with money which he fetched from his strong box. As he went into the compounding room, his apprentice said, "Got him at last, Master. Here we are. Aidan Fenchurch, Five, Bloomsbury Square."

"A good address."

The salesman having taken his money and his leave, the Apothecary returned to the back and lifted the street directory from Nicholas's hand.

"Yes, that's him, all right. There can't be two with a name like that."

"Are you going to call, Sir?"

"I might well. I have every excuse."

"Indeed you have. When will you go?"

"Now," said John, on a sudden whim.

"But won't he be at his office?"

"Even if he is, I can always leave my card. That should remind him of his broken engagement. Besides, I want to see what splendour this rich merchant lives in."

"Do you want me to get you a chair, Master?"

"No, I'll go to Piccadilly and pick up a hackney. I don't want to spend long over there. I intend to be back before the hour to dine."

"Very good, Master," Nicholas said, and helped John into his coat.

It was an enjoyable ride, the April sun, weak but sharp, lighting The Hay Market, then The Strand and finally Fleet Street and Drury Lane, from where the carriage picked its way through the familiarity of Bow Street to Bloomsbury Square, built round a delightful garden and lying close to two great mansions, Montague House and Bedford House. John alighted from the hackney and took a turn through the beautifully pathed and kept garden before he made his way to number five.

The house was large and imposing, that much he could see as he approached. But as he drew nearer, John suddenly stopped in his tracks. The curtains of every window were drawn closed and the brass streetdoor knocker was swathed in black flannel. These were the outward signs of a house in mourning and the Apothecary was seized by a terrible and constricting premonition. The need to get at the papers that Mr. Fenchurch had been due to deliver to him suddenly became of paramount importance. Despite the fact that he felt intrusive and rather lacking in good taste, John Rawlings climbed the steps and pealed the bell.

A footman answered. "Yes, Sir?"

"Forgive me for calling at such a time but I am seeking a Mr. Fenchurch. He was due to visit me last night but did not make an appearance. I can only trust and pray that no ill has befallen him."

The footman looked angry and sad simultaneously, no mean feat.

"May I enquire who you are, Sir?"

"My name is Rawlings, John Rawlings." And the Apothecary produced a card.

The footman took it. "I will show it to Miss Evelina, though I can tell you now that she is not receiving," and he started to close the door in John's face.

"One moment," the Apothecary demanded. "At least pay me the courtesy of telling me who has died."

The servant opened the door a crack and shouted through it. "Why, Mr. Fenchurch of course. He was set upon by two cutpurses just as he was entering his carriage. They bludgeoned him to death but ran off as they heard the watch approach. You are standing where he fell."

The door closed firmly and John was left to look down in horror. Sure enough the cobbles had been recently cleaned, but not sufficiently. Traces of blood still lingered and there were splashes on the steps leading up to the house. Dropping to one knee, the Apothecary saw that the spray covered a wide area, consistent with a violent attack to the head. Not quite sure what to do next, he stood up again and dusted his clothes with his hand.

Devastated by what he had just heard, John stood helplessly, staring at the closed door. Even though his acquaintanceship with Aidan Fenchurch had been of the briefest, he was cut to the quick by the shocking way in which the poor man had died. What a simply tragic end. And then Aidan's words came back to him. 'She'll finish me yet.' Suddenly full of suspicion, John looked at his watch, mulling over the idea of walking to Bow Street and putting the whole thing before Sir John Fielding, one of the sharpest brains in London even though he had been blinded in an accident at the age of nineteen, an event that might have made many people retire from public life.

His very indecision gave the Apothecary the answer. Bow Street it was. The whole story of Mrs. Bussell's obsession and her ex-lover's mysterious death at the hands of common thieves must be related at once.

The court had risen, it being four o'clock and the time to dine, and John was shown immediately into Sir John's salon on the first floor of the tall house in Bow Street. The downstairs rooms had been given over entirely to the work of the Public Office, and the Magistrate and his family, namely his wife Elizabeth and their adopted daughter, Mary Ann Whittingham, who was Lady Fielding's niece, lived above. This custom had been started some years previously by a former magistrate, Sir Thomas de Veil, a sexually robust and somewhat scandalous figure, who had first taken

24

up residence in Bow Street, thus setting the trend for others to follow. Now, as always, John bowed low as he came into the room, forgetting momentarily, as he frequently did, that Sir John was not sighted.

"Mr. Rawlings?"

It was an incredible trick for a blind man and one that he explained away by saying that he could smell the essence of his visitor and that each scent was individual to its owner.

"Yes, Sir John."

"My dear friend, I haven't spoken to you in an age. Not much, indeed, since that very sad affair which began in St. James's Palace. How are you keeping? I take it Mrs. Rawlings has not yet given birth or we would have heard of it."

"The child is due in approximately two weeks so Emilia is in Kensington at the moment with my father. I want her to get as much fresh air as she can before her confinement."

Sir John sighed, perhaps because of his own lack of offspring. "Exciting times. Your life will never be the same again, you know."

The Apothecary smiled a little ruefully. "I am fully aware of that."

The Magistrate rumbled a laugh, then said, "But I forget myself. Sit down, my friend. I trust you have not dined."

"No, Sir."

"Then you must join us. I insist. But first we will have some wine and converse privately. There is something in your manner that suggests to me you have a story of importance to impart."

Marvelling yet again at his mentor's perception, John took a seat. "There certainly is. I am greatly in need of your advice."

Waiting until a servant had brought a rich red claret and two glasses and they were once more alone, Sir John Fielding said, "Now, what is troubling you?"

Without hesitation, the Apothecary began his story with the arrival of Aidan Fenchurch in his shop, the pursuit of her former lover by Ariadne Bussell, the arrangement the two men had made for John to take possession of Aidan's papers, the missed appointment, then finally the discovery that the man had been murdered by common cutpurses on the very night he was to have seen the Apothecary.

"I presume the constable for the parish is dealing with the matter," said Sir John after a considerable pause.

"I imagine so."

"Then we must speak with him. For the whole thing stinks, does it not, Mr. Rawlings?"

"Meaning, Sir?"

"That it seems to me the so-called cutpurses could well have been hired assassins."

"There is nothing to prove that."

"Except that the victim had a vengeful Shadow. A fact, my friend, that you witnessed for yourself."

"Yes. Poor Fenchurch did not exaggerate. She is a frightening woman."

"It's a pity that the papers ultimately intended for the Public Office never got to you."

"I doubt, Sir John, that they said much more than the facts I have already told you. The victim truly opened his heart that day."

The Magistrate nodded slowly, then relapsed into silence, a sure sign that he was deep in thought. Indeed, John imagined that he could almost hear the great man's brain whirring in his head. Eventually Sir John's features changed and he looked extremely crafty.

"Of course, there is no one to say that they didn't, is there?"

The Apothecary was startled. "What do you mean?"

"Who's to tell whether the papers arrived or not? Only your good self. For if they had been delivered into my hands and contained the story of Mrs. Bussell's lunatic pursuit of Fenchurch, as you believe they did, then I would have every reason to question her about her ex-lover's death."

John laughed. "Well considered, Sir."

"It would not be the first time that the Public Office had used a little deception in order to achieve its ends."

"Nor will it be the last, I don't suppose. Do you want me to visit the Shadow, Sir John?"

"Mr. Rawlings, I couldn't presume."

"As a matter of fact it would give me a great deal of satisfaction, provided that I was carrying a letter of authorisation from yourself. It would be nice to see her in a position where for once she did not have the upper hand."

"You really took a dislike to her, didn't you?"

"Profoundly so."

Elizabeth Fielding appeared in the doorway. "Mr. Rawlings, what a pleasure. I trust John has invited you to dine with us."

The Apothecary rose and bowed. "He has indeed, Lady Fielding."

"Then I shall order another cover laid." Elizabeth wrinkled her nose. "I am still not used to being called that. I almost look round for somebody else when that name is spoken."

Her husband laughed. "You must try, my dear. There's no going back to plain Mrs. now."

Elizabeth sighed, nodding her head. "I know, I know. It's just that I have never been one for airs and graces."

"Nor ever will be," her husband said affectionately as he rose to his feet and took her outstretched hand.

It was a pleasant evening, ending long after darkness fell. Hiring a linkman, the Apothecary walked to the place where the hackneys plied for passengers, then was driven home, planning on retiring to bed early. But in this he was to be disappointed for no sooner had he gone into the hall than he was presented with a card on a tray.

"A lady has called to see you, Sir," murmured the footman who handed it to him.

"A lady?" John repeated. "Who is it? Anyone I know?"

"According to her visiting ticket it is a Mrs. Rayner and her face is not familiar to me."

John stared at the card, seeing that its owner had a fashionable address in the newly developed Mayfair.

"Where is the visitor?"

"I have shown her into the drawing room, Sir. She said she would wait an half hour for you but after that must return home."

"Then I'm glad I came back in time." And John crossed the hall to the room little used in Sir Gabriel's day but now, since the arrival of Emilia, the main reception room for the family and guests.

A woman stood by the fireplace, holding her hands out to the flames, a woman who turned as she heard John enter and fixed him with a cool stare. That she was Aidan Fenchurch's daughter he had no doubt, for the same, slightly small, crab-like eyes were looking at him, made somewhat more attractive by their feminine setting but not sufficiently so to render the woman a beauty. She was in her early thirties, John thought; a tall, thin, bony creature, at present clad from head to toe in black and even paler because of it.

"Miss Evalina?" he ventured.

"Mrs. Rayner," she answered haughtily. "Jocasta Rayner. And you are John Rawlings, I take it?"

The Apothecary bowed, very handsomely. "Yes, Madam. How did you know of me?"

"Because of this," she answered, and thrust towards him a packet which she had placed on the mantelpiece while she warmed herself.

John took it and went cold as he saw that it had his name and address written on it in a hand he did not recognise.

"How did you come by it?" he asked, but knew the answer even before she spoke. It was obviously the collection of papers that her father had been going to

29

take to Nassau Street had he not so brutally been done to death.

"It was in my father's coach," Jocasta answered abruptly. "It was not discovered until earlier today. I thought I would bring it to you and find out a little more about its contents and about you yourself."

John motioned her towards a chair. "Please sit down and let me get you some refreshment. Would you like a glass of canary?"

The woman shook her head, her face and lips drained of colour. "No. I doubt I could stomach it. Since my father's savage murder last evening I have not been able to touch a thing."

"Then allow me to give you some physick. I am an Apothecary and would suggest that you take some at once to help steady yourself. After that a drop of brandy would not go amiss."

Jocasta stared at him. "I had not put you down as a man of medicine."

"Oh? What had you thought me to be?"

"A nothing. A fop of fashion with plenty of money and no sense."

"Alas, no. Such a pleasurable life has been denied me. Though, on second thoughts, I believe I would hate to idle away meaningless days uttering silly oaths and sniffing snuff."

She barked a humourless laugh. "So there's more to you than meets the eye."

"So it would appear. Now, let me fetch you some restorative physick. Believe me, it will be of help to you throughout the days that lie ahead."

30

Jocasta seemed suddenly drained of energy. "Oh, very well. It would be impossible for anything to make me feel more wretched than I do now."

She closed her eyes and John hurried from the room and upstairs to a small cupboard in his bedroom in which he kept his pills and physicks. There he poured some powdered Feverfew into a glass, added some Oxymel and, taking the glass downstairs, mixed the whole with white wine.

"Here," he said, handing the concoction to Mrs. Rayner, "this should help you."

She eyed it with suspicion, looking extraordinarily like her father as she did so. "What is it?"

"A mixture to relieve melancholy and heaviness of spirits. If you send a servant to my shop in Shug Lane tomorrow I'll prepare some bottles for you."

She appeared to be finally reassured that John was actually what he claimed to be and downed the glassful in one deep swallow, then pulled a face.

"It has a bitter aftertaste."

"Things that are good for you often do," he answered wryly.

She smiled for the first time, looking quite attractive in her bony way. "A parallel with life, perhaps."

"Indeed." He took a seat opposite hers. "About these papers. Where did you say they were found?"

"In my father's coach. He had left the house and was just stepping inside when two robbers came out of the shadows and set about him."

"They were definitely thieves?"

Jocasta shot him a penetrating look. "What do you mean?"

"Did they rob him of his money and jewels or merely attack him?"

She frowned. "The watch disturbed them and they ran away, leaving him to die in the street."

"So nothing was actually stolen?"

"No."

The Apothecary looked thoughtful. "I wonder . . ."

"What?"

"Whether these men were actually hired assassins and theft was not their motive at all."

Jocasta Rayner looked utterly astonished. "But why? Why should anyone want to hurt my father? The very idea is beyond comprehension."

So she knows nothing of the Shadow, John realised. Aidan Fenchurch had confided none of his troubles to his children.

He looked vague. "One can never be sure of these things. However good a man one can never rule out the possibility of a jealous business rival or someone who imagines themselves slighted. Hardly anyone goes through life without upsetting somebody at some stage."

Jocasta nodded. "I suppose you're right. But personally I don't believe it. As far as I am concerned — and I am sure that I speak for the rest of the family as well — my father was killed by two footpads, chosen at random."

A slight colour had come into her cheeks as a result of the physick and she accepted the brandy that John now offered her. After a moment's silence, Jocasta said, "Mr. Rawlings . . ."

"Yes?"

"What was in those papers and why should my father pick you to give them to? Have you known him for some while in fact?"

The Apothecary weighed the situation carefully. To reveal everything about Ariadne Bussell to a daughter so recently and so brutally bereaved would be the height of cruelty. On the other hand, in view of the investigation that was about to start, most of the truth, if not all of it, would be bound to come out. He decided to be diplomatic.

"I haven't read them, of course, as you have only just now delivered them to me, but I have reason to believe that they might contain information of a nature very personal to your late father."

Jocasta looked immensely puzzled. "But why should he give them to you?"

John decided on a half-truth. "He came into my shop yesterday and said he thought me to be an honest citizen."

"Why on earth should he do that? Was it a joke?"

"Mrs. Rayner," the Apothecary answered firmly, "it was said in all seriousness. Your father asked me to take these very papers to Sir John Fielding of Bow Street in the event of anything untoward happening to him."

Jocasta seemed to shrink to half her size, crouching back in her chair as if she had been physically attacked. "What exactly do you mean by that?"

It had come and not at all as John had wanted it. Yet discretion must be paramount at this stage.

"Simply what I say. I think your father feared that someone had a grudge against him and might, just possibly, carry that grudge too far. So he had prepared a statement for the Principal Magistrate in the event of an accident befalling him. That is all I can tell you."

"So he was expecting an attack," Jocasta said, her voice very low.

"I think he was, yes."

"But from whom? He didn't have an enemy in the world."

"We have covered this ground, Mrs. Rayner. In the morning it will be my duty to take Mr. Fenchurch's statement to Sir John Fielding. It will then become his obligation to track down your father's killers and to discover the facts behind his death."

Jocasta was very quiet, slowly sipping her brandy, gazing into the fire. Then she shook her head. "Poor Father. I hope that this is all a horrible coincidence. That he imagined someone hated him enough to kill him."

"Perhaps it is just that. Perhaps he was done to death by cutpurses after all. Personally I think you should stop speculating until Sir John has made his decision."

She was silent again, then drained her glass and got to her feet.

"You are right, of course. No amount of conjecture can bring my father back. Incidentally, Mr. Rawlings, I shall be staying at Bloomsbury Square for the time being. My unmarried sister and my cousin are both in residence there and have asked me to remain until after the funeral. Millicent, of course, is coping but Evalina is completely hysterical."

"And which sisters are they? Older or younger?"

"Millicent is a cousin who lives with us. Evalina is the eldest of us three girls; my younger sister, Louisa, is . . . out of town at present."

Why had there been a slight hesitation in Jocasta's voice? John wondered. "Then she will not have heard the grievous news?" he asked.

"No. She is . . . touring . . . and I am not sure exactly where she is at present."

Again that hesitation. "Is she married?" John asked pleasantly.

"Yes. Yes, indeed." Mrs. Rayner started to move towards the door.

"You came by coach?"

"I did. It is presently round in Dolphin's Yard."

"I'll send a footman to fetch it."

They went into the hall together, listening to the sound of the equipage coming to the front door.

"You have been very kind, Mr. Rawlings. Pray will you call in person bringing some more of that excellent physick?"

He bowed and took her hand. "Of course I will. I shall arrive about noon."

"And if you have anything even stronger for Evalina I am sure the whole household will be mightily relieved."

He smiled irregularly. "I'll do my best."

Her coach had drawn up outside and a servant went to open the front door for her. Jocasta turned in the entrance.

"I wonder if Mrs. Bussell knows?" she said, more to herself than to her host.

John remained silent, determined to keep all secret until Sir John Fielding decided it was time to do otherwise.

"Do you think I should write to Father's friends?" Jocasta continued.

The Apothecary shook his head. "I think you will find that such a dramatic story concerning a well-known merchant will be reported in the newspapers tomorrow."

She smiled, very wryly. "I suppose we will then be overwhelmed by callers."

John gave an answering smile. "It is the way of the world, alas."

Jocasta Rayner curtseyed. "Goodbye, Sir. Thank you for your hospitality."

"It has been most interesting to meet you," he said, and accompanied her into the street where he handed her inside her carriage before going within to read the last words that her father had ever written.

CHAPTER
THREE

The papers, which John read and re-read once his visitor had gone, revealed little new. They simply recounted the tale of Mrs. Bussell and her obsessive love for Aidan Fenchurch which had turned to a dangerous hatred. But had it? John wondered as he finally resealed the dead man's statement. As he had said to the victim himself, it seemed to him that Ariadne was still besotted with the object of her affections. Would this, the Apothecary considered as he put on his nightshirt and got into bed, make her more or less likely to order an attack on her former lover?

He recalled her face; how affable she had tried to look when she realised that her fury was getting her nowhere. Yet the smile flashed by the overpowering set of teeth had been entirely without humour or humanity. Yes, John thought, blowing out the bedside candle, that woman could be a truly dangerous member of her sex, capable of handing out hurt to anyone whom she believed either stood in her way or had rejected her.

It seemed that Sir John Fielding was of a like mind. Having sat in total silence while his clerk, Joe Jago, read Aidan Fenchurch's statement aloud, his first comment was, "Poor fellow. I would not care for a harpy of that stamp to shadow me."

"Do you think she hired ruffians to take care of him, as it were, Sir?"

"If we are to believe all that he says, then yes, she would be prepared to do so if something upset her. But whether she did or not has yet to be discovered. However, on the evidence presented to us so far I would not hesitate to say that at the moment Ariadne Bussell is our principal suspect."

John spoke. "My offer to go and see her still stands."

The Magistrate drew in his breath, then relapsed into a further silence, clearly thinking things through. Finally he said, "I believe the only way to approach a woman like that is with bristling officialdom. I suggest, therefore, that you and Joe both go. If she refuses to cooperate, my clerk can order her to Bow Street where I will question her personally. Now, do we know where she lives?"

"No. But today I have to call on Mrs. Rayner, the victim's daughter, to take her some physick. She is bound to have her father's friend's address."

"Did you not say that she knows nothing of the scandal?"

"Nothing at all, Sir John," the Apothecary answered.

The Magistrate leant back in his chair, folded his fingers over his chest and allowed himself a smile. "I will despatch Runners Ham and Raven to see the constable examining Mr. Fenchurch's murder. They can offer their services in tracking down the assailants."

"Which they never will," put in Joe Jago grimly. "Be they cutpurses or hired assassins, either way they will vanish into the shadows, never to be seen again."

"Our only hope is that one of the peachers knows who they are."

"Do you want me to ask around, Sir?"

"If you would, Jago. Word is bound to be about by now."

It was an odd thing, John considered, that a man so mighty as Sir John Fielding, the principal upholder of the law in the teeming metropolis, should still use the peachers, those members of the criminal class prepared to inform upon their fellows, as sources of information. Yet he was realistic. Without the peachers — the term came from the word impeachment — there were certain cases that would not move forward at all. And this was one of them. Robbers or professional killers, whichever had ended Aidan Fenchurch's life, were both members of the same delinquent brotherhood. Therefore, to track them down, enquiries must be made amongst that brotherhood. There was no other way.

"I've a mind," said Sir John Fielding, a propos of nothing in particular, "to finish this case quickly. Joe and Mr. Rawlings, if you can interview Mrs. Bussell tomorrow and if Runners Ham and Raven can simultaneously follow any trails that the peachers might give us, it might well be over in a matter of days."

"Do you think Mrs. Bussell will confess then?" asked John, genuinely surprised.

"No. But she could make a slip or conduct herself in such a manner that our suspicions will be confirmed and she can be brought to me for further questioning."

"But how to tie her in with the assassins, if assassins indeed they were?"

"There are ways. Large amounts of money being drawn from a bank; suspicious meetings with strangers coming to the house. All that sort of thing. If she is our woman then we will nail her, never fear."

"He seems very confident," said John to Joe as they descended the stairs.

"It is very rare indeed, Sir, for a murdered man to leave behind the name of the person he believes will kill him, together with full details of the motive for so doing."

"Do you believe Mrs. Bussell is responsible, Joe?"

"Yes, Sir, I do. Cutpurses? I don't think so. Even if they were disturbed by the watch they'd have had the rings from the man's fingers even if it meant the fingers going as well."

"I'm sure you've hit on the right answer. Of course they would. So where are you off to now? To see Ham and Raven?"

"No, first Sukie and Little Will, two of our more reliable peachers."

"I remember them," answered John, grimacing at the memory of the kidnap of Mary Ann Whittingham, Sir John Fielding's adopted daughter, and the part the two peachers had played in rescuing her.

"And you, Sir?"

"To the shop to mix up some physicks for Mrs. Rayner and her hysterical sister. Then on to Bloomsbury Square to deliver them and at the same time find out where the ghastly Bussell resides."

"Will it be convenient for me to call for you in Nassau Street at nine o'clock tomorrow morning? Then we can proceed on to interview the suspect."

John smiled. "I wonder what she would do if she heard herself called that."

"Rant against authority, I dare say. Probably call Sir John and his men the most corrupt load of fobs ever to hold public office."

John laughed. "Do you know, I think you're right."

"Think of being married to such a blower," said Joe, looking grim.

"Perhaps," John answered thoughtfully, "as an act of self defence, Mr. Bussell has become just as nasty as she is."

As the Apothecary, carrying his medical bag and wearing serious dark visiting clothes, approached the house in Bloomsbury Square, a strange mixture of sounds greeted his ears. Distantly but penetratingly, a woman was screaming fit to bring the walls down, while another female voice was shouting the word 'Stop', presumably at the screamer. Meanwhile, yet another woman was calling out to both to be calm but becoming somewhat distressed herself in the process. It sounded like a scene from hell's kitchen and it was with a great deal of trepidation that John rang the bell to gain admittance.

As the door opened, the sound intensified, and the footman who answered looked apologetic. Despite this, he was opening his mouth to say that the ladies were not receiving and would have done so had not John forestalled him.

"I have an appointment with Mrs. Rayner. She asked me to call with some medicaments. My card." And the Apothecary swept it on to the tray.

"Very good, Sir. If you would step inside I will inform Mrs. Rayner that you are here."

"Thank you," John answered solemnly and put on his grave Apothecary's face.

The footman returned within a few minutes. "If you will follow me, Sir. Mrs. Rayner will see you in the drawing room. It is on the first floor."

The wine and spirits import business must certainly provide those who traded in it with rich pickings, John thought as he followed the servant upstairs. For the house was well appointed and had fine floors and decoration, and many beautiful paintings, some old and valuable, others merely of family members. Over the fireplace of the drawing room hung a full-length portrait of Aidan Fenchurch himself, probably aged about forty, his face less florid — unless this were merely the artist's flattery — but the crab-like eyes still staring suspiciously out upon the world. Just for a minute John gazed at it, wondering what it could have been about the man that had driven Ariadne into such a frenzy, then decided that Aidan must have had hidden charms and been a powerful performer in the bedchamber.

42

There was a rustle of skirts behind him and John, looking over his shoulder, saw that Jocasta Rayner had joined him. He bowed low.

"Madam, I have brought the physick that you requested."

"Then give me some now for the love of God. I'll ring for a glass. Truly, Mr. Rawlings, I am in dire straits and could do with a draught immediately."

She looked terrible, John thought. Her skin stretched tightly over her bones, her small eyes red with weeping.

"My dear girl," he said, forgetting himself, "you have not fared well since last we met."

Jocasta shook her head. "It's Evalina. She is driving me insane. She hasn't stopped screaming since news of father's death was brought to us."

"But that was the night before last. Surely you aren't serious?"

Mrs. Rayner laid her hand on his arm. "Listen. Be silent a moment. Do you hear that?"

He certainly could. The bellowing that had greeted him outside the door was twice as loud in the house.

"But surely her voice should have given up by now. By rights she should be hoarse."

"By rights, yes," Jocasta answered bitterly. "But there are no rights as far as Evalina is concerned. Because of her devil's mark she has ruled the roost since she was a toddling child."

"Devil's mark!" exclaimed the Apothecary. "What do you mean by that?"

"She has a birthmark on her cheek; some would call it a port wine stain. She blames it for all her ills. Says it precluded her from marriage and happiness. I told her to paint, patch and powder but she would have none of it. Father felt guilty about it, thought he was the cause, because he had a similar thing on his lower back . . ." She caught the Apothecary's eye and almost giggled. "Oh very well, his buttock. Anyway, he believed he had passed the blemish on to her and spoilt Evelina half to death as a result. Of course, the beauty of our family is Louisa but he hardly spared her the time of day. No wonder . . ."

"No wonder what?"

"Nothing. Anyway, my elder sister is going to bring this household to the verge of collapse unless you can do something drastic. Tell me, Apothecary, have you anything with you that can silence her?"

"A strong sedative, one that induces deep sleep, might well be the answer."

"At least it would give us a temporary respite." Jocasta sighed. "Now, please do attend to me. I am at the very end of my resources I assure you."

John asked a reasonable question. "What about Mr. Rayner? Could he not bring calm to the situation?"

Jocasta shot him a dark look. "Mr. Rayner is dead, Sir."

"I'm so sorry, I didn't mean to be tactless."

"It's not your fault. You weren't to know. I am remarkably young to be a widow so it was an easy mistake to make. I'll tell you about it one day but now is not the time."

"Of course not. Here let me ring for a glass. The sooner you swallow this down, the better."

44

"You're very kind," Jocasta answered, and gave him a glance that he could not interpret.

"Now, Madam, where is your sister at present?"

"In her bedroom. I will take you to her as soon as I have calmed myself."

The glass being brought and the physick consumed, Mrs. Rayner beckoned John to follow her, leading him up the stairs to the floor above. As they climbed, the sound of hysterics grew ever louder and the Apothecary marvelled at the stamina of anyone who could keep up such an unholy racket for an entire day and a night. Deciding that to be masterful was the only way, he flung open the bedroom door without even knocking.

An apparition reared up in the bed, an apparition that seemed to be composed entirely of black and white, dark hair almost obscuring a pale face, a white nightdress buttoned up to the neck respectably preventing even the merest glimpse of pink flesh. From beneath the veils of hanging hair a pair of mournful black eyes, quite unlike her sister's, gazed at the Apothecary angrily. Momentarily, the terrible screeching ceased as the apparition spoke.

"Get out! How dare you come bursting into my bedroom. Who the devil are you?"

"No. I do dare. And the name is John Rawlings," John replied crisply.

Evalina positively gaped, then she rallied and threw her pillow at him.

"Out, out, out!" she bellowed.

"For heaven's sake," Jocasta remonstrated, stepping into the room. "Evalina, get a grip on yourself. Mr.

Rawlings is an Apothecary and he has come to treat you."

"I won't be treated," she howled in response.

"So you just want to wallow in misery do you? Dragging the rest of us down in the process."

"Quite right," said a voice from the depths of the bed-hangings, and a woman that John hadn't noticed, standing in the shadow as she had been, stepped forward.

This, he thought, must be Millicent, for she was the epitome of a maiden cousin allowed to live with her rich relations because her own had fallen on hard times. Small, neat, earnest, far from beautiful but also not plain, she was an archetype of so many unfortunate unmarried ladies who relied on the charity of others.

"Don't you interfere," Evalina shouted, turning towards her. "Just because I am the only one that grieves for poor Papa while the rest of you shed crocodile tears."

"Oh how could you," Millicent remonstrated, and sniffed into a handkerchief trimmed with rather poor quality lace.

Jocasta lost her temper. "What a terrible thing to say. You should be ashamed of yourself, you witch. We are all cut to the quick but some of us control ourselves for the sake of the rest. Damn you, Evalina, you can fend for yourself. Come Millicent, Mr. Rawlings, let us leave her to her own devices."

Back went Evalina's head and out came a bellow fit not only to wake the dead but set them dancing.

John turned to Jocasta. "You're right. There's no dealing with her. I would suggest a total fast, though. Starving usually brings hysterics to an end."

Evalina shot him a malevolent glare to which he responded by pulling a hideous face, carefully moving away from the other two women as he did so. Weeping, Millicent hurried past him but the Apothecary, very gently, caught her arm.

"Please let me give you something soothing. I can see you are deeply distressed."

"Oh dear," the poor woman answered tearfully, and scuttled ahead of him and Jocasta down the stairs. They followed at a more sober pace.

"Did you really mean that?" asked Jocasta.

"About starving her? Yes, certainly. Obviously she is grieved to lose her father, especially in such horrific circumstances, but quite frankly I consider such a show to be attention seeking and no more. Order the servants to give her nothing but fluids for the next twenty-four hours and I am sure you will soon find a change in attitude."

"But I don't think I can cope with that noise much longer."

"Then I'll put a good dose of laudanum into some wine; that should render her unconscious for a while."

"It won't kill her, will it?"

"Of course not. An overdose would but I assure you that I will measure it out very carefully."

Jocasta gave a half smile. "Perhaps I should have some."

"You don't need it," John answered seriously. "I believe that you are possibly a very strong woman indeed."

In the drawing room into which he had first been shown, Millicent awaited him. Standing in a corner, back turned, shoulders heaving, she looked like a tragic little mouse. In a great rush of sympathy the Apothecary went to her side and put his arm round her. She jumped as only a maiden lady could, and moved away. Very contrite, John bowed.

"Madam, I did not mean to give offence. Only to offer comfort."

She turned to face him, all confusion, her small face working with emotion. "It is just that I am so upset, Sir. Aidan was very good to me, took me in when my father died, deeply in debt. Without my cousin I tremble to think what my future would have been. That is why his brutal death affects me so badly. If he had ended in his bed it would have been bad enough, but to go like that, bleeding in the street . . ." Millicent fought nobly to control her sobs but lost the battle.

"May I give you a soothing draught?" John asked. "I assure you that I am a recognised Apothecary and not some quack."

"Of course you are. I never doubted it for a moment." She looked bewildered. "An Apothecary I mean, not a quack." Her cheeks quivered. "Oh dear, I sound very foolish, don't I?"

"No," said Jocasta, coming to join them. "You sound just like our Cousin Millicent." She cuddled the older woman to her. "She was our governess, you know. She looked after us when our mother died."

Millicent, still clearly embarrassed, began to jabber slightly. "Of course it was most fortuitous — not dear Dorothy's death of course, I didn't mean that. No, it was just the timing. Papa went into debt — so very, very badly — and died in that horrible gaol just as Dorothy quitted this life. Naturally Aidan didn't want to put his girls into the hands of a stranger and as I had been a governess to the Delameres — such a good family — he asked me if I would consider the position. I was only too happy to accept, as you can guess, Mr. Rawlings."

"Indeed I can."

"I was twenty-six at the time but felt as if life had just begun when Aidan offered me a home."

It was a tale so similar to those he had heard from other poor relations that the whole story seemed familiar, yet the Apothecary's sympathies were stirred. Unless endowed with great physical charms, girls without means had little chance of securing a good match and were frequently forced to act as governesses to other people's children.

"How kind of him," he murmured.

Her eyes filled with tears. "And now he has gone. Poor Aidan. Whatever his weaknesses he did not deserve such a fate."

John was longing to ask what those weaknesses might have been but thought it more circumspect not to do so. However, he hazarded a shrewd guess that Millicent knew of her late employer's affair with Ariadne Bussell, a fact that she had kept secret from his daughters.

"It was indeed a most grim end," he said now. "But pray do not distress yourself. Allow me to give you some physick." And he fished in his medical bag, then poured out a deep measure which he handed to her.

Millicent sipped at it in true spinsterish fashion and John had a vision of her going through life like that, always taking little sips of everything, be it food, drink, or carnality. Never attacking anything with gusto, always careful, always cautious, a woman of small appetite in every way.

"It's a little sour," she said, and gave a timid laugh.

"Drink it down," advised Jocasta. "It did me good. Come on, Millie."

Her cousin took another tiny mouthful, then put the glass down and wept again. "Oh, what are we going to do without him?" she asked mournfully.

"If you're worried about your future, stop now," Jocasta said. "Papa has left Foxfire Hall to me — or so he always promised. I shall probably go to live there and, of course, you will be my companion."

"You will marry again," said Millicent sombrely. "I have no doubt of that."

Jocasta shrugged. "Perhaps. Who knows? I have certainly met no one to match Horatio as yet."

"How long ago did your husband die?" John asked.

"Eighteen months. It was very sudden. Admittedly he was older than I, but none the less it was unexpected."

"What happened?"

"He must have eaten something that disagreed with him, or so the doctor thought. He had violent stomach pains, sickness and laxes, and was dead by morning. Poor dear soul. It was considered that the mushrooms he consumed were poisonous. I had none because I have never been fond of them."

The Apothecary nodded. "One can't be too careful with fungi. You really must be able to differentiate between the toxic and the harmless."

Millicent spoke up. "When I was a girl — such a very long time ago —" She smiled a little archly. "We used to go picking in the woods. That was in the days before Father lost his fortune. Anyway, Mama would carefully examine everything we brought back. For poison, you see. She was most particular."

"Very wise," said John.

Jocasta exhaled her breath in a bitter sound. "Poor Horatio. I still can't think how it happened. Do you remember, Millie, how the cook took all the blame and left our employment hurriedly? But really it was misadventure."

The conversation was getting more sombre by the minute and tears from both women seemed imminent. The Apothecary frantically wondered how he could possibly lighten the situation but was saved by a wild gurgling scream from the upper floor. All three looked at one another.

"Evalina," said Jocasta, and, "I'll deal with her," said John, snatching his bag and sprinting up the stairs before the other two could even get a start. On the edge of anger, he entered the room of Aidan Fenchurch's eldest unmarried daughter.

"How dare you!" she expostulated.

"More to the point, have you no respect?" he answered furiously.

She hadn't expected that and gaped, not an attractive sight from a woman who had spent the last thirty-six hours in bed without attending to her toilette.

"You should be ashamed," John thundered. "With your father lying in the mortuary, you are now the head of the family. And what do you do? Lie slummocky in your sheets, wailing like a banshee and resembling a gorgon. You have the worst end of the staff, Madam. Rise up, wash, dress, and show a little dignity. Why, a child of twelve would behave in a more seemly manner than you can muster. Shame on you."

She glowered from beneath the hanging curtains of her hair. "Upstart, rogue. What are you doing in this house?"

"I come about your late father's business," he answered magnificently, and swept out.

At the bottom of the stairs Jocasta and Millicent waited anxiously.

"How is she?" asked the older woman.

"Play acting," said John. "I shall definitely barb her drink for her. Then you will get some peace. But no mercy, mind." He fixed the governess with a look. "I know you were called upon to be her mother, but do not give way. If she were smaller, she should be spanked. I am afraid, Miss Millicent, that in these dire circumstances you must be cruel to be kind. And now, ladies, with that advice I take my leave."

He bowed, then remembered the information that Sir John Fielding had wished him to obtain, rather spoiling his exit.

"By the way, do either of you know the whereabouts of Mrs. Bussell, Mr. Fenchurch's friend? She ordered some pills in my shop but forgot to leave her address."

Was it his imagination or did a silent ripple run between the two of them?

"Mrs. Bussell lives in Grosvenor Square," said Jocasta. "Number six, I believe."

"A very seemly address."

"Indeed it is. But then, of course, her husband is very, very rich so what else would you expect?"

"Aha," said Sir John Fielding. "It seems the Shadow lives most comfortably."

"So it would appear."

The Magistrate sighed. "I wonder at these husbands, truly I do. Was he aware of her affair and subsequent pursuit of her lover? Or is he merely an ignorant fool?"

John shrugged and shook his head. "Who knows?"

"Whatever the case, he has settled for keeping her into old age. Anyway, Mr. Rawlings, tomorrow you and Jago will ruffle her feathers. A woman like that needs to be called to order from time to time."

"Do you think she paid to have Aidan Fenchurch killed, Sir?"

"Yes, I do," said Sir John, sighing heavily. "The devil of it is going to be proving that she did so."

CHAPTER
FOUR

Having closed the shop for the night, John and his apprentice made their way home to discover that the post boy had brought a letter from Sir Gabriel with a postscript added by Emilia, assuring her husband of her improved health. The Apothecary read it through several times, the last reading being in bed before he blew out the candle and closed his eyes. But instead of falling asleep immediately he once more lived through the sequence of events precipitated by Aidan Fenchurch running into his shop hotly pursued by Mrs. Bussell.

What, John wondered, had she wanted in particular that would have driven her to run after her quarry in such a way? What could have been so urgent that she must see him then and there? Or was she just a crazed indulged woman whose every whim must be granted as soon as she so much as thought of it? Probably the latter, he considered, and fell to conjecturing what Montague Bussell could possibly be like and whether he would be at home when John and Joe Jago called at Grosvenor Square in the morning.

As it transpired, despite the earliness of the hour neither husband nor wife were in, a fact with which the representatives of the Public Office could not argue as no previous appointment had been made.

"Who shall I say called, Sir?" asked a footman, looking at Joe as if he had crawled from beneath a damp stone.

Sir John Fielding's clerk and right hand man showed his steel. With a flourish of hard, somewhat dangerous-looking fingers, he produced a card from within his sensible worsted coat and thrust it beneath the arrogant servant's nostrils.

Startled, the man read it aloud. "Joseph R. Jago, clerk to Sir John Fielding, the Public Office, Bow Street." He looked slightly taken aback. "And to what does this refer, Sir?"

"Mind your business," snapped Joe mightily. "I wish to see Mrs. Bussell and I shall return. My conversation with her is privy to the pair of us. Good day to you." And he stamped down the stone steps to where John waited in the street below.

"Upstart," said the clerk, none too quietly.

The Apothecary, who had grown accustomed to the ill manners of servants through years of calling on the sick, nodded sympathetically, then looked thoughtful. "D'ye know, he goes with his employer somehow."

"Is she of that ilk; rude and arrogant?"

"Horribly so. But I'd wager a goodly sum that when we finally pin her down she'll be in flirtatious mode, all grins, winks and teeth."

Joe shuddered. "Heaven forfend! I think I'd rather meet her aggressive."

"Are you sure about that?" said John, and burst into hilarious laughter, startling a passer-by.

They had come in the coach used for Bow Street business and now had it at their disposal. "Do you want me to take you to the shop, Sir?" Joe asked as they climbed aboard.

The Apothecary shook his head. "If it is no trouble to you, my friend, I would like to call at the mortuary. I have a feeling that I shall know more about Aidan Fenchurch's death if I can see the extent of his injuries."

"He's in a rough state, Sir. But then I have no need to warn you of that."

"I don't relish the task but I know I won't be allowed in without an official present so this will be my only chance to see him. What's the ruling regarding the body, by the way?"

"The coroner is due to release it to the family later today."

"Then we'd best make haste," John answered, wondering why he had set himself this loathsome duty.

The thing that he hated above all about mortuaries was the terrible smell of sweetness. Though the slabs were kept as cold as possible, still flesh had only one fate once the life force had left it and there was nothing that could be done about that. To counteract the stink of corruption and decay, herbs were scattered and rose water sprinkled by the mortuary keeper, but still the stench caught in the back of John's throat as he made his way down the central aisle to where lay the last mortal remains of Aidan Fenchurch covered by a stark white shroud.

That his skull had been split apart was obvious from the crude bandage that had been tied round what was left of his head. It was horrible, John thought, reminiscent of someone with violent toothache. The blood had long since been washed from the wounds but a pinkish seepage discoloured the bandage where it touched the skin, while the features of Aidan's face, including his crab eyes, now closed, had been rearranged by the blows which had been rained upon him.

John gulped, then braced himself. "Might I be allowed to examine the wounds?"

"I can but ask," Joe answered, attracting the attention of the keeper by a wave of his hand. "This is one of Sir John's assistants," he continued as the man approached. "He is an apothecary. Would it be possible for the bandage to be removed so that he can see the skull?"

The mortuary keeper leant over the body. "It's a terrible sight," he said over his shoulder.

"I'm ready," John answered.

But he wasn't, not quite. Brains oozed where there had once been a thatch of longish grey hair and the bones of Aidan's skull were visible through the hanging flesh.

"Christ!" said Joe, who clearly hadn't seen the injuries before.

John bent forward and somehow found the courage to raise his quizzing glass. "Whoever did this is worse than a savage."

"Can you see the work of two different hands?"

"Yes, I think so. The blows are coming from different directions. God help the poor devil, he must have died the most terrible death."

Joe turned away. "It's one of the worst I've ever seen, and I've come across a few in my time."

"I would describe this as crude butchery."

"So would I, Sir." The clerk shook his head. "What could the wretched fellow have done to deserve this? Was jigging Mrs. Bussell his only crime?"

"It certainly makes one wonder," answered John thoughtfully. He straightened up, pulling the shroud back to cover the face. "Perhaps he made other enemies on his walk through life."

"Or perhaps," answered Joe succinctly, "Mrs. Bussell was not his only woman."

They strolled in the park to clear the stench of death from their lungs, dodging the April showers beneath the trees and generally whiling away the time until it was three o'clock, an hour before the fashionable time to dine. Then they once more boarded the Bow Street coach and headed back for Grosvenor Square, certain that by now Mrs. Bussell would have returned to make a toilette. This time, just to confuse the issue, John rang the bell. The same superior servant answered.

"Mrs. Bussell, if you please," the Apothecary said crisply. "You may say that two representatives of the Public Office have called on the business of Sir John Fielding."

And with that the visitors presented their cards simultaneously and with a flourish.

"I shall enquire," the footman answered stiffly. "Kindly step within."

It was the type of self-conscious opulence that John would have imagined to be the taste of Mrs. Bussell, who clearly yearned to be associated with the arts. There were paintings and classical busts and pillars crowding the hall, together with an alcove devoted to chinoiserie, where horrible hangings depicting Chinese writing and nasty lanterns hung above vases of ugly twisted wood. Joe rolled an eye and raised a brow, while John sighed gustily.

The servant, who had disappeared, returned. "Madam is not at home."

"Then we will wait," announced Joe and sat down, folding his arms across his chest.

"I cannot allow that, Sir."

"You not only can but you will. I am here representing the Principal Magistrate who is quite prepared to summon Mrs. Bussell to Bow Street if she refuses to be interviewed. Therefore, my man, I would suggest that you find your mistress and ask her once more whether she will see us."

"And hurry up about it," John added for good measure.

Shooting them a glance of pure poison, the footman departed, heading up the stairs with a purposeful tread. A few minutes later, surging like a sailcloth in a somewhat transparent negligee — a casual fashion which had started in France — Mrs. Bussell herself appeared on the staircase, smiling coyly at her visitors and flashing her conker-coloured eyes for all she was worth.

"Prepare to be seduced," John muttered in an undertone.

"Heaven forbid," Joe answered from the corner of his mouth.

She was upon them in a flurry of frills and flounces, curtseying and smiling broadly. "Gentlemen, forgive my servant. He has been over-trained to protect me, don't you know." The Bath burr was very pronounced, so much so that the Apothecary presumed someone had once told Mrs. Bussell it was charming. "Now how may I help you? But I forget my manners. Pray come into the salon and have some sherry. Let us all be friendly."

Joe bowed, very deeply. "Madam, in other circumstances I would accept. But this matter is too serious to be treated frivolously. However, I would appreciate going where we may speak privately."

The brown eyes momentarily narrowed then grew over-wide as Mrs. Bussell fluttered her lashes. "La, Sir, what a fuss to be sure. What can I have done to merit such severity?"

John cleared his throat and she turned the beam of her attention on him. "Do I know you, Sir?"

"We met once, in my apothecary's shop in Shug Lane. You were pursuing a Mr. Aidan Fenchurch at the time. Now that same man lies dead in the mortuary, the victim of a savage attack in the street. Sir John Fielding is not satisfied that the killing was the random work of footpads. He believes that assassins may have been hired by persons unknown. Further, Mr. Fenchurch left papers — papers now lodged in the Public Office — in which he named you, Madam, as his potential killer. Now what say you to that?"

"Lies, all lies," shrieked Mrs. Bussell, waving her arms in the air and releasing the stale odour of one who bathed infrequently.

Joe took over. "This conversation really must be conducted privately, Madam. Of course, your husband can be present if you wish."

Her thoughts were as patent as if she had spoken them. She toyed with the idea of bluffing everything out and enjoying the protection of her husband's presence. Then she cast this plan away as the danger of what John might reveal became apparent to her. The question as to how much Montague Bussell knew hung in the air between Joe and the Apothecary though neither of them uttered a word; instead both fixed her with a stare and waited.

"He is asleep," she said eventually. "He always has a rest before dining." Once more she became arch. "I feel this is a brouhaha over nothing. Mr. Fenchurch and I were the best of friends. Why, I wouldn't have harmed a hair of his head."

Remembering the shattered skull beneath its long grey mane, John shuddered. "That is not what he believed," he said dryly, and followed her as she led the way into another affectedly artistic room that attempted a careless abandon as to its arrangement but succeeded only in looking contrived.

Mrs. Bussell settled herself on a profusely embroidered square-backed sofa, then smiled largely. "Now then," she said.

Joe became the height of officialdom. "You did realise, did you not, that your friend, Mr. Fenchurch, was done to death in the street on the very day that you pursued him into Mr. Rawlings's shop?"

The conker eyes snapped. "I did not pursue him. I had an urgent message for Mr. Fenchurch and I thought I saw him go into your shop, Sir. But he was not there and, if I may say so, your manner towards me on that occasion was extremely offensive."

"And so was yours to me," John answered nastily.

Joe laughed, so suddenly that it was quite shocking. "The truth is, Mrs. Bussell, that he was cowering in the back of the shop on the point of tears. He also told Mr. Rawlings that he thought you would do for him one day, meaning that he believed you quite capable of killing him."

At last he had got through. The big mouth closed and the woman lowered her gaze. All pretence at flirtation ceased.

"Are you accusing me? Because I have witnesses as to where I was that night. My husband was by my side from dusk till nightfall."

Joe made a derogatory sound. "Of course you couldn't have killed him directly. I doubt that even a woman of your build . . ." She glared at him. ". . . could have hit him with the savagery that the poor devil endured. No, as I said, the deed was done by two men, supposedly cutpurses, but they took nothing, not even a ring from his finger. Now, what do you say to that?"

Mrs. Bussell was silent for a moment, then she rallied. She looked up, hard-faced. "I say that I know nothing about it. If these men were paid to murder, then I did not hire them."

John's heart sank. She would never break, not a woman of that stamp. The great grins and provocative eyes masked a creature hard as horseshoes.

Joe must have felt something of this but still he fought on. "Are you prepared to come to Bow Street and swear that on oath?"

Her chins rose. "Yes I am."

She was game, John had to give her her due. "How do you explain away Mr. Fenchurch's written statement that if he were to die in suspicious circumstances then you would be responsible?" he asked.

"Hallucinations," she snarled, giving him a withering look. "The man was probably suffering from delusions."

"Were you once his mistress?" Joe put in. "And did you then become his Shadow, driving through the night to hurl things at his front door?"

She did not reply, then she tightened her expression. "He did me wrong. He told me he loved me, deceived me cruelly. I became upset and might indeed have returned his love letters in anger." Her big lips trembled and she started to weep loudly.

"And what did your husband have to say about all this?" Joe asked bluntly.

"He didn't know about my affair. He was away at the time. I was in Aidan Fenchurch's thrall. I couldn't help myself. His power is so great."

"Was," said John pointedly.

She shot him a look but continued to cry and babble. "I loved him. I loved him. I couldn't help myself. But he was a cruel bastard. He left me for someone else. Oh merciful heavens, my heart was fit to break, so it was."

Joe stood up. "Mr. Rawlings, I suggest we take our leave. We are clearly going to get no further sense from this lady. Madam, Sir John Fielding will no doubt be in touch with you. If you intend to leave London please be so kind as to let me know."

"Of course I intend to leave," the weeping woman answered mutinously. "You have shotten my nerves to shreds with your horrid insinuations. I need the tranquillity of rural life in which to recover myself."

"And where and when do you plan to go?" Joe asked, pleasantly enough.

"That," said Mrs. Bussell, trembling violently, "is entirely my own affair."

"Were the killers hired assassins and, if so, did she employ them?" asked the Apothecary as the coach rattled its way back to Bow Street.

Joe's trenchant profile, etched by the light spilling from the street, turned towards him. "I've never known robbers fail to rob, Sir, even if they were disturbed by the watch. So yes to the first part of your question. As to the second, I'm not sure. She's not the kind of woman that I could take to personally, but whether that makes her a murderess is a different matter."

"You're right, of course. She's horrible but one can't hang her for that. Yet why was Aidan so convinced that she would do for him?"

"Because she's crazy and capable of anything," Joe answered succinctly. "But those facts alone do not prove her guilt."

"So what's the way forward?"

"I think Sir John should see her. If anyone can break her down, it will be him."

"Is that what you are going to tell him?"

"Yes, Sir, it is. Now, I've an idea. Can I drop you at Bloomsbury Square, ostensibly to enquire after the health of the bereaved but also to find out where the Bussell woman might be likely to bolt to? For bolt she will, I feel it in my gut."

"Of course you can. But would it be tactful? Aidan's body might have arrived."

"I doubt they'll bring it before tomorrow morning. He has to be shrouded and coffined, remember."

John shivered. "Oh, don't remind me. Not a task I would relish."

"Come now," said Joe. "You're a medical man and used to death."

"Not like that I'm not."

"No," said Sir John Fielding's clerk, and within the confines of the coach there was sudden stricken silence.

The physick had clearly worked for there were no screams from the upper floor of the house. In fact a deathly calm hung over the place. Feeling that he was truly trespassing, John handed his card to the footman almost apologetically.

"I simply called to see if any of the ladies required medical care. I have no wish to intrude."

"Mrs. Rayner said that you might visit, Sir. She and Miss Millicent are in the drawing room. Please to step this way."

They were speaking quietly together as John went in but two snatches of conversation were distinctly audible. Millicent was saying in that intense little voice of hers, "How could she? How *could* she? And with an upstart like Mendoza. The girl deserves to be whipped."

"And so does he," answered Jocasta. "Why, if Papa had still been alive I swear he would have done it."

Millicent gave a loud sniff and it was at that moment that John walked into the room and all conversation ceased. Jocasta stood up.

"Mr. Rawlings, how very nice to see you. I thought you might come to visit us. Will you stay and dine?"

So poor Aidan's shattered body had not yet returned home.

"It would be a pleasure."

"It will only be very simple, in view of our mourning."

"I would have eaten lightly had I gone back to Nassau Street."

"You live alone?"

"Temporarily, yes. My wife is staying in Kensington with my father."

"Oh," said Jocasta.

Millicent spoke up, her eyes shining earnestly. "My dear Mama — before she was taken from us, of course — was a great believer in keeping up one's strength through regular meals. This is not a time to neglect oneself. Would you not agree, Mr. Rawlings? — you being an apothecary and all."

"I certainly do, Ma'am. I have always believed that a hearty breakfast is the only way to begin one's day."

"There, Jocasta, there," Millicent said triumphantly. "You must do more than sip tea, dear."

"Would you care for a sherry, Mr. Rawlings?" asked Jocasta, determinedly changing the subject.

"Are you ladies going to have one?"

"If you are," they chorused.

John nodded and bowed and all three sat down to have a glass of the very finest vintage, presumably imported by the late Aidan Fenchurch himself.

"Such a pleasure to have your company," said Millicent enthusiastically.

"Yes, it really is," Jocasta added, and it suddenly struck the Apothecary that there had been a great deal of sadness in this household, even without the added sorrow of the brutal murder of its head.

"So," said Sir John Fielding, guiding a cup of tea to his lips without spilling a drop, "Mrs. Bussell was defiant, was she?"

It was still only eight o'clock in the morning but already the Magistrate, John and Joe Jago were gathered round the great man's breakfast table, eating the

Apothecary's favourite meal and discussing the murder of Aidan Fenchurch at the same time.

"I believe you'll have to call her in to Bow Street, Sir John. But I don't think you'll break her, mind. She denies having anything to do with the murder and she won't be budged."

The Magistrate made an impatient sound. "That is farcical in view of the papers that the victim left behind him."

"But it could just be true," John put in.

"I wondered about his other woman," ventured Joe. "Mrs. Tre ... what was it?" He turned to the Apothecary.

"Trewellan. She who wouldn't marry him because of her ghastly son."

"It did occur to me," Sir John's clerk persisted, "that she might know something. Perhaps she and the victim had quarrelled recently. Perhaps she should be questioned."

"Yes, yes." Sir John waved a hand. "But my money is firmly on the Bussell woman. She sounds marvellously deranged to me."

"She's still in love with him. I'm sure of it," the Apothecary answered.

Joe chuckled. "Then she's sure to have had him put down. There's nothing like a woman slighted to be full to the eyes with vengeance."

"Hear, hear," said the Magistrate. "I'll send a Runner to request the pleasure of her company in the Public Office."

"She might have left London," John pointed out. "Apparently she has a place in Surrey, some ten miles or so from Aidan Fenchurch's own abode."

"Where? Do you know?"

"Mrs. Rayner said West Clandon. A house called Merrow Place."

"And where did Fenchurch live?"

"A village with the grand title of Stoke d'Abernon. He has apparently left his middle daughter that property, while the eldest inherits the London house."

"And the youngest?"

"I don't know. There's a mystery about her. She's travelling at the moment and is, apparently, still unaware of her father's death. All I can tell you about the girl is that she is called Louisa and is the most beautiful of the three according to her sister."

"Um, an odd tale. Do you think she's run away from home?" said Sir John thoughtfully.

The Apothecary considered the idea. "Probably, yes."

"Another thread," said Joe. "Had she fallen out with her father? Could it have been she who hired the killers?"

"Jago, you are impossible," answered the Magistrate, swallowing down his food rather noisily. "Just for once we are presented with a case in which the murdered man has actually written down the name of his killer. But does this satisfy you? No. You must run round after other ideas like a bloodhound with six simultaneous scents. We have our principal suspect and she is the guilty party, mark my words."

Joe stood his ground, despite his employer's formidable reputation. "None the less, Sir John, would you object if I saw this Mrs. Trewellan and asked Mr. Rawlings to find out all he can about the disappearing daughter from the other ladies of the house?"

"Of course I wouldn't object," answered the Blind Beak, somewhat angrily John thought. "If you wish to waste your time, my dear Jago, please feel at liberty to do so."

He was very truculent and, in a way, the Apothecary could see Sir John's point of view. A man stalked by an unstable woman dies most violently, the apparent motive of robbery hardly credible. Papers which, in the event of his death, the victim asks to be delivered to Bow Street, appear to suggest a case that is open and shut but, for all that, the Magistrate's clerk insists on pursuing loose ends. And yet, John thought, it was the Beak himself who had taught both him and Joe never to take anything at face value.

He spoke up. "I think I would like to discover more about Louisa, Sir. Just for my own interest."

"Of course, of course. We might be able to help her sisters find the girl in time for the funeral. Go to it, Mr. Rawlings. And Joe . . ."

"Yes, Sir?"

"I want Mrs. Bussell brought to Bow Street today. I am tired of this conjecture. Let the wretched female answer to me."

And with that the Magistrate plucked his napkin from under his chin, threw it on the table, and with his cane tapping before him left the room.

Joe turned to John. "Oh, dear. We are not in the finest of humours, are we?"

"No." He looked the clerk straight in the eye. "Joe, do you think Mrs. Bussell is responsible for Aidan Fenchurch's death?"

"Yes."

"Then why bother to look further?"

"Just because," said Joe Jago, and shook his head at his own foolishness.

CHAPTER
FIVE

It was not far to walk from Shug Lane to Bloomsbury Square and having closed the shop for the night and sent Nicholas home to dine, John decided to make his way there to pay his respects, aware that Aidan Fenchurch's body would have by now arrived home. Much as he had expected — for to attend lyings-in-state was the very height of fashion amongst the beau monde — as he approached the Square he saw that a queue had formed outside the house of the deceased, silently plodding forward to gain admittance. Aware that probably only half the people moving in this miserable parade had even known the dead man, the Apothecary joined on the end and made his way towards the house.

Signs of mourning were everywhere, all the curtains being drawn, a mute standing solitary and black at the door, sable cloth draping the walls, tallow candles lighting the hall, which John could dimly perceive as he shuffled forward. It was also clear that the house, being only of normal size, was not equipped to hold such numbers and mourners were literally waiting on the steps while one person was admitted and let out again for a second to enter. Eventually, it was the

Apothecary's turn and he removed his hat, simultaneously putting on a solemn expression.

The two sisters and their cousin, Millicent, stood at the bottom of the stairs shaking hands with the visitors and receiving their whispered condolences. Evalina, scorning any form of paint, looked terrible, her dark hair scraped back beneath a stark black cap, her port wine stain livid on her left cheek. Her jet-coloured eyes seemed to burn in their sockets as she looked at each caller malevolently, as if they had been personally responsible for the violent and early demise of her father.

John bowed before her and she literally hissed, "What are you doing here?"

"I have come to pay my respects," he answered with great dignity and passed on to Jocasta, who was standing second in line.

"Mr. Rawlings, do stay for cake and claret," she murmured. "We are serving to special visitors in the drawing room. If you would make your way there once you have seen my father."

"Certainly. Thank you."

"We cannot ask everyone, just look at the numbers." She cast her eye nervously over the crowd outside the street door.

"Mr. Fenchurch was obviously a much loved man."

She gave him a genuinely warm smile. "They have come for the sensationalism, you know it as well as I. Few here actually knew poor Papa."

John smiled crookedly. "Fashion really does take the oddest forms. Are you hurt by it?"

"I have learned to live with it," Jocasta Rayner answered very simply, and turned to the next arrival.

Aidan Fenchurch's coffin was laid out in the largest salon in the house, supported by a trestle table, yellow candles flickering at its four corners. Further tapers had been lit in sconces round the walls but the beautiful candelabra that hung from the centre of the ceiling was in darkness. The entire effect was sombre and somehow slightly sinister for the coffin, contrary to custom, was closed and draped with a stark black cloth. Aidan's injuries had obviously been considered too severe to be disguised by flowers and the lid had been ordered nailed down.

Because of the crush only two people were walking round at a time, John's companion being a hatted, cloaked female figure whom he was sure he recognised as a person of high society known to attend lyings-in-state for a hobby.

"Good evening," he ventured in an undertone.

"Good evening," she replied in a sibilant whisper, ostentatiously bowing to the coffin. Somewhat amused, John had to straighten his features as he solemnly walked past the mortal remains of Aidan Fenchurch, a man who had made the mistake of loving unwisely and paid the highest price of all.

It would seem that as well as those who had come merely out of morbid curiosity, there was also a goodly number of genuine mourners, for the drawing room was full of people partaking of the customary claret and ale, biscuits and cake. Much to John's delight and amazement, he saw that Joe Jago was present,

74

respectfully dressed and wearing a wig which sat ill upon his foxy curls. "We meet again," said the Apothecary, bowing politely.

Joe returned the salute. "Mr. Rawlings. I came representing the Public Office and Mrs. Rayner invited me to take refreshment. Sir, much has happened since I saw you this morning."

"Oh? What?"

"The Beak, who was in ugly mood as you yourself observed, despatched Runner Munn to bring in Mrs. Bussell only to find that she had already flown the nest."

"She'd left for Surrey?"

"I don't think so. Her servants seemed to think she had gone to an address unknown. However, Sir John, nothing daunted, as soon as he has ascertained her whereabouts, is going to send the two Brave Fellows with instructions to fetch her back, by force if necessary."

"Her actions are certainly those of someone guilty."

"They are indeed."

"What about Mr. Bussell? Where is he?"

"Gone with her."

"I wonder just how involved he is. Perhaps he organised poor Fenchurch's death in a frenzy of jealousy."

"But why after all this time?"

John shook his head. "It makes no sense, I agree."

"Nothing does, because the woman at the crux of the matter is totally without any. That's why."

John sipped his claret, deep in thought. Finally he said, "Do you remember my friends the de Vignolles?"

"You mean Comte Louis and his beautiful wife?"

"Yes I do."

"How could anyone forget them?" Joe said. "I shall always think of her as the most outrageous and delightful gambler in London."

"When she was the Masked Lady. Yes, those were the days."

And the Apothecary thought back to the time when he had been in love with the elegant Serafina and how, many years later, he had delivered her second child for her, a boy now three years old.

"So what of them, Sir?"

"They have a country place in Surrey, not far, I believe, from West Clandon. I'm wondering whether to beg an invitation and see what I can find out about Mrs. Bussell and her entourage."

"That, Sir," said Joe enthusiastically, "sounds like a mighty good plan. One can discover more through neighbours' gossip than ever one can through direct questioning."

He would have said more but at that moment they were joined by an elderly couple, both very sad-faced and red-eyed.

"Dear Aidan," said the woman. "I don't know what we shall do without his expert guidance on fine wines."

"A lamentable loss," agreed her husband. "Fenchurch imported the most excellent port to be had in London. Would you not say so?"

It was easier to join in than explain their real reason for being there and by mutual, silent consent John and Joe allowed the conversation to dwell on wine and its merits rather than the loss of Fenchurch and their involvement in investigating his death. However, the elderly woman did give a sigh and say, "And to think he was killed by footpads. It is hardly safe to leave one's house these days."

"Indeed, Ma'am," said Joe. "However, Sir John Fielding and his fellows are doing their best to stem the tide of violence."

"Unfortunately, a Runner is never there when you want one," answered the old chap. "Why, d'ye know, I was sitting in my own house t'other night when I heard a cry of 'Stop thief!' A highwayman, would you believe, had attacked a post-chaise in Piccadilly and it was not yet eleven o'clock at night. Anyway, chase was given, but the wretch rode over the watchman, almost killing him, and escaped."

"Did you report the matter to the Public Office?"

"No, Sir, I did not. I saw but little, having hurried to my street door rather too late."

"Insufficient to describe the robber?"

"Alas, yes. Where will it all end?"

"On the gallows," said Joe determinedly. "Such audacity as to rob in the very heart of town will bring him down eventually."

The conversation was reaching the end of its course and John was just wondering how they could move away without causing offence when a sudden hush fell over the room. The two sisters and Cousin Millicent had finally come in. It would appear that the great queue of mourners had at last departed and only those who had been invited to stay on remained.

Millicent held up her hand for silence. "Ladies and gentlemen, as the governess of the girls as well as their cousin, they have asked me to thank you all for coming to pay respects to poor dear Aidan. We have a gift of mourning gloves which we hope you will accept. Of course nothing can fit everybody — that is, we are all different in hand sizes are we not, if you follow my meaning. But for those of you who are exceptionally big or small — I refer to your hands, of course, not your build . . ." She giggled nervously, ". . . we shall order special pairs to be made. After all, Shakespeare's father was a glover, was he not," she added completely inconsequentially. Somebody laughed, which seemed to make Millicent more anxious than ever. "Now, more claret and cake will be served, except for those who are drinking ale and eating biscuits, that is. Oh dear me, I do hope I have made myself clear."

"Very," said Joe Jago, and bowed deeply. "A good speech, Madam."

Millicent went scarlet, then white, and sat down hurriedly in a corner. Meanwhile, Mrs. Rayner and Miss Fenchurch began to move round amongst their guests.

"I am so glad you came, Mr. Rawlings," said Jocasta, arriving before him. She turned her eyes on Joe Jago. "How do you do, Sir."

He kissed her hand very gallantly. "Jago, Madam. I am here representing Sir John Fielding."

78

She grew very pale. "Of course, I keep forgetting. The Public Office believes that killers were hired to do my poor father to death."

"There is much that would indicate so," Joe answered, adding swiftly, "Of course, we have no evidence as to who could be behind such a terrible act."

"It could only be a business rival," Jocasta stated firmly.

"Dare I ask," John said quietly, "if Mr. Fenchurch's affections were ever engaged elsewhere after your mother's death?"

She gave him a level look. "He courted a Mrs. Trewellan for a while, but she turned him down I believe. Papa and her son did not see eye to eye."

"And that was all? There were no further alliances?"

Jocasta looked suddenly fraught. "Why do you ask? Do you believe a woman could be behind this terrible business?"

"It is possible," John answered diffidently.

"But who? Unless . . ."

"Unless what?"

"I know I shouldn't gossip," she said, taking a glass of claret from a passing tray, "but I always thought that that obnoxious Mrs. Bussell gave Father the eye."

"Really?" said John, noticing that Joe had most discreetly removed himself so that she and the Apothecary could be absolutely private.

"Yes, but you wouldn't know her, of course. She became a friend of the family shortly after my mother died and was always hurling herself at him, like a great marmalade cannonball."

The description was so accurate that John's crooked grin appeared briefly, then vanished. For this was the moment of decision. The most intelligent and well-disposed member of the family was telling him her observations. To dissemble with her would be a disservice indeed.

"Mrs. Rayner, do you remember me telling you that your father came into my shop in Shug Lane and told me he thought me an honest citizen?"

"Of course I do."

"On that occasion he was being pursued by Mrs. Bussell and actually asked me to conceal his presence. I did so, hiding him in my compounding room at the back. Please don't be shocked because a man is only a man when all is said and done . . ."

Why, he thought, had she suddenly gone rigid? What was it that made her momentarily appear elsewhere?

Jocasta collected herself. "Go on."

"He admitted to me that he had briefly had an affair with her, when he was lonely and bereft, missing your mother desperately. He also told me that he ended the relationship, when Mrs. Trewellan came on the scene. It was then that Mrs. Bussell took to following him about, full of hatred and spite, making his life a misery."

John hesitated, not wanting to make further trouble, but Jocasta was there before him. "Do you mean that she could be responsible . . . ?"

He shook his head. "I don't know. Nobody does. But it is a path of enquiry that Sir John Fielding is most anxious to pursue."

"What is John Fielding pursuing?" asked Millicent in her odd little voice, having left her corner and silently joined them.

"Nothing, dearest."

"Did I hear Mrs. Bussell's name? Such a jolly woman, is she not? Always laughing and joking and so very clever with her brushes. Of course, I paint a little but nothing in her field of endeavour."

John looked round the room. "She is not here I see."

"Oh you know her!" said Millicent, clapping her hands. "Is she not a wit?"

The agony of answering such a question was spared for it was at this moment that Evalina, having no doubt decided that people were relaxing too much, let out a spectacular howl and swooned, knocking a tray of wine from a passing servant's hand. There was general uproar as glasses shattered, showering to the floor in tinkling pieces, and a deaf old gentleman yelped as his hand was cut and gouted blood. John and Joe exchanged a glance, then acted as professionally as they possibly could. The clerk administered salts and attempted to heave the fainting woman into a chair, no mean feat, while the Apothecary bound the old man's wound with his handkerchief.

Millicent and Jocasta appeared, looking anxious.

"Oh Evalina," her sister said impatiently. "How I wish that you would get a grip on yourself. Do the words respect for our visitors mean nothing to you?"

"There, there, Evie," fluttered the cousin, patting Evalina's large white hands. "Come on, dear. It's the strain, you know," she said to the group who had gathered round, staring at the prostrate form with a certain degree of malicious enjoyment. "She's taken her father's death very hard, haven't you, pet?"

"We all have," snapped Jocasta.

"Unfeeling, unfeeling," moaned Evalina, then rolled her eyes up once more.

"I wouldn't advise taking her to bed," said the Apothecary very loudly. He turned to a hovering footman. "Could you get me some ice and water in a pail. That should do the trick."

One of Evalina's lids twitched slightly.

"Yes, in severe cases of the swoon my old master always held the patient's head in a bucket of freezing water. Failing that, he threw it over them. Rough treatment admittedly, but most effective."

"Drag her to one side of the room. I do not want the Turkey rug ruined," said Jocasta, clearly delighted by the whole idea.

Evalina groaned and sat up, clutching her brow. "Oh the heat, it is too much for a body to bear."

"Why not take a turn in the garden?" suggested Millicent kindly. "I'll go with you."

"Yes," said Evalina, clambering to her feet and leaning heavily on her cousin, who buckled under the strain. "I must have air."

The guests politely drew apart to make way for her and she was in the process of performing an extremely elaborate and wildly theatrical exit when from downstairs came a scream that far outshone anything Evalina could do. Indeed this scream held a note of genuine terror and despair and was so heart-rending that even the murmured conversation was hushed. Running feet could be heard on the stairs and then the door to the drawing room was flung open. A small girl with a mop of tossing red hair topped by a cheeky hat, stood in the entrance. Her terrified gaze swept round the company and finally came to rest on Jocasta.

"The coffin," she said breathlessly. "Whose is it?"

"Father's," Mrs. Rayner answered briefly.

"Oh no, oh no," the little thing gasped and reeled back into the arms of a dashing young soldier, all red coat and jet black curls and not a white wig in sight, who was coming into the room behind her.

Everybody stared and there was a moment of even more intense quiet, then Jocasta spoke once more. "Lieutenant Mendoza, I presume," she said icily.

"At your service, Ma'am," the young man responded, and clicked his heels and bowed with aplomb despite the fact that he was the only thing preventing a fainting girl from falling to the floor.

Everything considered, it had been a most interesting night, John thought as he finally entered the quiet of his own home and with a sigh of relief went into the library to sit down. To see the hysterical Evalina behaving just as badly when she was up and about as when she was bed-ridden had been quite a revelation, but to meet the missing Louisa in such circumstances had been even more fascinating. Though nobody had uttered a single word of explanation, it seemed apparent that the girl had either eloped with the dashing Lieutenant Mendoza or had been on the point of doing so.

83

Whatever, there was yet another skeleton in the Fenchurch family cupboard that needed investigating.

And where, the Apothecary wondered, were the biggest skeletons of all: the Bussells, husband and wife? If they had not gone to their Surrey retreat, they were clearly hiding out somewhere else. But why? Was their absence a coincidence or had they deliberately left London to avoid Ariadne being questioned by Sir John Fielding? This brought him back to the question that puzzled him most of all. Did Montague Bussell know that his wife had indulged in an adulterous affair with the late Aidan Fenchurch? And, if so, was he aware of her subsequent obsessive shadowing of the dead man? Could it even be that Montague loved that most unlovable of creatures and was gamely trying to protect her from the processes of the law?

"Strange," said John aloud, and picked up the newspaper. But his mind was roving, refusing to concentrate on the printed words before him. He closed his eyes, thinking that he might doze before supper, for it was too late to dine, so much time having been spent attending to the fainting women of the Fenchurch household. Millicent had been very competent throughout, he thought. She had removed Evalina, who had started to berate Louisa, shouting the word 'slyboots' over and over again, before she could scandalise the few remaining guests, hovering in the hope of hearing further gossip. Then she had returned and in her funny little way organised those family members who were not weeping or yelling into having a meal. They all owed her a lot, John considered. And he wondered whether she had secretly loved Aidan; a tradition for poor plain female relatives taken into the household out of pity, particularly if the head of the family were a man of powerful personality.

Considering deeply as he was, the Apothecary was abruptly dragged back to reality by the sound of Irish Tom's voice in the hall.

"I know he's reading but I've a letter from Mrs. Rawlings that he will want to see."

The Apothecary got up and put his head round the library door. "I certainly will. Can you bring it in, Tom?"

"At once, Sir."

"And how is she?"

"Round as a rosebud and just as blooming."

"What a nice description."

"But she won't be coming home for a few days yet. Mrs. Alleyn has arrived and begs a while yet in the country before they both return to London for the birth."

"Oh dear, I hope she doesn't leave it too long. I was planning on going to Surrey and taking Emilia with me."

The coachman frowned. "I don't know about all this travelling, Sir. I think when Mrs. Rawlings gets home she ought to stay put until that child arrives."

This was utterly beyond the bounds of polite conversation between employer and servant but the hulking Irish coachman, who had been given to John as part of his wedding present and who had shared several adventures with him, meant far more than an ordinary hired hand and was therefore accorded all the privileges of someone deeply trusted.

The Apothecary nodded. "You're right, of course."

"I take it the visit out of town might be connected with the Public Office."

"You take it correctly."

"Then why not go now, Sir? Before Mrs. Rawlings returns. In that way everybody will be satisfied and no harm done."

John stroked his chin, an old habit when thinking. "You're right as usual. There's only one snag. I want to visit the Comte and Comtesse de Vignolles while I'm in Surrey but I'm completely unsure of their present whereabouts. I mean are they in town or country?"

"Should I go round to Hanover Square and make enquiries? I fancy a night in London to be honest with you and would like a good excuse."

The Apothecary looked at the clock. "It is getting rather late but let me pen a swift note to the Comtesse which you can deliver if she is home. If not, I will write to her tomorrow, then follow up with a visit."

"We mustn't be away too long though, Sir. I reckon Mrs. Rawlings will be heading back very shortly now. I feel in my bones that that baby is anxious to enter the world."

He left the room and John crossed to the writing desk, then paused a moment before he picked up his pen. Irish Tom's words echoed in his head and he felt a sudden and exhilarating surge of excitement. His son or daughter was anxious to come into life, to know him and his friends, to be part of their circle and communicate with them as soon as he or she could. Swift tears came and he wept silently at the immense thought of the person, so very nearly born, who was coming to be part of all their futures and to take part in the great adventure that they were currently living.

CHAPTER
SIX

Nestling most improbably in the green Surrey countryside was a truly delightful Italian villa, Palladian in design, and which, though not large or pretentious, possessed its own small park, a lake like gleaming glass, formal gardens and meadowland, and an imposing, though short, drive. Fashionable to a degree, it could only belong to his friends the de Vignolles, John thought, as Irish Tom clipped stylishly through the gates and made his way to the half-moon carriage sweep which lay directly below the two flights of steps leading to the front door. The Apothecary put his head out of the window to get a better look at the pretty little palace before he disembarked.

Though he had known the de Vignolles for many years, indeed since that time when he had stumbled across a body lying in the Dark Walk at Vaux Hall Pleasure Gardens, when he had also first met the Blind Beak — an unforgettable experience — their country home, Scottlea Park, was utterly new to John. But then, he considered, it had only been completed less than ten months ago and despite several invitations to inspect the new premises, the dates had not been convenient for him. But now he was here, uninvited, hoping that they would ask him to stay, hoping that from this base he could find out not only more about Mrs. Bussell but possibly the scandal surrounding Louisa and Lieutenant Mendoza. Joe, meanwhile, or so he had told John before they had parted company on the previous evening, was off to call on Mrs. Trewellan, who lived at a rather less fashionable address than her late suitor, namely in Liquorpond Street, Holborn, not so smart yet only a short walk from Bloomsbury Square down Theobalds Row and The Kings Way.

Irish Tom had returned from his visit to Hanover Square with the news that the Comte and Comtesse had left London for their country seat, and the Apothecary had made up his mind there and then that he must call on them on the following day, before Emilia came back to await the birth of her child. So early the next morning, after he had seen Nicholas leave to open the shop, he had written to Emilia telling her of his plan and asking her to join him at Nassau Street in four days time. Then he had set off, bag packed, hoping that he would be invited to stay in Surrey.

But there could be no doubt about that. The front door was flung open even as he was getting out of the coach and two small children, followed by their mother, came rushing down the steps to greet him.

"John," said Serafina, "what a wonderful surprise. Have you come for several days? I do hope so."

The Apothecary shot Irish Tom a brief grin. "Bring my bag into the house, would you?"

"Yes, Sorrh," the coachman answered, leaping down from the box.

Italia, Serafina's daughter, stretched up to her full height and pulled the Apothecary down to her level so that she could kiss him on the cheek, but the boy suddenly lost courage and hung back, clutching his mother's hand, younger and shyer than his sister.

John bent down to him. "Well, little fellow, do I get a kiss as well?"

He was very solemn but very endearing, approaching cautiously, giving the Apothecary the cool dry kiss of childhood. Over the boy's head, Serafina looked at John and smiled.

She was as stunning as ever, he thought, her tall, fine figure unaffected by childbearing, her unusual looks enhanced by maturity. Her hair swept up in the latest fashion still kept its rich hue, as yet unaffected by grey. But it was her mouth he had always adored, with its curving lips and slow spectacular smile. When she had been the Masked Lady, the most spoken-of gambler in town, hiding her features behind her customary covering, it had been her mouth he had fallen in love with. That and her husky voice. Now, when she spoke, he remembered those times with fondness, recalling the warmth that he had felt whenever he had been in her presence.

"John, my dear, this is such an unexpected pleasure. But where is Emilia? Surely you haven't left her at a time like this."

"She is in Kensington with my father and her mother. She will be back in four days time and after that I shall not leave her side until the baby is born. So now I am here for a few days holiday, if that is convenient to you."

She looked at him suspiciously. "You are sure there is no business involved? No little errand that you are running for Sir John Fielding?"

He smiled crookedly. "Well, there might be."

"I thought as much. Now, my dear, come in. Louis is out riding but will be back to dine. So when you have refreshed yourself we shall walk in the grounds a little. I know the children will want to show you their own small garden. Your godson, Jacques, is particularly keen on planting things and caring for them."

"Jacques? Is that what you call him?"

Serafina laughed and slipped her arm through the Apothecary's, pressing close to his side and making him feel immensely comfortable and at home.

"As you delivered the child into the world, we named him John, after you. But what with that and Sir John into the bargain, it all grew too confusing. So we called him Jack, which Louis insisted became Jacques. So there's the story of your godson's name."

The little boy, who still held his mother's hand while Italia, John's other godchild, ran on ahead, looked up and spoke to Serafina in French.

"We have taught them both languages," she said, smiling again. "Thank God that terrible war that has had the whole of Europe in uproar for the last seven years is over. So now travelling abroad will resume once more. Then to speak more than one language will be useful."

"It is always useful," John answered. "But I agree with you. I think visiting the Continent will become the height of fashion. I shall certainly go. I feel quite starved of travel."

The Comtesse's mouth curved up. "But you will be a family man, John. How will you manage? Will you take them all?"

He frowned. "Perhaps. I don't know. I must confess that I hadn't really thought about that."

"How typical of a man. Well, you'll have to start thinking, John. There are going to be three of you from now on."

"Actually, I look forward to it. Rawlings and Son, Apothecaries."

"And what if it is a girl?"

"There are no women apothecaries in England but that doesn't prevent me teaching her all I know."

"If she wants to learn, that is."

"Of course."

Serafina laughed. "Don't look so serious, John. Whether she is scholarly or whether she is a little gadfly, she will still be delightful."

"Provided she isn't a boy."

"Oh stop it," she said, and nudged him in the ribs.

They walked round the lake, chattering and laughing, recalling old times and fond memories, the children running ahead of them. Eventually, though, the two adults sat down on a stone seat beneath a willow while the young people fed the swans with pieces of bread which they had brought with them especially.

"Well, my dear," said Serafina, her beautiful mouth smiling, "why are you really here?"

He answered with another question. "You are only a few miles away from West Clandon. Do you know anyone who lives there?"

"Of course. It's no distance from us."

"And the people of Stoke d'Abernon village? Are you familiar with any of them?"

Serafina narrowed her eyes. "This, I take it, is connected to the little errand for Sir John Fielding?"

"You take correctly. The people I am interested in are the Bussells of Merrow Place and the Fenchurchs of Foxfire Hall, Stoke d'Abernon."

The Comtesse pursed her lips. "Strangely, the name Fenchurch is familiar. Did I not read in the newspaper that a merchant of that name had been done to death by footpads?"

"You did."

Serafina was a jump ahead. "But the Public Office believe that there is more to it than that. That is why you are here."

"Utterly correct. There is evidence pointing to the fact that Fenchurch was killed by hired assassins. And there is other evidence linking Mrs. Bussell with the whole thing."

And then because he knew her so well and trusted completely both her integrity and ability to keep her own counsel, John told the Comtesse everything, even to the dramatic reappearance of Louisa and Lieutenant Mendoza at the lying-in-state of her father.

"So the poor girl didn't even know who was in the coffin?"

"No."

"And had she eloped with the Lieutenant?"

"I rather imagine so but didn't have time to ascertain. There were bodies everywhere." John grinned naughtily. "That remark sounds in very poor taste but truly there were fainting females as well as the deceased."

Serafina laughed, then frowned. "I've certainly heard of the Bussells. In fact I believe I was asked to dine by friends in West Clandon — the Onslows who live in Clandon House — and she was present. Is her name Ariadne and does she come from Bath?"

"Yes to both. What did you make of her?"

"I felt she wore two faces. One all smiles and laughs and another, much more ominous, lurking beneath. She's not the type that I could make a friend of, or would want to for that matter."

"I think she's highly dangerous."

"Did she murder her lover?"

"Yes, I think so. But the point is that she has left town and appears to have gone into hiding. Sir John is mustard sharp to interview her personally. I think he is hoping to break her story down and get a confession."

"And will he?"

John slowly shook his head. "I don't believe so. For all her silly accent and big grins, she's as tough as an old hunting saddle."

"Then she'll get away with it?"

"More than likely. If it cannot be proved that the killers were hired men and, if they were, who hired them, then there is no case to answer."

"I see. Well, my dear, we shall visit West Clandon tomorrow morning and take a good look round. We shall go in my carriage."

"Do you mind taking me there?"

"On the contrary, I shall positively enjoy it," said Serafina with relish.

The evening was pleasant, passed in the company of two such dear friends as Comte Louis and his wife; though over dinner, the host made an alteration to the earlier plan.

"I love to ride when I am out of town so shall you and I go to West Clandon on horseback, John? Serafina can follow in the coach."

"Serafina can do no such thing. I'll ride with you," his wife replied.

This decided, they set off after an early breakfast, through the glades of Surrey that reached in an unbroken vista to the weald. To the east, in sweeps of woodland and copse, lay the downs and the villages of West and East Clandon, the de Vignolles' residence being some five miles away. From the time of the Domesday survey, Clandon had always been two villages, the name coming from Clenedune, meaning clear of scrub. Thus, East Clandon had been Clenedune and West, Altera Clenedune. However, in the thirteenth century the names had changed to Clandon Abbatis for East and Clandon Regis for West, one being under the patronage of the church and the other under the patronage of the crown. Now, the two villages were simply West and East.

As they climbed a small hill, Serafina pointed. "There, that's Clandon House, where our friends the Onslows live."

"And Merrow Place?"

"I presume it must be that other large house on the far side of the village." Serafina shaded her eyes with her hand. "There's someone at home. Look, there's smoke rising from the chimneys."

"Yes," said John, and sat very still for a moment, his horse not moving either, echoing his mood. Something, his instinct for trouble perhaps, told him that he was about to discover an important fact.

"What is it?" asked Louis, sensing his friend's change of mood.

"I have the uncanny feeling that she's there. Mrs. Bussell I mean. Lying low. Not letting herself be seen."

"Will you arrest her?"

"Certainly not. I will simply report back to Sir John Fielding and let him take action."

"But how are you going to find out?" Serafina said. Both men silently turned to look at her. "Oh no," she added.

"Oh yes," Louis replied. "Call and invite her to dine."

"She won't fall into that trap. From what John says, she's cunning as a vixen."

"But if you gain entry to the house there might be some giveaway sign. A pair of gloves tossed carelessly aside, an opened letter on a tray."

His wife let out peals of laughter. "You should write novels, my dear. Your imagination is running riot."

Louis looked as severe as only a Frenchman can. "That's as may be. Now, will you call or won't you?"

"Very well. But what will you and John do in the meantime?"

"We shall repair to the tavern."

"At this hour of the day?"

"Yes," said Louis grandly. "At this hour of the day indeed."

They trotted through the village, scaring the hens from the track, reining in outside the tavern, The Onslow Arms, where a gaffer sat on a stool, smoking a long pipe.

"Is that Merrow Place?" asked John, pointing to the distant gates.

"Aye, that's the one. Nobody there, though."

"Oh? How do you know?"

"My daughter cleans up there. Only the servants in residence."

"There are a lot of fires burning," Louis commented dryly.

"Perhaps they like to keep warm," answered the gaffer and wheezed with laughter, slapping his thigh and shaking his head.

"Let me buy you some refreshment," offered John, a great believer in using local information.

The gaffer tugged his forelock and laughed again.

"This, my darling," Louis said to Serafina, "is where you brave it out."

She pulled the skirt of her riding habit out of the mud of the track, still churned up by the April showers, and adjusted her hat to an incisive angle. "Wish me luck."

"If she is there you will nose her out," the Comte replied, and gallantly raising one of her hands to his lips, kissed it, then watched as she sped off, her back straight and strong, towards the gates of Merrow Place.

The gaffer turned out to be a wagonload of information. His daughter who cleaned at the big house knew much of the way of the rich folk, as he quaintly called them. Apparently, Montague and Ariadne did not share sleeping quarters, a fact which made John raise an eyebrow at Louis, who spoiled everything by laughing. But the truly interesting piece of news was that the couple had two sons, Justin and Greville, who frequently came to Surrey and lorded it round the place.

"And how old might they be?" asked the Apothecary, refilling the old man's ale pot.

He scratched his head, a thick red thatch with very little grey in it. "Don't know exactly. Both in their twenties would be my guess. They say that they have a contest between the pair of them as to how many village girls they can get into bed."

"At the same time, do you mean?"

The gaffer wheezed another huge laugh. "Might be, for all I know. But I think they mean a list each. If you follow my meaning."

"And do these boys resemble their parents?"

"No, big as blacksmiths, the pair of 'em. Tis said their mother came from humble stock, from some place close by Bath, and that her father was a smith. So they've probably got their grandpa's looks, hulking great brutes."

"How very interesting. Do they spend much time here?"

"A fair bit. But they've got some other dwelling in London town where they gamble and womanise and live like the sons of a gentleman."

"They sound dreadful."

"I'll say this for 'em," said the gaffer, "if they get a local girl in trouble they pay up and no questions asked."

"I suppose that's a point in their favour," Louis remarked dryly.

"It certainly is, Sir. There's a lot that don't, you know."

The Comte, who had had quite a racy past before he settled down and made a success of his marriage, sighed. Perhaps at old memories, John thought.

"So where are the lads at the moment? Are they in residence?"

"Not they. I told you, there's nobody there."

The Apothecary stared closely, trying to decide whether the old man was lying. "Well, when are the Bussells expected back? Surely your daughter must have some idea."

The gaffer gave them a very crafty look. "She only cleans up there. She's not the housekeeper."

He was either much cleverer than he seemed, or else telling the simple truth, but it was hard to know which. John decided on one last attempt.

"You've been very helpful," he said, producing a handful of shillings. "But I am anxious to make contact with Mrs. Bussell so could you send word to me if she returns? I shall be at Scottlea Park for the next few days." He held a guinea between thumb and forefinger. "I'll offer this to the first person who brings me news of her."

The gaffer bent his head over his ale pot so that his expression was hidden. "Why so anxious, Sir?" he asked between swallows.

"I have some business to discuss. London affairs," the Apothecary answered smoothly.

Louis came in. "If my friend has returned to town I shall be sure to pass any message on."

The gaffer squinted meaningfully. "But it may be before he goes," he said, then finished his ale, held the pot out for a refill and refused to say any more.

Serafina joined them thirty minutes later, sweeping into the tavern on her own, turning every head in the place.

"Well?" said Louis.

She indicated the gaffer by the merest inclination of her head. "My darling, I must return home. The children will be missing me." Then, when nobody but her husband and John were looking, she slowly winked one eye. Sensing something positive, the Apothecary grinned.

Once outside, though, Serafina said nothing. She allowed Louis to lift her into the saddle and immediately set off at a pace, not turning her head to look at the two men who cantered along behind.

"She knows something," shouted John with elation.

The Comte grinned Gallicly. "She most certainly does. Come on, let's overtake her."

But try as they would, Serafina, accomplished horsewoman that she clearly was, led them all the way and finally clattered into the stable yard ahead, lowering herself into the arms of the hostler, then hurrying into the house. By the time they had dismounted, she was nowhere to be seen.

They found her in the drawing room, dressed in her riding clothes, her hat now at an extremely jaunty angle indeed. She raised a glass of champagne in their direction.

"You saw her," said Louis, pouring a glass for John and then one for himself.

She smiled mischievously. "Not exactly, no."

"*Mon Dieu*, don't torture us. Wife, I beg you. What happened?"

Serafina drained her glass and sat down. "Well, I did not bother with the stables but went straight to the door, securing my horse to a pillar the meanwhile. This so disconcerted the servant who answered that I believe he took me for someone either mad or tipsy."

"Which you are, frequently — both."

The Comtesse ignored this and continued. "I presented my card, he ushered me into the hall. I said I had come to visit the lady of the house with an invitation to dine. He told me she was not at home. Then . . ."

"Yes?" said John.

"I heard the faintest scuffling, as if someone were still ascending the stairs, above my head, out of sight. And then . . ."

Louis thrust his head into his hands. "For heaven's sake, Serafina. I shall have a seizure in a minute."

"I smelt it."

"What?"

"Her perfume. It came wafting down the stairwell on a cloud. There was no mistaking it. It is made by Charles Lillie and is sold to ladies of *bon ton*."

"Well, he made a mistake with her then," said John, and laughed uproariously at his own joke.

Serafina tutted disapproval. "Really, Mr. Rawlings, how could you interrupt thus?"

"I beg your pardon. Pray continue."

"It is the sort of perfume that could not possibly be worn by a servant, however highly placed. No, she's there all right, hiding out on the upper floors."

"Well, well," said John. "I thought as much. I shall write to Sir John this very afternoon and Irish Tom can take the letter immediately to Bow Street. Then before the journey back he can call at Nassau Street and bring with him any messages."

"But what about Emilia? How will she get home from Kensington if Tom is here?"

"As soon as I return I shall send him to fetch her. I don't want her to delay a moment longer."

Louis looked thoughtful. "I wonder if the old gaffer knows that Mrs. Bussell is in hiding."

"I'm sure he does. He'll probably be round for his guinea before nightfall."

"Crafty old devil."

"Enough of him," said Serafina. "What about me? Have I helped your enquiries Mr. Rawlings?"

"You will have assisted in bringing a villainess to justice. At least I hope that you will."

"What do you mean by that?" asked Serafina.

"That even if Sir John Fielding frightens her to the best of his mighty ability, we have yet to see whether she will crack under the strain."

"And if she doesn't?" asked Louis.

"If she doesn't, then she will get away with murder."

CHAPTER
SEVEN

Much as they had expected, just as the April evening fell, soft as a woman's glove and full of the heady scent of flowers, the gaffer plodded up the drive in a dilapidated cart pulled by an old but serviceable horse. The three friends, who were sitting on the terrace, drinking in the gentle twilight, not saying a great deal but comfortable in one another's company, exchanged cynical glances.

"I thought as much," Louis remarked, watching the old fellow draw to a halt and make his way to the back of the house.

"He's tempted by the guinea but I don't think he'll tell us everything," John answered. "He'll want to keep in with the rich folk when all's said and done."

And he was right. The gaffer, who refused to enter the main part of the house because of his boots, said nothing about Mrs. Bussell but did offer the information that Justin and Grenville had arrived from town that very evening.

"They're bucks of the first head, they two. They're in the tavern now, sinking bumpers and playing bumble-puppy."

Serafina looked thoughtful. "I've a mind to invite them here for cards. Tomorrow night perhaps. What do you think, my dears?" She turned to the two men.

"Excellent plan," said John. "I imagine they're the sort who'll get drunk and grow loose-mouthed."

"As long as they behave themselves and don't vomit," answered Louis, "I have no objection."

The gaffer looked hopeful. "Have I told you enough, Sir?"

"No," said John, "you haven't. I think the Bussells are in residence and that their sons have come to join them for a few days. I also think that you are a prime example of one who runs with the hare and hunts with the hounds. What's your name?"

"Rob, Sir."

"Well, Rob, here's your guinea. You haven't earned it, mind. But you might be of use to me in the future so I am going to give it to you out of the goodness of my heart. Now, keep your eyes open."

"I will, Sir. You can rely on me. Watchful, that's what I am." And after a great deal of forelock-tugging, he was gone.

They returned to the terrace and watched the moon rise.

"Tom will be back in London by now," said Serafina, rather sleepily.

"Yes, and drink all night with his Irish cronies but still be back here by noon. That man has the constitution of a dray horse."

"I wonder if he'll have word of Emilia."

"I wonder," John answered, and suddenly felt an urgent need to see his wife and tell her that all was well with him and that he would not leave her side again until the baby had been born.

He didn't know whether he was reassured or not when the coachman returned with a letter from her. Rather anxiously, John broke the seal.

My Dear and Loving Husband,

Hoping that you are in Good Health as I Am at the Writing Thereof. Despite This, I am now so Heavy that Walking is Hugely Difficult for I do Believe That the Babe has Started to Move Downwards.

For This Reason, and Also For the Reason that I Miss Your Company, I and My Good Mother shall Proceed to Nassau Street Within the next Two Days, There to Remain until I have Travailed.

Your Loving and Affectionate Wife,

Emilia Rawlings

There was also another letter, a letter which brought the Apothecary to his feet, calling out for Tom, who was taking his ease in the servants' quarters. It was from Jocasta Rayner, informing John that her late father was to be buried not in London but at Stoke d'Abernon church, by mutual decision of the family. Gazing at the date of the funeral, John realised that it was that very day at two in the afternoon. Obviously the letter had arrived on the morning he had left London.

Hearing his master call, the coachman came running into the hall. "What is it, Sorrh?"

"Tom, borrow some of the Comte de Vignolles's horses. We're off to a funeral."

"And whose would that be?"

"Aidan Fenchurch, the man who was killed outside his own house in Bloomsbury Square. Which reminds me, what did they say to my letter in Bow Street?"

"I took it to that old fox Jago. He told me to tell you that the two Brave Fellows would be setting off this morning to bring the woman concerned in for questioning."

"God's teeth, they may well be here by now."

Tom shook his shaggy Irish head. "I doubt it, Mr. Rawlings. If there is one thing I pride myself on it's my speed. Flying Runners they might be, but they will never outpace me."

John nodded. "You're probably right. Now, do you feel up to turning out again?"

"Oh yes indeed, Sir. I like it when we go to funerals. There is usually a good alehouse close to the church and besides the happenings are so exciting. There's nearly always someone vomiting or fainting."

John yelped a laugh. "Well, if that's your idea of fun. Anyway, Miss Evalina is bound to do a really good swoon today. She's probably been practising at home."

It was the coachman's turn to grin. "Why is it, Mr. Rawlings, that the burials you go to are attended by such a rum bunch of coves?"

"Usually because there's a murderer amongst 'em," the Apothecary answered succinctly, and went to change into the darkest clothes he had brought with him.

Stoke d'Abernon, which despite its grand name proved to be little more than a hamlet, lay some ten miles or so north of West Clandon, yet despite its proximity was difficult to get at for want of a road. Therefore, having taken directions from the de Vignolles's coachman, Irish Tom followed the course of the River Wey, which meandered serpentine through verdant pastureland, then eventually turned away from the stream and on to a well-beaten track. In the distance John could see the spire of the church, from which a solemn bell was already tolling, filling the countryside with a gloomy reminder of man's mortality.

"Oh, I think this is going to be a fine one," Tom called from the coachman's box.

"Why do you say that?"

"I feel it in my bones, Sir."

"I wonder why they decided to bury him in the country. It must have been a terrible effort to bring the body all the way."

"Perhaps he came down by water, Sir. It would be much easier."

"Yes, I suppose it would. What a depressing thought."

"What?"

"That a river journey which should be so pleasant and sparkling, particularly in this green month, should actually be the one he never sees at all."

108

At that moment John had a vision of Aidan Fenchurch's anxious crab-like eyes and felt genuinely angry about the way in which he had met his end.

"Let's hope the Brave Fellows find Mrs. Bussell and take her to Bow Street without too much difficulty," he called up to Tom.

But even as he said the words the Apothecary knew that there was no hope of that happening. That Ariadne would start by being flirtatious and end by kicking and screaming as they hauled her away to London.

"Wretched woman," he muttered as they rounded the corner and drew up outside the church. Then he froze in horror, his jaw arrested in mid air, his brain questioning what his eyes were actually seeing. For standing at the end of the church path, clad from head to toe in deepest black and leaning on a small, water-rat kind of man for support, was the woman he had just been thinking about. Ariadne Bussell had come out of hiding and was about to attend the burial of the lover whom she had most likely ordered to be killed.

"Drive round the front, Tom," John whispered loudly, and crouched down on the coach floor as the equipage swept round and out of sight. "That was her," he continued, straightening up and adjusting his hat.

"Who? The Bussell woman?"

"The very same. You were right. This is going to be an extremely interesting occasion."

The main door was at the other side of the church and already some mourners had gathered there to await the arrival of the dead. Disembarking, John joined them, glad that Mrs. Bussell had decided to stay at the back of the building, presumably to avoid contact with the family for as long as possible. Or had she, wondered John, become nervous of leaving her hiding place, and was presently trying to remain away from prying eyes?

The crowd of mourners must be locals, the Apothecary thought, looking them over and not recognising a single face. He bowed to everyone in turn, putting on his good-citizen-in-sorrow expression. Many bowed back and one woman greeted him as if she knew him.

"So good to see you again, Sir. But what a sad occasion."

Long experience had taught him never to correct such a misapprehension and John smiled, then lengthened his features even more. "Terrible, Madam, terrible. My heart is with the family."

"And mine, and mine. I pity poor Jocasta. First husband, now father, and all within an eighteen month."

"I was in Scotland when . . ." John clutched wildly at his memory and plucked the name out of thin air. ". . . Horatio died. It was an accident with mushrooms I believe. Did it happen down here or in London?"

"Down here. Why, he is buried in the churchyard yonder." A skinny arm gesticulated. "Poor soul. What a painful end. Dear Dr. Best could do nothing."

"Humph," grunted a figure standing beside her. "Horatio Rayner was a philandering goat and deserved everything he got."

"Henry!" remonstrated the woman, clearly shocked. "How could you speak ill of the dead so?"

"Easily," responded the man, who spoke so familiarly that he must be her husband. "It's the truth, ain't it? He was up the skirts of all the village girls and many more beside."

John stood agog, amazed by this latest piece of information. It had never occurred to him that a striking woman like Jocasta could have been betrayed by an older husband. The next question came automatically.

"Horatio was considerably older than his wife, was he not?"

"Yes, some twenty years I believe."

"He was still a stinking whoremonger," her husband repeated doggedly.

"You must tell me . . ."

But he was silenced by the sight of black coaches drawn by horses with tosing black plumes arriving at the church gate. A country parson, red-cheeked and with matching nose, stepped forward to greet Evalina, who came crashing out of the first carriage, Cousin Millicent hovering like a small dark moth beside her. Jocasta Rayner was the third to descend, looking terribly thin but somehow gauntly attractive in her mourning clothes. From the next coach stepped the errant Louisa accompanied by Lieutenant Mendoza, redcoated but with a black armband. The third carriage disgorged elderly people; a brother, cousins perhaps? But it was the fourth coach, following closely those of the family but not quite with them, that caught the Apothecary's attention. Momentarily he thought that Mrs. Bussell was stepping out and wondered how she could manage to be in two places at once. But then he saw that it was a woman very similar to her in appearance, yet not quite so crass in manner. Preceded by a young man of about twenty, his face positively seething with yellow-encrusted pimples, who offered a hand to help her out, came what could only be Mrs. Trewellan. Large and really rather stupid looking, her expression bland, her black clothes floating about her so that she resembled a dark feather bed, she was very like the woman whom she had succeeded in the affections of the late Aidan Fenchurch. That is except for her eyes, which were a colourless blue, like the ocean in dull weather. The Apothecary spared a moment to debate the question that lovers repeatedly go for the same type, then thought of Coralie Clive, his former mistress; Elizabeth di Lorenzi, who had never been his mistress at all; and the angelic Emilia Alleyn, whom he had married. It was not true at all, he decided.

In Aidan's case, though, the similarity between the two women he had loved spoke for itself. It was going to be a clash of heaving breasts, John thought, when the pair of them faced each other over the coffin. But Mrs. Trewellan, the spotty man — presumably her son — in tow, was bearing down on Evalina.

"Oh my dear," she whispered in a wee, far-away voice. Aidan's eldest daughter responded with a mighty eye roll. "Mrs. Trewellan," she said icily, and gave the curtest inclination of her head. So she had not approved of her father's choice.

112

It was just at this interesting moment that Mrs. Bussell, arm linked firmly through that of her water-rat husband, appeared sailing round the corner of the church. On sight of her rival, however, she stopped short, her mouth working. Then she hurried forward, red in the face, her entire demeanour suggesting that she was about to slap Mrs. Trewellan hard. This, John decided, was the time to intervene. He stepped directly into Ariadne's path and bowed.

"Mrs. Bussell."

She stopped short. "You! What are you doing here you horrible little man?"

The Apothecary adopted the grimmest expression in his repertoire. "I come to honour the dead, Madam. And you?"

Montague Bussell spoke up. "Who are you exactly, Sir?"

"My name is Rawlings, Mr. Bussell." John bowed once more. "By trade I am an apothecary but I have another interest which I am currently pursuing."

"And what is that?"

"I work with Sir John Fielding on behalf of the Public Office in Bow Street."

"Oh," said Montague Bussell, and gave the Apothecary a long hard stare.

He was quite slight in build and not particularly tall, giving the impression that his wife was twice as big as he was, which, strictly, was not true. The whiskery look was created by the fact that whoever shaved him did a poor job, leaving small patches of facial hair, all of which were grey. These hirsute clumps joggled when he talked, a fact that John found absolutely fascinating. However, despite his rattish features, Montague did not have the bright eyes of a rodent. Instead his were pale; a watery grey. Yet belying his insipid colouring, John got the feeling that a hard man lay beneath this dull exterior, that a certain set to Mr. Bussell's jaw indicated that he was not to be trifled with. Yet again, the question of how much he knew about his wife's affair and subsequent stalking activities rose in the Apothecary's mind.

Mrs. Trewellan, in response to her son's whispering, turned round and regarded her rival, her expression hesitant. Ariadne's vast teeth were bared in a travesty of a smile, though her conker eyes remained ice cold. The two women bobbed in each other's direction, then turned away. But further confrontation was impossible for the hearse was weaving its way up the track towards the church. Behind it, led by a groom and all tricked out in black, came a riderless horse — presumably Aidan Fenchurch's — his hat on the saddle, his riding boots, crossed, beneath it. If he had been an army man, no doubt his sword would also have been there, and John could only feel thankful that no one had suggested putting up a bottle of fine port to represent the deceased.

The hearse drew to a halt and some very feeble and ancient male relatives stepped forward to shoulder the coffin into church. Hoping to God that they weren't going to drop it, the Apothecary was relieved when the dashing Lieutenant Mendoza left the crowd of mourners and courteously moved a bow-legged octogenarian to one side, taking the burden himself.

"Not family," hissed Evalina in a loud whisper.

"He is now," answered Louisa, and pulling of her glove flashed a wedding ring beneath her elder sister's nose.

So they had eloped, thought John, but then his attention was wrenched back to the matter in hand as the coffin began its perilous journey up the aisle, wobbling dangerously at every step. Behind it, as custom decreed, came the eldest child, accompanied by poor Millicent, weeping copiously into a black trimmed handkerchief. Evalina, grim-faced, marched steadily however, presumably relishing the fact that every eye was set upon her. Thin as a reed, Jocasta walked behind with Louisa, who even despite the solemnity of the occasion had a hat with bobbing feather set on her sweep of red hair.

Thanks to the efforts of a sweating Lieutenant Mendoza, the coffin arrived at its resting place and at a sign from the parson, the congregation sat. There was a lot of subdued coughing and then the service began. John, as was his wont, made for the back of the church where he could see but not be seen. Two rows in front of him sat the Bussells, immediately in front of them, Mrs. Trewellan and son, an unhappy arrangement to say the least of it. Indeed, Ariadne went so far as to strike her rival with a bible, all under the pretence of accident, of course.

John's mind was far away, in the coffin with the shattered remains of Aidan Fenchurch. Whoever had inflicted those blows, be they robbers or hired killers, had dark hearts and even darker souls, that much was clear. Yet could a woman have been behind such savagery? Was it possible that a female could have ordered such a dreadful execution? Shivering, John stared at Ariadne Bussell's studiously turned back, and wondered, as she raised a handkerchief to dab her lips, whether she might perhaps be smiling behind its concealing veil.

Unusually, the scene at the graveside revealed nothing. Evalina was relatively calm, only letting out one enormous shriek as she threw a large clod of earth, which landed with a plop, on to her father's lowered casket. Louisa leaned heavily on her new husband as they did the same, while Millicent scuttled like a miserable mouse, avoiding looking down into the grave's greedy maw as she tossed in not earth but a bunch of rosemary woven round with wild forget-me-nots. After that the mourners filed past like a line of dark rooks. Mrs. Trewellan cried, while her son looked sly, like a dog who had stolen a string of sausages. Mrs. Bussell got her shoe caught in a fissure and stumbled at the grave's edge, much to John's delight. The water-rat husband, having rescued her, wobbled his whiskers in what was, presumably, a show of emotion, and then it was all over. Wondering if the Brave Fellows were going to appear at any moment and drag the principal suspect into their awaiting coach, John trudged up the church path, thinking that it hadn't been as dramatic a funeral as he had hoped for.

Jocasta glided up to him, so silently that it made him jump. "Mr. Rawlings, you will come back to Foxfire Hall for the wake, I trust."

He snatched off his hat. "Madam, I would not presume. You are family and neighbours. I am a mere outsider."

"But you did so much for Father."

"I only met him once."

"But he trusted you, confided in you. Felt he knew you well enough to put his papers into your safekeeping."

"I did what any other citizen would have done."

"Not at all. I insist that you join us. Is your coachman here?"

"Waiting with the others."

"Then I will give him directions how to find us."

With that she walked away, leaving John no opportunity to argue further.

"So we're going on, are we, Sir?" Tom asked as the Apothecary approached.

"It would seem so."

"Did anything fine happen at the funeral? Was anybody taken ill?" the coachman continued eagerly.

"No, not really. Let's hope the wake will prove more interesting." John became serious. "Any sign of the two Brave Fellows, Tom?"

"Not a sniff of 'em, Sir."

"When you've dropped me at the Hall could you have a look round the local tracks. They probably got as far as the Clandons and then lost themselves."

"I'll do what I can. How long do you expect to be?"

"One hour. No more."

"Very good, Mr. Rawlings." And Tom saluted with his whip as they turned through the gates and up a drive towards an imposing mansion. "By God, was this man titled?" the Irishman called out.

"No, all this was achieved through the consumption of fine wines and spirits."

"Then we're all in the wrong profession, so we are."

And the Apothecary felt inclined to agree. For Foxfire Hall was vast; a huge Tudor edifice with curling chimney pots and mellow brick, built in the traditional E shape that indicated the reign of Elizabeth. Roses, in bud and leaf but not yet flowering, rambled over the walls in profusion. In summer, John imagined, the entire place must be filled with their fragrance to an overpowering degree. Where roses ended, ivy took over, so that the whole place seemed alive and bursting with growth. For once in his life, John felt that he could live in such a house with total happiness.

The heavy front door stood open, a footman on duty within the porch, another beyond who took John's hat and cloak. Ushered within, the Apothecary almost immediately found himself amongst the other mourners, who mingled in an oak-panelled, tapestry-hung Great Hall. A table on which cakes and some sort of punch had been prepared stood to one side, the visitors not yet touching the refreshments but forming a line to pay their condolences to the family members who stood on the raised dais at the end of the hall. As luck would have it, John found himself immediately behind the couple he had met at the church door.

John bowed. "Madam, Sir, we meet again. The name is Rawlings, John Rawlings, apothecary of Shug Lane, Piccadilly."

"Gilbert," replied the other. "Henry Gilbert and my wife Martha."

Everyone bowed once more. "You have known the family long?" John enquired politely.

"I was a childhood friend of Dorothy Millard, who married Aidan Fenchurch. Foxfire Hall was her home you know, but her father sold it to Aidan when his debts became too crippling, so the old place has stayed in the family. They were a bad lot the Millard brothers, inveterate gamblers and profligates, the pair of 'em."

"I see," said John looking wise and thinking to himself that somewhere within these recollections there might lie a valuable bit of information.

"Anyway, Aidan was steady enough, restored the Hall where old Millard had let it fall into disrepair. The girls were here a lot when they were small."

"So you know them well too?"

"Yes. Of course, little Louisa is my favourite . . ."

"That's because she's the prettiest," interrupted Martha.

"But it seems she's married another ne'er-do-well."

"Lieutenant Mendoza? Is he a bad lot then?"

"Very poor family, so they say. Church mice. Anyway, Louisa will be a wealthy young woman now that her father is dead. I believe he left substantial amounts to all three girls, to say nothing of Foxfire and the London house. Rich pickings for someone." He rubbed his hands together.

"You shouldn't gossip, Henry," Martha reprimanded. "We're here to grieve not gabble."

John decided on a direct approach. He looked musing. "So, many people stood to benefit from poor Mr. Fenchurch's death it would appear."

"Many indeed," came the reply.

They were nearing the top of the queue and John saw Ariadne Bussell, conker eyes abrim with tears, step up to Evalina.

"Oh my dear," she said, Bath accent rich.

The eldest of the three sisters flashed her father's ex-mistress a dark, unfathomable look. "Mrs. Bussell," she said between clenched teeth.

This day Evalina looked terrible, the port wine stain seeming redder and more noticeable than ever. If one added to this the redness of her eyes and the flush in her unblemished cheek, she looked like a study in crimson. Despite her penchant for swooning, John felt genuinely sorry for her.

Aidan's Shadow seemed unable to realise the woman's wretched state, however. "Know that you have all my sympathies," she said loudly, as if delivering a speech to the rest of the room. "If ever you need a mother to talk to, then you may rely on me."

Evalina looked stricken but made no reply and it was left to Millicent to say, "How kind of you, Mrs. Bussell."

Jocasta's voice, sharp with suspicion, came in. "I know how close you were to my late father, Madam."

She gave Mrs. Bussell what the Apothecary could only think of as a dark look from eyes that were so

120

reminiscent of his except in their colour. Nor had she finished yet.

"Mr. Bussell, you must comfort your wife. Why, her grief is as profound as if she had lost a husband rather than a friend," Jocasta continued.

John caught himself thinking that Mrs. Rayner might well have been lying. That she had always known of her father's attachment to Mrs. Bussell.

Montague gave a silly laugh but the Apothecary could see he was put out by the remark.

"Grief affects us all differently," he answered shortly.

"Indeed it does."

They passed down the receiving line, Mrs. Bussell raising an eyeglass to inspect Lieutenant Mendoza more closely, then simpering at him before she returned to the body of the Hall where a footman served punch to those who had paid their respects. It was very strong, John thought, as he took a sip.

"So," said Henry Gilbert, "a new chapter begins in the history of this great house. Who is to inherit, do you know?"

"I think Mrs. Rayner. She intends to live here with Miss Millicent, I believe."

"That should liven the place up!" the old rogue said sarcastically.

"You are impossible!" his wife remonstrated. "Poor Mr. Rawlings."

John spread his hands. "No, really, I . . ." But he got no further. There was a sudden commotion at the back of the Hall and in company with everyone else, all mingling and refreshing themselves by now, the family dutifully serving their guests to help out the servants, the Apothecary turned to see what had caused it.

He stared, his eyes, popping. Runners Dick Ham and Nick Raven, totally ignoring the two protesting footmen who were trying to stop them, had entered the Hall. Runner Raven, who was small and dark and totally suited to his surname, strode in and bowed to Evalina.

"Madam, is there a Mrs. Ariadne Bussell present?"

The poor woman went redder than ever and gasped out, "Yes, there," and pointed a trembling finger.

Nick crossed the Great Hall, seemingly oblivious to all the staring faces. "Madam," he said in ringing tones, "I must ask you to accompany me peacefully. I have the power of arrest but prefer not to use it."

"What is all this?" she demanded furiously.

"Sir John Fielding wishes to see you at Bow Street. It is in connection with the death of Mr. Aidan Fenchurch."

"My God," said Ariadne and fell backwards onto her husband, who promptly lost his balance and crashed to the floor, where he lay, looking dazed.

"I'll not accompany you anywhere," she said contemptuously, glaring at the Runner from her supine position.

"Then I arrest you," Nick answered calmly. "Madam, come with me."

CHAPTER
EIGHT

It was quite extraordinary, thought John. Walking into Serafina's salon, lit by candles, all of which were reflected in the many gilt-edged mirrors that hung round the walls, it was as if the dramatic events of that afternoon had never taken place. For there, lounging back in chairs, trying to look like negligent young men about town and not quite succeeding, were what could only be Justin and Greville Bussell, totally unaware of their mother's arrest and the subsequent undignified scene which had ensued. Slightly aghast, John walked up to the table.

Serafina looked up, saw who it was, and flashed the Apothecary a signal with her eyes. He signalled back that he must speak to her in private. She understood and got to her feet.

"Gentlemen, if we could halt play for a few minutes. Allow me to introduce my house guest, John Rawlings. John, may I present Justin and Greville Bussell."

Neither of the brothers Bussell got to their feet, obviously considering themselves too versed in the ways of high society to bother with ordinary courtesies. They did, however, look up from the hand of cards that each was holding. Justin, John saw, was tall, with thick dark features and the same conker-coloured eyes as his mother. He gave a half-hearted smile in the direction of the new arrival and the Apothecary saw that he had also inherited the formidable teeth of his dam. Teeth which had positively gnashed the air as Mrs. Bussell had been manhandled, kicking and yelling, out of the Great Hall and into the waiting Bow Street coach.

Greville, on the other hand, was slightly smaller, though that didn't say much. John guessed that the pair of lumpkins must both loom over six feet in height. But still the snapping eyes dominated; a family characteristic that John did not care for at all.

"How do?" said Justin lazily.

Greville tried a little harder. "A pleasure, Sir."

The Apothecary was furious, so much so that he actually felt his heart beat speed up. He gave the most stylish bow in his repertoire, kissed his fingers into the air and said, "Gentlemen, your reputation precedes you. You are the toast of West Clandon. I salute you."

They stared at him suspiciously, vividly reminding John of a pair of plough-pulling oxen, and not too bright into the bargain. He couldn't help it. "Moo," he added.

Serafina fluttered brightly. "John, my dear, pray step outside a moment. I must find you a book. We are involved in whist but are due to have supper soon."

It was a feeble excuse but it got them out of the room and into the passageway, beyond earshot.

"What happened?" she whispered. "Did you get to the funeral?"

"I did indeed. And, my dear, it was more than dramatic. The Runners arrived at the wake and arrested the mother of those two oafs — or is it oaves? — who was hauled off without further ado."

Serafina's eyes widened and she clasped her hands in excitement. "What did her husband do?"

"At first he looked like an astonished rodent."

"I've never seen one of those," interrupted Serafina with a smile.

"Now don't start," admonished the Apothecary. "Then he suffered some sort of change of heart and muttered 'Nemesis' beneath his breath, but loud enough for those closest to hear. After that he rallied and became the concerned husband, asking the Runners where they were taking his wife and whether he could accompany her."

"What did they say?"

"No. But he was at liberty to follow them to Bow Street from whence he would be allowed to escort Mrs. Bussell home, providing Sir John Fielding saw fit."

"Meaning?"

"That the Magistrate has the power to hold her in custody."

"Gracious me. What happened next?"

"The wake turned into a near riot. Evalina swooned in style, Cousin Millicent quivered, Jocasta attempted to restore order with no success, and for no reason that I could see, Lieutenant Mendoza drew his sword. The rest drank as rapidly as they possibly could."

Serafina suddenly looked serious. "What do we do about the sons? Tell them?"

John thought in silence, then said, "Best not. Let it come from their father. They've no idea of my connection with the case, have they?"

"None at all. I invited them here as a neighbourly gesture, saying that Louis and I would love to play cards with them."

"Have you shown them your mettle yet?"

"I've held back but now they are beginning to bore me so after supper I shall concentrate."

John laughed. "God help them. A mother under arrest, a father muttering 'nemesis', and you playing them at whist. I wouldn't wish it on my worst enemy."

Serafina did not smile. "I wonder what Bussell meant by that. Do you think it indicates that he knew all along about his wife's affair with Aidan Fenchurch?"

"That was the impression I got, yes."

"And does he think she had Fenchurch murdered?"

"That I couldn't say."

"What a strange affair it is," said Serafina as they returned to the salon.

John sat apart while the others played on, ostensibly reading but in fact not seeing the words at all, turning the events of the wake over and over in his head. What had brought about the sudden change in Montague Bussell's attitude? There was no doubt that momentarily the mask had slipped and the affable husband had been replaced by someone else; someone who considered that Ariadne deserved all she got. But did that extend to believing she had murdered the former object of her affections? John wondered. Deciding that somehow or other he must talk to the duped Mr. Bussell and find out more, the Apothecary attempted to concentrate.

Behind him he heard Serafina call out, "Gentlemen, let us pause for supper. If you would follow me . . ."

But she got no further. From the drive came the sound of horses' hooves clattering at speed and a coach being driven recklessly towards the house.

Louis shot to his feet. "What the devil . . . ?" And he hurried to the front door.

The brothers Bussell, roused at last from their act of blasé young bucks, looked round in some surprise but still remained too lethargic to leave their chairs. John, sensing danger, left the room and joined Louis, standing with his footmen, watching the carriage hurl itself towards the entrance. As it drew nearer, with a shock he recognised it.

"It's the Runners!" he exclaimed. "What in heaven's name are they doing here? They should be half way to Bow Street by now."

Louis shook his head, as startled as John, as the conveyance drew to a halt with a rear of horses and Runners Ham and Raven jumped down from the coachman's box.

"What's going on?" called John. A mad idea occurred to him. "Has she escaped?"

"It's a bit worse than that, Sir," said Dick, giving the briefest bow to John and Louis.

"Then what . . . ?"

"She was taken ill on the way to town. And I mean seriously ill, gentlemen."

With that he threw open the door of the carriage and the foul smell of vomit and excrement hit the nostrils like an evil gas.

"God's grace," said John. "What happened?"

"First of all she was violently sick. Repeatedly so. We tried to keep her head out of the window but she became too weak to stand. Then she lost control of her bowels and soiled herself."

"All the while she was rolling in agony," put in Dick Ham. "God's life, Mr. Rawlings, but we had no alternative but to take the wretched woman home."

"Is she there now?"

"Yes, we managed to get her into the hall but there she collapsed."

"No doubt they'll send for a physician but I'd better go to her meanwhile," said John, already turning to race upstairs to fetch his medical bag.

"You can't travel in the coach, Sir," answered Nick Raven firmly. "It's like a midden. Tomorrow, by daylight, we must swab it out and somehow try to make it sweet-smelling again."

"Take it to the stables but stand it well away from the other carriages," Louis ordered. "Then, gentlemen, make your way to the kitchens. I'll see to it that you are given some good brandy. You look in need of something strong."

John turned to him. "The sons. What do we tell them?"

"Simply that a messenger has come from the big house and that they are to return home immediately."

"But won't they find out?"

"It will be too late by then." Louis gave a Frenchman's shrug.

Serafina joined them in the hall. "What's going on?"

"Fetch those two bumpkins," her husband answered. "Mrs. Bussell was taken ill in the coach. John is going to her now. They must leave immediately."

Hoping for a lift, the Apothecary's wishes were dashed. On Louis's instructions, two large horses were brought round and the brothers swung into the saddle and were off, with their customary lack of charm leaving John to sort out his own transport.

"I don't feel like taking an unknown road in the darkness."

"Could you drive a gig?"

"Yes."

"You don't sound too certain. I'll send one of the servants with you."

So it was that the Apothecary, in company with one of Louis's stable boys, set off in the direction of Merrow Place, wondering what he would find there and what could possibly have caused Mrs. Ariadne Bussell's sudden and violent attack of sickness.

As soon as he entered her bedroom, John knew that she was dying. She was drained of all colour and the snapping eyes were closed. The great mouth was open, however, and through it she was breathing in shallow gasps. Luckily for the Apothecary, the family physician had not yet been found and so he was able to make an examination for himself.

129

Very quickly, he drew back the bedclothes, recoiling at the smell of Ariadne's napkin, a large version of the type put on babies. He spoke to her maid, more tersely than he meant to.

"Change this. Give the poor creature a little dignity."

"But it's such a struggle, Sir, and she'll only fill it again."

"I don't think so. Change it and send for her sons." A thought struck him. "Where is Mr. Bussell?"

"In his study."

So he hadn't gone to London in pursuit of his wife. Or had he seen the Runners' coach turn round? Whatever, it was as well that he was present.

John took Ariadne's pulse and raised one eyelid. A conker eye regarded him glazedly. Then, as the maid turned her back, searching for fresh linen, he examined Mrs. Bussell's lips and tongue. Neither were swollen. Yet though this ruled out any of the Wolfsbane venoms, John felt utterly convinced that this was not simply an attack of severe food poisoning. In fact he was sure that Ariadne had been deliberately poisoned. With a lurch of his heart, the Apothecary realised that the principal suspect in the case of the murder of Aidan Fenchurch was about to die herself, thus sending all their neat conclusions reeling. But there was no further time to think; the brothers, one on each side of their father, were coming into the room.

Justin eyed John suspiciously. "What are you doing here?"

"I am an apothecary, Mr. Bussell. I came to offer your mother any help I could give. But, alas, she is too far gone."

"What do you mean by that? What are you saying?"

"That your mother is dying, Sir, and is beyond my skills."

"But why?" asked Montague. "She was all right this morning." He eyed John suspiciously. "Who are you anyway? Ain't you something to do with that wretched Fielding fellow?"

"I assist Sir John occasionally," John answered. "But this is not the moment to go down that path, Sir. Save your thoughts for your wife."

Montague went to the bedside. "I can't believe this," he said. "What could cause this change to happen so suddenly?"

"I would imagine that something was administered to Mrs. Bussell. That, other than food poisoning, is the only explanation."

The little man faced John truculently. "I think you're a fraud and a fake, Sir. Out of my house, d'ye hear? Let's get a physician to her at once."

"Dr. Bowles has been sent for, Father. They're out looking for him now."

"Meanwhile, you are to leave at once."

"Certainly, Sir," answered John, and was just about to make a dignified exit when there was a huge gasp from Ariadne.

The three men turned back to the bed, though John remained exactly where he was. But there was no need to examine her closely to see that the Shadow had breathed her last. With that final exhalation the dark eyes flew open and one hand, tense a second before, hung limply over the side of the bed. It would seem that from beyond the grave, Aidan Fenchurch had been avenged.

"*Mon Dieu*," said Louis, shivering as John described the scene. "What happened then?"

"The boys looked suitably grim but did not cry. As for Bussell, he struck the maid."

"He what?" exclaimed Serafina, shocked.

"He clouted the maid. Blamed her for not sending for help sooner. Said Ariadne would be alive but for her. Then he hit her again and walked out of the room. I think he would have struck me too but I managed to get out ahead of him."

The Comtesse looked pensive. "That suggests to me that he has a very nasty streak. He probably poisoned her himself and thought that that was a clever way of deflecting the blame."

"Strangely enough, my dear," said John, downing a strong brandy, "that is exactly what I thought too."

"I believe this case is simpler than we all reckoned," Louis remarked, stretching his long legs towards the fire and placing his folded hands behind his head. "I think Bussell paid two assassins to remove his wife's lover and then got rid of her by poisoning her food or drink."

"That would suggest a certain amount of expert knowledge."

132

Louis shrugged. "If he didn't do it himself he probably paid someone else. He's rich enough."

John nodded. "You may well be right. It certainly makes a neat pattern. My God, there's a lot to report to Sir John."

"Will you leave tomorrow?" Serafina asked.

"Yes, bright and early. Much as I have enjoyed your delightful hospitality, I have been here too long as it is. I only hope that I get back before Emilia. She will not be best pleased if she and her mother return to an empty house."

"No," the Comtesse agreed, "she won't. John, you must put her first from now on. I know you love solving mysteries for the Public Office but that is not the most important thing in your life any more."

He nodded. "I know. Believe me, I am a reformed character. Once I have reported the latest turn of events to Sir John, I shall devote myself entirely to my family."

"Yes," said Louis, his voice suspiciously expressionless, "I'm absolutely sure you will." Then he and Serafina exchanged a glance in which lay both fondness and exasperation.

"Will you be going to Bow Street first, Sir, or shall I take you straight home?" Irish Tom called down from the coachman's box.

"Bow Street," John answered. "The court should soon be rising for the dining hour. I'll make my report to Sir John, then I can devote myself totally to home duties."

"I wonder if Mrs. Rawlings is back yet."

"I hope not. I want to be there to welcome her."

"She'll be very close to her time, won't she."

It was a statement not a question and John, hearing the words, felt such a thrill of apprehension that he almost countermanded his instruction to go to the Public Office. But then good sense prevailed. Better by far to get the last bit of business over so that all his time could be devoted to Emilia and the child that was to come.

The Blind Beak had just arrived in his first floor salon, the room that John knew and loved so well, and was allowing himself a preprandial glass of sherry. Elizabeth Fielding was in the chair opposite his but the precocious Mary Ann, their adopted daughter, was elsewhere, somewhat to the Apothecary's relief. He did not find it easy to relate some of the more lurid details of a case in front of her, yet as a guest was not really in a position to suggest that she leave the room.

Sir John listened in his customary silence but Lady Fielding reacted amazingly, looking utterly astonished at the news that the principal suspect had died.

"Do you think she was poisoned?" the Magistrate finally asked.

"Yes, I do. No stomach complaint could manifest so quickly and claim a life, other than for genuine food poisoning, of course."

"And you believe that impossible?"

"I can't say for sure. I don't know what she ate that day but I imagine that as they were going to a funeral both she and Mr. Bussell would have eaten lightly."

"Um. Where are the Runners at present?"

134

"They have retired to the inn awaiting your instructions, Sir John."

"I'll get word to them straight away. I want them to check with the cook exactly what Mrs. Bussell consumed before she left for the funeral. But I tend to agree with Comte Louis."

"In what regard?"

"I think that originally we went down the wrong track. In hindsight I believe that Montague Bussell seethed with jealousy, that he knew all about her affair with Mr. Fenchurch and her subsequent unrelenting pursuit of her victim. I think he is responsible for both their deaths."

"But why poison Mrs. Bussell at the wake? For it must have been then if the timing of her falling sick is anything to go by."

"To deflect suspicion from himself. Anybody could have tipped something into her glass or sprinkled a substance onto her food in that crush. You say that there was a goodly crowd present?"

John nodded. "Yes, Sir."

"Then that will be his story, mark my words. That somebody with a grudge against his wife took it into their head to kill her."

"As an act of revenge for Fenchurch's death?"

"Precisely."

It was John's turn to become silent.

"You do not agree?" asked the Beak.

"It could have been just that, Sir. Any one of the family could have hated Ariadne sufficiently to want to see her off."

"You have a point, Mr. Rawlings. But none of them would have wanted to kill their own father, now would they? No, this second murder points to one person and one person alone. My further instruction to the Runners will be to bring Bussell in for questioning."

"You're probably right," said John.

And indeed the fact could not be argued against. Who else would want to kill both Aidan Fenchurch and Ariadne Bussell? One, perhaps, but not the other. Most certainly the entire focus of the enquiry had changed. Yet the Apothecary could not help but feel that there was some thread, some obscure fact, that he should have noticed by now but which at the moment lay beyond his grasp.

John had not requested a fast drive home but Irish Tom gave him one regardless of the fact. They positively sped through the streets, irritating several hackney coach drivers who shouted abuse. The Irishman ignored them and positively whirled up The Hay Market, then cut across various smaller alleys, a feat not achieved at quite such top speed, then clattered along Gerrard Street and turned left into Nassau Street with a thunder of wheels. He drew to a halt outside number two and John dismounted. But before he could cross the space leading to his house, the front door flew open. The Apothecary stared, for there stood the last person on earth he had expected to see. Sir Gabriel Kent had come to town.

"Father," said John, running to him and hugging him. "What are you doing here?"

"Taking your place, my son. Where in heaven's name have you been?"

"In Surrey actually . . ." He stopped explaining. "Where's Emilia?"

"Within."

The word was said solemnly and with much import and John felt his stomach heave. "Oh my God, is she all right?"

"She is very tired but other than for that she is well enough."

"I must go to her at once."

Sir Gabriel laid a restraining hand on his adopted son's arm. "No, my boy, she is asleep. You will be doing her no favours by waking her up. However, there is another visitor here whom I would like you to meet. Come into the library."

John felt a faint flicker of irritation. "What is going on? Visitors calling and Emilia sound asleep. Is this some kind of joke?"

"No, it's quite serious I assure you. Now follow me and sit down. You must be tired after your journey. Have you dined?"

"Not as yet."

"Then let us have some champagne." Sir Gabriel motioned John to a chair then rang the bellrope. "Some champagne and three glasses, if you please," he asked the footman who answered. "And could you ask Mrs. Alleyn and Miss Rose to step this way."

The servant grinned, quite broadly. "Certainly, Sir Gabriel."

"Who's Miss Rose?" John asked, then momentarily closed his eyes as the warmth of the fire combined with the early start to the day and the strain of the previous evening, made him suddenly overcome with exhaustion.

He opened them abruptly as what felt like a lacetrimmed cushion was placed on his lap. John looked downwards and a pair of bright blue eyes gazed back into his. He quite literally couldn't believe what he was seeing. An infant lay on his knees, an infant quite newborn and yet with that look of ancient wisdom, of knowledge and understanding, that was almost shocking in its unexpectedness. Yet it was not to the baby's knowing expression that John's gaze was drawn, instead he looked at her hair. It was red and gold and curled round her head in whorls and spirals. It was the longest, thickest hair he had ever seen on a baby and this, together with her rosebud mouth and creamy skin, made her the prettiest infant he had ever seen.

John's voice came out as a croak. "Is she mine?"

Sir Gabriel and Emilia's mother, Maud Alleyn, laughed gently. "She is yours and Emilia's."

"When was she born?"

"Yesterday. Just after daybreak. She came into the world like a spring flower. Her mother named her Maud Phyllida Rose because of it. Do you approve of that?"

"Rose Rawlings," said John in wonderment. "She couldn't be called anything more apt."

He picked the child up in his two hands so that her face was on a level with his and they looked at one another long and hard for several minutes. Of course those who knew about such things would tell him later that the child merely twitched with a flatulent spasm, but John knew differently. There was no doubt in his mind whatsoever that as they stared at one another, each one getting the measure of the other, Rose Rawlings quite deliberately winked at him, sweeping long dark lashes onto her snow-drop cheek.

That night the whole house seemed alive because of the presence of the newcomer: candles and fire burned more brightly, snatches of cheerful song came from the servants' quarters, wine sparkled in goblets, laughter seemed to come from every room.

Emilia had woken much refreshed and had sat up to feed her child, somewhat alarmed at the prospect but greatly comforted by a decoction of leaves and roots of marsh mallow boiled in water with parsley and fennel and applied warm to her breasts. Nicholas, who had come home from the shop early, had compounded it himself and was delighted that his Master had sanctioned the mixture as fit to be used by Mrs. Rawlings. As for John, he could hardly bear to leave Rose for a second, amazed by her minute hands and feet, by her perfect little body, by the luxuriant growth of hair upon her head.

"I wonder where that colour comes from?" said Emilia, as the child suckled peacefully.

"Your father?"

"No, he was brown before he went white. I thought your mother perhaps."

"No, she was dark. Midnight hair, Sir Gabriel used to call it."

"Perhaps it is from your real father, John."

"It could be. I know nothing of him at all, not even what he looked like."

"Perhaps you'll find him one day."

"Do you know," said John thoughtfully, "I used to care about that. But now that Rose is here I have a blood relative again and I no longer have the desire."

"Do you like the name?" asked Emilia, snuggling into his arms where he sat beside her on the pillows, supporting her as she fed their child.

"I can think of nothing more appropriate. I know you chose Maud and Phyllida out of courtesy to the two grandmothers but please let her be known as Rose, by us at least."

"Rose Rawlings it is," said Emilia.

"Rose Rawlings," echoed John, and knew with certainty that this was one of the turning points of his life.

CHAPTER
NINE

John Rawlings woke suddenly, wondering as he lay in the darkness what the sound was that had broken his sleep. Then he heard it again. Somewhere in the house a baby was crying. Just for a moment he thought he was at Serafina's Palladian villa in Surrey and that one of her children was in tears, then he realised that this was the cry of an infant, not an older offspring, and his memory returned. He was a father, Emilia had given birth, and it was Rose Rawlings herself who was shouting to be fed. Smiling, John lit a candle and got out of bed.

He was sleeping in a room no bigger than a box, usually reserved for the personal servant of a house guest, but for which he had volunteered in order that Emilia should get her much-needed rest. It was at the top of the house, close to the bedrooms of the regular staff, and as he started to pad downstairs in his nightshirt, a door opened and Dorcas, Emilia's maid, appeared.

"I'll see to the baby, Sir," she whispered.

"No, I'll do it. I'd like to. Go back to bed."

"This is her feeding time, Sir. She wants her mama."

"Then I'll take her."

"Very good, Mr. Rawlings."

She yawned, gave him a look that was an exquisite mixture of resentment and gratitude, and went back to her room.

Very rich families with larger dwellings than number two, Nassau Street, had nursery suites staffed by servants whose sole job it was to care for the babies and children of the household. But John's establishment being far too small to warrant such an arrangement, Rose lay in a cradle in the same room as her mother. As John went through the door, Emilia was just beginning to stir as the baby cried, but when he picked his daughter up she stopped wailing and his wife went back to sleep.

He realised with enormous pleasure that he wasn't in the least afraid of his child. Most new fathers hardly dared touch the newborn for fear of dropping them but John felt utterly confident with her and wondered why. Then he realised that in the many years since he had become a fully-fledged apothecary, he had handled and treated so many children and infants that they no longer worried him.

"Rose Rawlings, you do not daunt me," he said quietly.

She gave him that wise, knowing look of hers, then tested him by crying again. John carried the noisy bundle over to Emilia who sat up, still half-asleep, and started to feed her. Everything went quiet again.

"Do you like her?" Emilia whispered.

"No. I love her," he whispered back. "Sweetheart . . ."

"Yes?"

"I apologise for not being in the house when she was born. Though other men may not care, I do. Very much indeed. But the case of Fenchurch and the Shadow has become even more convoluted and I truly could not leave Surrey until yesterday."

Emilia nodded her head resignedly. "It was ever thus."

"Don't be angry with me, please darling."

"What would be the point? I would have left you on honeymoon if I had allowed one of Sir John's enquiries to come between us."

"It is a ridiculous hobby for a man to have."

Emilia shook her head. "No, not at all. It is public-spirited of you to help track down wrongdoers."

"But I don't do it for that. I do it because it is both exciting and challenging."

She smiled and suddenly looked very tired indeed.

"Has she finished? Shall I remove her?" John asked.

"A few more minutes and then you can."

"Would you mind if I took her down to the library for a while? I want to talk to her."

Emilia gave her husband a loving smile. "You are quite mad and utterly sweet. Take her by all means."

The library fire was almost out but John threw on another couple of logs and blew the embers with bellows, while Rose observed him with interest. Then they sat together and watched the flames flicker up. He felt that he had always known her and wondered if this was a belief common to all new parents. Then he decided that it was not, that it was especial to him and Rose, that they were friends of centuries standing.

Finally they both fell asleep at the same time and did not wake until the fire went out again and the room grew cold. Holding her close, John tiptoed back upstairs and put her back in her cradle without waking Emilia. Then he retired to his box bedroom and lay awake, wondering again what it was about the deaths of Aidan Fenchurch and his mistress that he should be noticing but still had not yet managed to grasp.

After the high drama of the last few days it was reassuring to get back into the shop and work amongst all his familiar things. Compounding and mixing, crushing herbs into a paste, putting the ash of burnt vines into pots to sell as tooth whitener; all these things John found quite relaxing. Therefore he was somewhat taken aback when a voice from the shop called out, "Is Mr. Rawlings within?" and he left the back room to see that Lieutenant Mendoza, very dark and dashing without his wig, had come to visit him.

John wiped his hands on a towel. "My dear Sir, how nice of you to call."

The Lieutenant lowered his voice. "I need to speak to you privately, Sir. There is much to tell."

"Then come into the compounding room. Or would you prefer to go out somewhere?"

"Walls have ears," said the Lieutenant. "Is your room utterly private?"

"Utterly. My apprentice will look after the shop and the door between can remain closed. But first, can I offer you some refreshment? Would you care for tea?"

144

The Lieutenant looked shifty. "Have you any brandy?"

"A little. I'll pour you a draft."

"Thanks. I feel I need it." The Lieutenant took the proffered glass and downed it in one. "I don't know where to begin," he said, taking a seat at the wooden table.

"Why not start with your connection with the Fenchurch family. Were you and Louisa childhood sweet-hearts?"

"Hardly. My uncle brought me up with his children because my father died tragically at the age of nineteen. Anyway, uncle and Aidan were business rivals. We are Portuguese, by the way, though my father settled here when he was very young and I was born in this country. Be that as it may, rivalry brought about bad blood between the two families. Accusations were hurled about stealing customers, that sort of thing. Then my uncle started to lose money, rather suspiciously I thought."

"What do you mean by that?"

The Lieutenant held out his glass for another brandy and John refilled it. "I could never prove it, of course, but I had the feeling that obstacles were deliberately put in his path."

"I see," said John, thinking that here was a possible motive for murder.

"Anyway, any hopes I had of following my uncle into the family business were firmly scotched. There was no business left to follow him in to! So I joined the army instead. Then, to pay the Fenchurchs back I started to court Louisa. I intended to seduce her and leave her; make them suffer a bit in return for all they had done to us. But you've seen the minx for yourself. The boot was on the other foot. She ran rings round me and I was hopelessly lost."

The Apothecary burst out laughing. "I know the feeling."

"It was she who decided to elope. Not the other way round."

John chuckled.

"But the tale takes a nasty twist. Rumours are now being circulated, emanating from Evalina I imagine, that it was I who hired the assassins to kill the girls' father. That I had planned some magnificent revenge which involved not only stealing the youngest daughter but murdering her parent, and that I put it into train, thereby inheriting Louisa's share of the will into the bargain."

"And did you?" asked John in a guileless voice.

"I resent that, Sir," said Mendoza, standing up.

"Please don't. It is my duty as an associate of Sir John Fielding to say that kind of thing. If he had been questioning you he would have asked the same."

The Lieutenant sat down again. "The answer is no, quite definitely. It's true that I did not like Aidan Fenchurch. But I most certainly would not have killed my sweetheart's father. However, it seems that the number of people who believe that I would have done is growing. That is why I came to you for advice. Apparently you have the ear of the Magistrate. I wondered what I should do next."

146

"Does Louisa believe you innocent?"

"She most certainly does. We were eloping at the very time he was killed. My mind was on other things and she knows it." He laughed, somewhat harshly.

John looked thoughtful. "Tell me, did you know Mrs. Ariadne Bussell?"

"Aidan's mistress? Yes, at one stage she was cultivating me. She told me that she collected people. I presume that I was to be added to the assortment."

"What a terrible thought."

"Isn't it? I remember that she kissed me secretly, giggling the while. It was like being sucked by a codfish."

"You know that she is dead?"

Lieutenant Mendoza looked astounded. "Is she? Good God! The last I saw of her was at the wake being taken away by those two men. Almost immediately afterwards I had to leave for London myself. But Louisa stayed behind to help her sisters." His expression changed. "She's a good girl despite her flighty appearance. A loyal heart who would do anything for me. But what of Bussell, how did she die?"

"I believe she was poisoned," John answered slowly.

"This is deep," said Mendoza, pinching his nostrils together and sighing out a breath. "Do you mean . . ."

"By a person unknown? Yes, I do. I cannot credit that it was an accident and nobody would choose such a ghastly suicide."

"But who?"

"That is the question. At the moment nobody has an idea."

"The husband," said the Lieutenant. "He must have hated her for her infidelity and her public pursuit of Aidan."

"So you know about that?"

"Everybody did. Well, perhaps not everyone. Evalina certainly. The only one who may have been in the dark was poor Millicent, who is so ingenuous that she tends to see the best in people."

"How interesting. Thank you for telling me. I had rather thought Miss Millicent knew."

"So what will happen next, regarding Montague, I mean?"

"He will be questioned by Sir John Fielding who, I presume, will try to get a confession out of him. If he doesn't, it will be an almost impossible case to prove."

"Why is that?"

"Because if the poisoning was done at the wake, the lethal substance could have been adminstered by anyone present. Unless someone actually witnessed Montague in the act of tipping something into his wife's glass or onto her cake, then he will probably get away with it."

"But that's preposterous!" Mendoza said angrily.

"Preposterous but true, I'm afraid," John answered, and had the sudden dread feeling that the circumstances he had predicted would shortly come true.

That afternoon a letter arrived from Bow Street. Reading it, the Apothecary was somewhat shocked to learn that Runners Raven and Ham had returned to London without Montague Bussell despite Sir John's

148

instructions sent by special messenger. It seemed that the recently widowed husband had thrown an apoplexy at the very suggestion and that the family physician had backed him up and ordered immediate bed-rest. The oafish sons had been forced to take over the funeral arrangements and the general running of the household, a fact which had gone down badly with both of them. As a result they were drinking too much and making a thorough nuisance of themselves in the village tavern, both by day and by night. It seemed that there was no alternative but for Joe Jago to travel to West Clandon and question Mr. Bussell in situ, as it were.

Sir John wants me to go too, John thought helplessly, but there is no way that he can persuade me to leave Emilia and Rose.

Then he realised that, as yet, nobody knew Rose had arrived, and so he spent the rest of that day writing letters to various friends and relations, especially Louis and Serafina, and his old and greatest friend, Samuel Swann the goldsmith. That done, he instructed Nicholas to lock up the shop and stepped out into the April evening.

It was fine, filled with a golden light only visible in spring. On the trees, green buds looked on the very point of bursting forth and there was a softness in the air that not even London's most noxious smells could spoil. John filled his lungs and was just luxuriating in the splendour of the sunset when a sedan chair, held up by a slow-moving cart, drew to a halt alongside him. Without really meaning to, the Apothecary glanced towards it. A hand shot up to pull the little curtain over the small window — but not quite quickly enough. Hidden beneath his hat but visible for all that was the whiskery rodent face of the widower. Despite all statements to the contrary, Montague Bussell had returned to town.

John's legs took control and started to pursue the chair, walking as fast as they could without drawing the attention of the chairmen to the fact that he was following them. Down The Hay Market they swept, then along Pall Mall, finally stopping outside a house in St. James's Square where they set their passenger down. Glancing round furtively but fortunately not seeing John, who had flattened himself against a tree, Bussell paid them off then rang the bell and went within as soon as the door was answered. The Apothecary noted the number, then proceeded home, not wanting to delay his return any further and longing to cuddle both his wife and daughter, the two most beautiful females in the world, in his eyes anyway.

Emilia certainly looked rested and bright, the old sparkle back in her angel's eyes, her skin returning to its former creamy texture. As for the baby, the Apothecary swore that she smiled at him, though her mother maintained that the child was flatulent.

"I don't smile when I have wind," John protested.

"On the contrary, you glower."

"There you are then. That proves the point."

"Rubbish. John . . ."

"Yes?"

"Talk to me this evening. I am getting bored with my own company. Besides I am dying to hear the latest developments regarding Aidan Fenchurch. Tell me everything."

So he sat beside her on the bed after he had dined with his father and mother-in-law, and told Emilia all that had taken place, right up to Lieutenant Mendoza's visit to the shop and the sighting of the new principal suspect craftily visiting a house in St. James's Square.

"How extraordinary it all is," John's wife remarked when he had finished.

"What?"

"Well, everything was so neat. It really seemed clear that Mrs. Bussell had ordered her former lover's death, then all of a sudden she is killed as well and the blame shifts untidily to her husband."

"Of course he could be innocent. It could have been anyone at the wake."

"But why should one of them want to kill Aidan? He was the head of their household and they all seemed genuinely fond of him."

"There were other people there as well."

"Who for example?"

"Mrs. Trewellan and her spotty son."

"They should be questioned, John. Suppose Spotty decided to remove his mother's suitor and Aidan's lady love just for good measure. My money is on him. Does he have a name, by the way?"

"No, just Spotty."

She roared with laughter. "John Rawlings, you are incorrigible."

"But I make good babies, don't I?"

"You most certainly do." And they both gazed fondly at the cradle in which Rose slumbered peacefully, occasionally giving her strange windy smile.

Shortly afterwards, Emilia grew tired and John went downstairs to compose an urgent letter to Sir John Fielding which he intended to take to Bow Street very early next morning. Now that Montague Bussell was back in town the ideal opportunity to question him had presented itself and the Apothecary was determined that the rat-like little man shouldn't wriggle out of the net yet again.

He woke early and left the house shortly afterwards, heading for Bow Street, where he dropped off his letter. After that John made his way to Shug Lane and arrived just as Nicholas got there to open the shop. He turned to look at his apprentice.

"Well, my friend, your days of doing this are very nearly over. Next year I shall release you from your indentures. You will be free to open your own premises."

Nicholas shook his head. "I can't quite envisage that, Mr. Rawlings. But I have hopes." And he winked a russet eye.

"Of what?"

"Of you opening a shop in Kensington and putting me in charge."

John laughed. "Well, thank you for telling me. It's nice to know that others have made plans on my behalf. But I suppose that now I have a dependant I should be thinking of expanding my business. I'll consider it, Nick."

"Considering will be fine for now," the Muscovite answered cheerily, and went about his work whistling.

A reply to John's letter arrived by midday, though, somewhat to his surprise, it said little other than to request his company at Bow Street on his way home that evening. So he was quite unprepared for the flowers, for the beautiful rattle of silver and coral, for the bottles of champagne that the Blind Beak and his family had waiting for him in their salon on the first floor.

"Oh, my dear," said Lady Fielding, kissing the Apothecary on both cheeks. "What wonderful news. And you say she is to be called Rose. A delightful name if ever there was one."

"To Miss Rose Rawlings," said the Magistrate, moving deftly amongst them with a tray of champagne glasses, the contents of which he spilled very little.

Everyone took a glass. "Rose Rawlings," they chorused.

"And her delightful mother," Elizabeth added. "When may I call on her?"

"Any day," John answered. "She is starting to get bored and would greatly appreciate a visit."

"Then I shall make it tomorrow."

"May I go too?" Mary Ann enquired.

"Provided you behave yourself," her uncle, the Magistrate, answered automatically.

The girl was now sixteen and utterly beautiful, all her early potential having been realised. She was the sort of young woman who could not walk down the street without every head turning, without all who passed her, both male and female, staring after her. At the theatre, at the shops, in fact wherever she went, she was constantly surrounded by gallants declaring their love for her. Poems were dedicated to her, songs were written about her, she was the toast of London and had she been a member of the aristocracy would have secured one of the finest matches in the kingdom by now. And this, John felt certain, is what the girl was aiming at: a marriage that would give her all the privilege and position she desired. For this reason and this reason alone, he was sure, she kept herself to herself, scorning all suitors, waiting for that golden moment when the heir to a dukedom would lower himself to court the adopted daughter of the Principal Magistrate and she would graciously accept him. Meanwhile, she would continue to play cruel games of rejection with lesser mortals, bestowing smiles and occasional kisses but nothing further.

Feeling John look at her, Mary Ann gave him a dazzling glance. "So you're a family man now, Mr. Rawlings."

"And growing middle-aged, alas."

"I think thirty is an interesting age, Sir."

"Let us hope you continue to think so when you get there."

"That time is a long way off," Mary Ann answered serenely.

"Ladies," boomed Sir John, "let me refill your glasses and finish this bottle. For we must not keep Mr.

Rawlings from his duties. But before he goes I would like a word with him in private. If that is acceptable to you, my friend?"

"Provided I am not home late, it is, Sir."

"How well trained you are," said Mary Ann, but John ignored her.

They drained their glasses and the two women, after congratulating the Apothecary all over again, left the room.

"I'll come straight to the point," said Sir John. "Runners Raven and Ham went to the address in St. James's Square this morning but found nobody at home. However, enquiries reveal that the house belongs to a Mr. Tobias White who, so it seems, went to school with Montague Bussell."

"Do you think he intends to hide out there?"

"Probably. I imagine he feels the country is not safe, that the Runners will go back for him."

"But he has to attend his wife's funeral. Where and when is that to be held?"

"I have no idea. West Clandon, I imagine."

"If those two louts are in charge they will do the thing that gives them least trouble."

"Then West Clandon it is. Mr. Rawlings . . ." Sir John lowered his voice.

"Yes, Sir?"

"You are sure that the Shadow was poisoned?"

"As sure as I can be without an autopsy, yes."

"And what do you think was used?"

"Not one of the Wolfsbanes. They make the tongue and lips swell. No, my guess — based on the violence of the symptoms — would be Water Hemlock. Easy to administer — it looks like parsley — it could be added to food or, chopped fine, put into a drink. I think it was given to Mrs. Bussell at the wake by a person unknown."

"The husband?"

John made a slight face. "Not necessarily. Remember, all the family were there, to say nothing of Mrs. Trewellan and Spotty."

"Who?" said the Blind Beak.

The Apothecary turned a laugh into a cough. "Her son. None of them liked Ariadne if you recall."

And he repeated all that Lieutenant Mendoza had said, including the rumours that were being spread about the Lieutenant himself.

The Magistrate sat silently, then said, "Mr. Rawlings, may I ask a favour? In time that you would not be devoting to your wife and child would you go and see Mrs. Trewellan for me? I would not like it thought that we blamed Montague Bussell without enquiring further."

"Yes, I'll do that, Sir. I saw her at the funeral and thought her quite intriguing."

"Why?"

"Because she was terribly similar to Ariadne in type; large and untidy and not particularly attractive."

"The sort of woman poor Fenchurch went for, it would seem."

"Yes." John paused, then said, "I think you're right to question others, Sir."

"But you would agree that everything points to Bussell?"

"Yes, his being guilty makes total sense. He would have known all along that his wife was unfaithful but waited his moment to get rid of them, wife and lover, both in such very different ways. None the less, you are doing the right thing by asking further afield."

"Can you see Mrs. Trewellan tomorrow?"

"Of course I can."

"I can only express my gratitude, my friend."

"And what of Mr. Bussell? How will you find him?"

"I'll leave that to Jago and the Runners," said the Blind Beak, and finished his glass of champagne with a certain satisfaction.

The minute he left Bow Street, hailing a chair so that he would not be late home, John had the strangest feeling that a weird chain of events had clicked into motion and that however hard he might try to escape them, he was going to get caught in the web. Yet when he stepped into his house all seemed quiet enough, other than for the laughter of Sir Gabriel and Maud Alleyn, surely the happiest pair of grandparents in the kingdom.

"I'm back," he called, and his adoptive father stepped into the hall to greet him.

"You have a visitor, my dear."

John raised his eyebrows. "Who?"

"A Mrs. Rayner. She said you knew her. I have shown her into the small parlour." Sir Gabriel smiled.

157

"She seemed surprised to see me. I think she was under the impression that you lived alone."

"I doubt that. However, I was by myself when she called previously. She's Aidan Fenchurch's daughter," he added by way of explanation, for his father still wore a slightly whimsical expression of amusement.

Jocasta's back was turned as the Apothecary entered the room and he saw by the heave of her shoulders that she was crying. Instantly, he went to her.

"Mrs. Rayner, please don't distress yourself. I know that you have been through a very difficult time but it's over now. You must put the past behind you."

"Is it though?" she asked in a low sibilant voice. "Is it over? I wonder."

She turned to face him, her face bleached ice white, her black clothes accentuating the thinness of her spare frame.

"Jocasta," he said, throwing convention aside, "what is the matter? Terrible things have happened recently, I know. But what in particular has upset you so much?" she collapsed into a chair, weeping bitterly, quite unable to speak, and it was at that fraught moment that Sir Gabriel Kent put his head round the door. He gave John an extremely startled look and inwardly the Apothecary groaned.

"My dear Madam," said the older man, hurrying to Jocasta's side. "You are clearly unwell. What may I fetch you?"

She gazed at him piteously but still could not utter.

"A brandy," said John shortly. "That should help."

"Of course, of course." Sir Gabriel paused in the doorway. "So sorry to interrupt but your wife is asking for you, my boy."

Jocasta found her voice. "I am being a nuisance. It is best that I go." She got to her feet.

John put out a restraining arm. "Please don't leave. If you can just give me ten minutes to sort things out, you and I can have a long chat."

She gave him a look in which lay concealed a hidden message.

"I will speak with you another time," she murmured. "I have moved back to my house in Mayfair. This is my address." She passed him a folded piece of paper.

John put it in his pocket without looking at it. "Please, Jocasta. Wait until you have recovered your spirits."

She shook her head. "No, I have called most inconveniently. I know you mentioned a wife, Mr. Rawlings, but somehow or other I had formed the impression that you and she lived apart. But now I find you in the very bosom of your family. For me to arrive without an appointment was both inexcusable and inconsiderate."

"I might do the same to you one day," he answered, trying to raise a smile.

Jocasta looked him straight in the eye. "That would be different. I live alone," she said, then swept into the hall and out through the front door.

"Oh dear," said Sir Gabriel.

"Oh dear indeed," answered John.

He drew the paper from his pocket, determined to call on the widow shortly and find out what it was that she wanted to say to him. Then he stared at the message for a moment before thrusting it back into his pocket. For no address had been written there: simply the words, 'There is a poisoner in our midst'.

CHAPTER
TEN

John truly knew what it was to feel on the horns of a dilemma. All his training at the hands of London's Principal Magistrate, Sir John Fielding, cried out for him to speed up the road after Jocasta Rayner, to persuade her back to his house, and there to comfort and placate her until she told him what she had meant by the stark message written on the piece of paper she had handed to him. All his instincts as a husband and a new father, were to leap up the stairs to the main bedroom and there to cuddle and kiss his wife and play with Miss Rose Rawlings, that interesting and attractive new addition to his household.

"Oh God!" he said aloud.

His father overheard him. "What did that piece of paper say?"

"See for yourself," and John handed it to him.

Sir Gabriel's golden eyes grew wide. "How very interesting. I wonder what she means."

"She must have seen something at the wake. Something that only now that Ariadne has died does she recognise as a poisoning. Oh 'zounds, but I need to speak to that woman."

"Obviously. But this is not the moment, John. She has trailed her coat cleverly but I do not think this is the right time to follow it."

"What do you mean by that?"

"If she had been putting on an act — I repeat the word *if* — she could not have done so more adroitly. She has you thoroughly intrigued and ready to do anything to find out what she meant by that cryptic note."

"That's true enough."

"Supposing she were bluffing. Have you thought of that?"

John stared at Sir Gabriel aghast. "No, I haven't. What do you mean? How could she be bluffing?"

"Because she might be the poisoner, hiding herself in the depths of this fog that she has conjured up. Surely, is it not a ruse of the guilty party to arouse suspicion about another? Oh my dear boy, leave Mrs. Rayner to her own devices. She will come to you, sure as fate."

Much as the Apothecary would love to have denied every word, liking Jocasta the best of Aidan's daughters, there was a ring of reality about Sir Gabriel's words that stopped him in his tracks. If Montague Bussell were innocent . . . But he dismissed this thought. The case against the man was strong indeed. He was the principal suspect and must be treated as such.

"Damnation," said John loudly and at that moment, in the manner of a truly silly piece of theatre, the front door pealed.

Samuel Swann stood there, large as life, his features mobile, prepared to look joyful or serious depending on the mood within the house. In his arms he carried a large parcel, its paper breaking to reveal what appeared to be the head of a wooden horse. On top of this were flowers, above this again, Samuel's grin as he saw that both Sir Gabriel and John were jolly.

"Is Miss Rawlings in?" he asked.

"Do you have an appointment with her?" asked John seriously. "I'm her father and I'll have no unwanted suitors calling I'll have you know." Then he laughed and embraced his old friend, who came into the hall smelling of the April evening and quite pink in the cheeks with the excitement of it all.

They had known one another for ever, or at least that was how it seemed to the Apothecary. Starting as neighbours, both the boys' mothers dying young, they had been thrown together and had become the firmest of companions from then on. The same age, they had both attended the Reverend Mr. Johnson's school for twenty pupils, situated in a house on the edge of Kensington village. But after that they had gone their different ways, John as an apprentice to Richard Purefoy, Apothecary of Evans Row; Samuel Swann to Edward Hall, Goldsmith of West Cheap. Yet they had remained as close as was possible and now John clasped his friend to him with a great deal of emotion.

"Champagne," said Sir Gabriel, appearing with a bottle and with Mrs. Alleyn who was smiling profoundly.

"I'll go upstairs and check on my ladies," said John. "Then, when they are prepared, you will be allowed to visit them."

"Splendid," answered Samuel, and followed Sir Gabriel into the library, his arms still bulging with parcels, his face a moon of delight.

"Dear Samuel," said Emilia, drawing him down and kissing him.

She was sitting up in bed, having prepared her face and hair and looking as angelic as the day that John had first set eyes on her. The wooden horse was now almost totally visible through its wrapping paper but both she and the Apothecary expressed great surprise and pleasure when it was fully revealed and put on the floor at the end of Rose's cradle. Then they both wept a little at the sight of their large friend leaning over and extending a finger, which the infant promptly grabbed and put in its mouth.

"She's beautiful," Samuel said earnestly.

Neither Emilia nor John made jocular remarks about his turn next, knowing that the Goldsmith's most recent romance with Christabel Witherspoon, sister of the famous artist Julius, had come to an end. It seemed that for such a totally loveable fellow, he was totally unlucky in love. And John wondered if that were part of the trouble. If Samuel were too nice and too kind, and that the majority of young women wanted something a little more challenging. But he kept his own counsel and decided to wait until such time as they were private together before he expressed an opinion — and only then if he were asked for it.

Rose began to make hungry noises and Dorcas appeared. At that the two men departed and made their way downstairs, only to find that Sir Gabriel and Maud were celebrating further before dinner.

"Do stay and dine, my boy," John's father invited.

"I'd love to, Sir."

"Then why don't you two go into the parlour. John is involved in one of Sir John Fielding's affairs at the moment. I'm sure he would love to discuss it with you."

The Apothecary was feeling too benign to argue but inwardly he groaned a little. Samuel adored taking part in enquiries that stemmed from the Public Office, considering himself rather good at interviewing witnesses — a fact which couldn't be further from the truth — and John was utterly sure that with an investigation as involved as this, Samuel would not hesitate to offer his services.

Sure enough, the Goldsmith said, "Consider me in," when John had finished recounting the whole convoluted tale.

"Of course we'll have to get Sir John's permission first."

"Of course. But he's always welcomed me in the past. I think he has quite come to rely on me."

John controlled his features admirably, more than aware that the Magistrate was too kind to rebuff Samuel out of hand but sometimes found it hard to give him a job that was virtually foolproof.

"Indeed," he said noncommittally. "Now, how are things with you?" the Apothecary continued, anxious to change the subject.

Samuel looked gloomy. "My betrothal to Christabel Witherspoon is at an end."

"I didn't realise it had even begun."

"It had not yet been formally announced, that is true. But promises had been made privately. However, after they moved back to London from Islington, and as her brother's reputation as a painter continued to grow, she suddenly found herself the toast of the town." Samuel gave a deep sigh. "It went to her head, I fear. I suppose by comparison I looked too plodding and dull, too ordinary a sort of chap." He emptied his glass in a gulp. "And I am, John. That is my trouble. I am a plain, honest citizen and boring into the bargain. No woman will have me. Think of all the beautiful girls I have known, all of whom have passed me by as soon as they have got to know me. But what am I to do? How can I change?"

He was so kind and so loveable and so distressed that John could have wept. The Apothecary leant forward in his chair so that his face was close to his friend's.

"I don't think you should change, Sam. You are a true delight just as you are. The fault lies with the women, believe me. They are too young to realise your merits. They crave nothing but excitement and glamour, little realising that that plays out soon enough. Besides, you are not boring. Look at the works of art you create with your hands. Your reputation as one of the finest goldsmiths in London grows daily."

"But that does not fill the empty corners of my life."

John's heart bled for his friend. Mankind's cruel enemy loneliness was obviously no stranger to him.

"I hate to give unsolicited advice . . ."

"But John, I need it."

"Then, my dear Samuel, I would suggest that you look amongst women of your own age or, maybe, even a little older. A more mature female will appreciate your qualities far more than a flibbertigibbet."

"But I would like to have a family."

"Oh 'zounds, Sam!" said John crossly. "I said mature, not ancient. Now behave yourself."

His friend cheered up. "Tomorrow I shall go and see Sir John. An investigation is just what I need to help me get over Christabel."

"Yes," answered the Apothecary resignedly. "I'm sure it is, my dear."

It was a journey of memory to be returning to Liquorpond Street in Holbourn, for that was where the enigmatical Dr. Florence Hensey, whose path had crossed with John's on more than one occasion, had lived before the web of intrigue, of which the physician had been the centre, had finally enmeshed him. Remembering how they had first met in a post-chaise heading towards the mysterious Romney Marsh, the Apothecary smiled. He had always liked the man, regardless of everything that had transpired, and nothing could ever erase the genuine concern that the doctor had felt for the suffering of others.

Strangely, Mrs. Trewellan lived but three doors away from Dr. Hensey's old home, and John could not help but glance over his shoulder as he knocked vigorously, half-expecting to see the physician come walking up the street.

An elderly servant answered the door. "Yes, Sir?"

"Is Mrs. Trewellan in? I do not have an appointment but am calling on behalf of Sir John Fielding of the Public Office, Bow Street," said John, cutting straight to the heart of the matter.

"I will see if she is at home, Sir."

He shuffled off only to be replaced by Mrs. Trewellan herself, looking like an unmade black bed in her mourning clothes. "Yes?" she asked in her tiny voice.

"John Rawlings, Ma'am. I represent Sir John Fielding and would like to ask you a few questions regarding the recent tragic events."

She flapped a hand in front of her face as if she were fanning herself. "I don't see how I can help, but do come in."

She was indeed oddly like Mrs. Bussell in appearance, other than for the teeth which, in Mrs. Trewellan, appeared to be of normal size.

"Now, how may I help you?" she asked, when they were seated in the parlour.

"I believe that at one time you were considering marriage with the late Aidan Fenchurch. May I ask why you did not proceed?"

Mrs. Trewellan looked slightly annoyed. "Surely that is my business."

John put on his sympathetic-but-call-of-duty face. "It is, of course, Ma'am. But the fact is that Mr. Fenchurch is dead and so is his former mistress. Therefore we at the Public Office are bound to ask questions. Some of them may appear not to have any bearing on the matter in hand but, believe me, when they are all added together they form a picture."

Mrs. Trewellan emitted a tiny sigh. "Oh very well. I decided against marriage for several reasons. Mr. Fenchurch and my son Sperling . . ."

For one side-splitting second John had thought she was going to say Spotty and had hardly known where to look.

". . . did not see eye to eye. Further, I am partial to the feline species and Aidan could not abide my little pets. Finally, I did not care for the omnipresent Mrs. Bussell. Oh, she pretended great friendship towards me but I was not at ease with her."

"May I ask why?"

Another wee sigh. "I did not trust her. I feared she might do me an injury."

"But you remained friends with Mr. Fenchurch."

"Yes. He was kind enough in his way. I did not wish to fall out with him."

"But you no longer regarded him as a marriage partner?"

Mrs. Trewellan actually simpered. "You seem a very understanding young man."

"Thank you. Tell me, what was your reaction when he was killed? Please speak frankly."

"I thought Mrs. Bussell had done it."

"How interesting. Why?"

"Because I did not believe for one second that her feelings for him had gone away. I thought she was still dangerously entranced with him."

"So what did you think when Ariadne herself was poisoned?"

Mrs. Trewellan looked horrified. "Poisoned, do you say? I was told by Evalina, who called on me yesterday to give me the news, that she died of natural causes."

John shook his head. "We do not think so."

The childish voice quavered. "Then she got what she deserved. Whoever did it rid the world of a horrid, horrid woman."

Unmade bed or no, Mrs. Trewellan certainly did not lack the courage to voice her convictions.

"Have you any idea who that someone might be?" John asked, accepting the cup of tea which his hostess had been pouring for him.

"No. It could have been anyone. She was not well liked."

John nodded. "Perhaps you could clear up a point that has been bothering me. When I first met Mrs. Rayner she refused to believe that her father had an enemy in the world, yet later she said she recalled Mrs. Bussell's infatuation with him. Recently, another party told me that the whole family were aware of Ariadne's pursuit. What, in your opinion, is the truth?"

Mrs. Trewellan sipped her tea. "I think Jocasta might well dissemble. She, more than any of the other girls, put her father on a pedestal. She might well act a part rather than let his memory be besmirched."

Remembering the piece of paper that Mrs. Rayner had handed to him, John asked, "Are you saying that Jocasta would lie in order to protect someone she loved?"

Yet another little sigh. "Lie is such a strong word. Let me say that all the truth might not be revealed."

170

"I understand," said John. He put his cup down. "Mrs. Trewellan, do you think Montague Bussell murdered his wife?"

"Quite likely," she answered. "He knew all about Aidan and Ariadne, even though pretending not to helped preserve his amour propre. I find with those small smelly men, one can never be quite sure when they are going to explode into ill-temper. And that is what I believe must have happened. He had suddenly had enough of both of them. So he arranged for hired killers to do away with Aidan, then poisoned Ariadne himself."

"But surely that would mean he would have to have knowledge of such things. Does he know about poisons, do you think?"

"Couldn't he just have obtained some from the killers?"

"But why not ask them to do it? There's something wrong here," said John, thinking aloud.

"Perhaps he wanted the satisfaction of killing his faithless spouse personally," said a voice from the door. Sperling Trewellan had entered the room.

His mother got to her feet. "Dearest, this gentleman is John Rawlings, who is here on behalf of Sir John Fielding, following on the visit of Mr. Jago. We are discussing the death of Aidan and Mrs. Bussell. It seems that her demise was no accident but deliberate poisoning."

Sperling flicked some invisible dust from his lapel. "The only surprise regarding that is the fact that somebody did not do it years ago."

"I take it you did not like her?" asked John, his crooked smile appearing.

"She was a spoiler," answered Sperling succinctly. "She could not bear to see anyone else having fun. She would move heaven and earth to stop them. And now somebody has stopped her — for good."

The Apothecary realised with a lurch of his heart that he was duty bound to report to Sir John that the field was open, that to nail Montague as principal suspect was hardly fair without a full investigation of everybody else.

"Did she ever do anything to you personally?" John asked, the question out of his mouth before he had time to think.

Sperling did not give a direct answer but continued the story. "She believed that my mama was the cause of her downfall. She thought that Aidan tired of her because he had met someone else. In truth he had been off her for some considerable time but was too frightened to tell her. Then she started to shadow him. But no doubt you know all about that?" John nodded. "Then she turned her attentions to Mother. Threatening her with God knows what if she didn't leave Aidan alone."

The Apothecary turned to Mrs. Trewellan. "Is this true?"

"Oh yes. But I saw her off. Aidan and I told her that we would reveal everything to her husband — every last detail — if she didn't go away."

Sperling gave a bitter laugh. "She was actually afraid of that, imagining herself without the man who had

172

paid for every aspect of her dilettante life. But she could not let the matter drop entirely. So she turned her attentions to me."

"What did she do?"

"Sent her two horrible sons to fleece me at cards." Sperling changed colour, his face going white so that his spots stood out like shimmering red eruptions. "I'd always considered myself a reasonable player so I played deep — too bloody deep. I lost every penny that my father had left me. All was gone except the clothes I stood up in and the roof over my head. If it had not been for my mama's charity I would have become a pauper overnight."

John felt certain without any evidence at all, that here lay the cause of Sperling's quarrel with Aidan Fenchurch, who had probably called him every kind of fool and accused him of sponging off his mother. Emilia's words, 'My money's on Spotty', came back and rang in his ears hollowly.

Mrs. Trewellan heaved herself out of the chair, her strange robe-like garment rippling as she did so. "Poor boy," she said. "It was so unfair that he was punished."

"Was Mr. Fenchurch sympathetic?"

She opened her mouth to answer but before she could do so, Sperling spoke for her. "No, he was not. Said that I was mad to get involved with two professional gamblers like that."

Making a mental note to tell Serafina of this development, John said, "Was that when you two fell out?"

It was Mrs. Trewellan's turn to speak even though the question had been directed at her son. "I thought Aidan's attitude was cruel and unjust. That is when I began to see him in his true colours, yes."

"So in a way Mrs. Bussell succeeded," the Apothecary said to himself.

"What was that?"

"I said Ariadne won the point. You and Aidan decided not to marry."

The widow lost colour. "I never thought of it like that. But you are right. She out-manoeuvred all of us. By God, what a cunning creature she was."

"Cunning but stupid," said her son. "Remember that, Mother. Creatures that rely on cunning have no intellect."

John cleared his throat and changed the subject. "Did Evalina say when Mrs. Bussell's funeral is to be?"

"The day after tomorrow in West Clandon. It seems they want to get it over as quickly as possible."

"I wonder what the Coroner said at the inquest?"

"No doubt you'll find out. Now, can we be of any further assistance to you?" Sperling was obviously anxious to draw the interview to a close as Mrs. Trewellan's somewhat soggy eyes were starting to brim with tears.

"No," said John, standing up. "You have been more than helpful. I am most grateful." He went to the door and Sperling escorted him into the hall. "Tell me, will you attend the burial?"

The young man grinned. "But of course. I wouldn't miss it for the world."

"Did you kill her?" the Apothecary asked suddenly.

"Only in my mind. But then, I expect, so did a lot of other people."

"Yes, I'm sure you're right about that. Well, good day to you."

"Until we meet again," said Sperling, and for a moment looked quite unbearably sad.

He should have gone back to the shop but everything kept nagging at him. Thoughts flew through his mind like arrows, particularly the question of Jocasta and her extraordinary message. Was she the poisoner, hiding herself in a fog of deceit? Or had she seen something of enormous significance? In the end John could stand it no more and walked the short distance to Bloomsbury Square.

Everybody was out except for Miss Millicent, he was informed, and she was lying down with a megrim. Furious with himself that he was not carrying a medical bag, John hired a hackney coach, rushed to Shug Lane, picked up a jar of powdered Pellitory of Spain, hurled himself back into the waiting carriage and returned to the invalid, all of this achieved in under thirty minutes. As a reward for his efforts he was ushered into the sick room.

Millicent lay in the dark, the curtains drawn against the bright spring sunshine.

"May I?" asked John, and pulled one back in order to throw enough light to move around. She winced. "Oh, my head. I cannot remember a more savage attack than this."

"Nervous tension," he replied, nodding wisely. "You have all of you been through the most enormous ordeal of late." He handed her the jar. "Here, try some of this."

She peered at it cautiously. "What is it?"

"Pellitory of Spain, one of the best purgers of the brain that grows. Chew the powdered root, Miss Millicent, or sniff some up like snuff. It will clear the megrim in no time."

"Oh I do hope so." She put some into her mouth and chewed. "I must be well to support Evalina through the funeral."

"You refer to Mrs. Bussell's?" Millicent nodded. "I did not realise Evalina was so attached to her."

"Oh she was, in her way. Of course, Evalina is not prone to attacks of sentiment, but dear Ariadne was so good to her."

"Good gracious," said John, genuinely astonished.

Millicent burbled on. "Evalina can get so depressed, about ..." She whispered the next three words. "... the devil's mark. But Ariadne was always tremendously bright, you know. Told her that looks are of no significance; that it is the beauty within that counts."

The Apothecary felt sick but grinned feebly. "How nice."

"Anyway, we are rallying behind Montague and going to the funeral."

"All of you?"

"Yes, Jocasta is taking Louisa and Lieutenant Mendoza. They are staying with her at the moment."

John seized his opportunity. "Jocasta asked me to call but I don't have her address."

"Oh, she's in Curzon Street. Number seventeen. But I believe she's out today and leaves for Surrey tomorrow."

"I'll probably wait until she returns in that case," said John, scribbling the address on a piece of paper and putting it into his pocket. "Now, how's the head?"

"I do believe it's better," said Millicent, raising herself carefully from the pillow.

"Just keep chewing until the pain goes."

"So kind of you to bother."

"Part of my job."

"Is it? Oh yes, I'd almost forgotten. Will you be at the funeral, Mr. Rawlings?"

"No. Despite the fact that I'm always around I'm not really part of the family."

"Of course you're not. How silly of me." She laughed nervously.

Feeling that this really was not the moment to ask her anything further, John bowed politely and made his way out.

The need to talk to Sir John Fielding, to tell him of Jocasta's note, to ask the great man's opinion, was so strong that the Apothecary found himself heading for Bow Street, regardless of the fact that the court might be in session and more than likely he would have to wait. Hurrying down Drury Lane, the Apothecary had a sudden sense of urgency, as if it were imperative that he got there quickly. So much so that he had almost broken into a run by the time he had reached Russell Street and doubled back to the entrance to Bow Street. Consequently, he was out of breath by the time he rushed through the front door and into the Public Office.

The place was in pandemonium, Court Runners scurrying about as if they had taken leave of their senses.

"What's going on?" John asked Runner Munn, a veteran of the old days when Sir John's half-brother Henry had been Principal Magistrate.

"A man has been taken ill, Sir. A man who walked in and asked to see Sir John. A physician has been sent for but has not yet arrived."

"Where is he? Perhaps I can offer some assistance."

"He's in that room over there." Runner Munn pointed. "It's a bit of a mess within, Sir. He's purging and casting."

John rolled his eyes. "Oh no. I've got a decent coat on."

Runner Munn grimaced. "Best take it off, Sir. There are some types of stain that will never come out, you know."

Removing the garment then bracing himself, John opened the door. Lying on the floor in the midst of his own vomit, the state of his breeches indescribable, lay Montague Bussell.

"God's tears," said the Apothecary, running to him. "What has happened to you, man?"

But the poor creature could not speak. He clutched John's shirt, holding fast to it as if it were a lifeline, and tried to mouth a word. Bending his head close, despite the appalling smell, the Apothecary strained to hear what was being said.

Montague's lips moved. "Rake."

"What?"

"Ake."

It was no good, the word was unintelligible. Frantically rummaging in his medical bag, John sought anything that might alleviate the man's suffering. But the only thing he could find was a strong sedative which he was reluctant to give lest Montague fall asleep and choke. Feeling more helpless than he had ever done in his entire life, John just held poor Bussell close.

The door opened again and John felt the arrival of the Magistrate rather than saw him.

"Well?" said Sir John.

John shook his head. "There is nothing I can do."

"Do you mean . . . ?"

But the answer was provided by Montague Bussell himself, who, with one final scream of agony, gave up the struggle and died in the Apothecary's arms.

CHAPTER
ELEVEN

In all the years he had known him, John Rawlings had never seen the Magistrate so silent. This was a silence far removed from his old ploy of sitting completely still, uttering not a word, frequently giving the impression that he had fallen asleep. This was something far more profound. Sir John Fielding was like a statue, only the slight rise and fall of his chest showing that he breathed at all.

Today he had on a dark grey suit and a shirt of white cambric, his long white wig falling in curls to his shoulders, his strong features composed and still, the black bandage he always wore concealing his sightless eyes from the world. Yet he was not composed, John knew that, for his mouth twitched very slightly as the muscles around it pulled with tension. Indeed, in all his many recollections of the man he regarded as his mentor, the Apothecary had never seen him so strained.

Eventually Sir John Fielding spoke, his voice a rasp in his chest. "You say that Bussell has died?"

"Yes, Sir."

"Dear God, what a terrible thing for the Public Office. That a man comes in, quite freely and without duress, to speak to us, and then dies in agony in one of the rooms. John, what have we come to?" He sunk his head into his hands and made a noise that sounded suspiciously like a sob.

"But, Sir, the poor bastard was dying anyway. From what I can make out, Montague Bussell grew tired of hiding in St. James's Square, decided to come to Bow Street and tell us what he could but on his way must have called in somewhere and there he was poisoned."

The Magistrate raised his head. "You are sure of that? There is no way in which he could have died of natural causes?"

"He exhibited identical symptoms to that of his wife. My guess is they were killed by Water Hemlock, sometimes called Dropwort. It grows all over the place, is completely lethal, bringing about death within three hours."

Sir John sighed wearily. "What a fool I am. I had put the poor wretch down as our principal suspect."

The Apothecary shook his head. "Sir, this case is much more complex than that. I have felt recently that there are far more strands to it than meet the eye. The other night Mrs. Jocasta Rayner called on me. Under the pretext of giving me her address, she left a note which read, 'There is a poisoner in our midst'."

"God's wounds, what did she mean?"

"Just that, I imagine. I took it that she had seem something at the wake which she later realised was poison being admistered to Ariadne Bussell. However, I feel it only fair to tell you that my father took another view. Namely, that that could have been a deliberate ploy on her part; that Jocasta herself was guilty and this was her way of disguising herself."

Sir John shook his head. "Aidan Fenchurch, Ariadne Bussell and now her husband. These crimes are beginning to resemble those of a Jacobean tragedy."

It was the Apothecary's turn to remain silent. Eventually he said, "I know the first has to be linked but yet it is so different from the other two. Is it possible that they are not related?"

The Magistrate exhaled breath slowly. "No. All my experience, all my instincts rebel at the thought. These three are connected by one of the oldest emotions in the world."

"Revenge? Jacobean indeed."

"Quite. Still, I agree with you that the brutal bludgeoning of a man to death is far removed from the subtlety of a poison that regards specialist knowledge to employ. But for all that these murders are linked, take my word for it."

"Yet, Sir, you must admit that the murder of Aidan Fenchurch raises many unanswered questions."

Sir John Fielding lifted his head and the black bandage turned in the Apothecary's direction just as if the Magistrate were looking at him. "Mr. Rawlings, there is something very complex here. So complex that neither of us as yet can begin to credit what it can be."

"You're right, of course, it is all very strange. Now, what is to be done with poor Bussell's body?"

"It is to be taken to the mortuary. There a physician will look at it. But that is a mere formality; he will be able to add nothing to what you have said yourself."

"I think I'll clean him up a bit before he goes. Nobody should have to bear the shame of soiled breeches. Do you have anything fresh we can put on him?"

Sir John rumbled a half laugh. "Strangely, yes. A child thief came in the other day, its speciality thieving from cascades of clothes hung out to dry. We put his cache in a cupboard somewhere. I'll get a Runner to dig out some breeks."

"What did you do with the boy?"

"Sent him to train for the sea. Prison would have killed the child."

"The navy probably will as well."

"At least he'll stand a fighting chance."

"Yes, poor soul."

With this thought of justice, rough but fair, the Apothecary left Sir John's salon and went down to the room, now locked, in which Montague Bussell lay dead.

Admitted by a Runner, John stood looking at all that was left of the wretched fellow, somehow made even smaller and more vulnerable by death. He may have been a whiskery rattish being in life but everything about him was now less noticeable, as if his features were already taking on the mask-like cast of someone who was no longer there. The Apothecary realised that he had forgotten to close the man's eyes and bent down to do so. As he did, he looked into them and saw that they were empty, void. Was there, then, John asked himself, such a thing as a soul that had already gone on its way? Had the essence of the creature who had once been Bussell started on a new quest? In an age of strong religious beliefs, the Apothecary felt, unlike his fellows, that he knew nothing and accepted nothing, his only certainty that the eyes of the dead become so still and empty.

With a sigh, he set to work; preparing Montague's body to go decently to its coffin and the room in Bow Street to be fit for interviewing people once more.

Thoughts of the soul returned to John that evening, long after he had firmly put the whole sad and sordid business of Montague Bussell's demise from his mind. It was the way in which Rose Rawlings, newborn though she might be, gurgled with joy at the sight of Joe Jago. If she had been strong enough to have held out her arms she would have done so, her father felt sure of that. As it was, dandled on her grandmother's lap, her eyes moved round as Joe came into the library and she let out a cry of delight.

"Hello, Miss," said the clerk.

She gave the smile that everyone said was flatulence, everyone except for John that is.

"She knows you," said the Apothecary.

"What nonsense," answered Maud Alleyn.

But even she could not explain the way the small bundle wriggled and squirmed and started to cry and would not be content until her father, rather moist of eye, handed her to Joe, who held the infant against his rugged cheek and talked to her in a strange child's version of cant, the language of the street people that few could understand.

184

It was then that he thought of the leaping soul and wondered, briefly, if this was the journey that it made, so that those who had known each other before might have a momentary glimpse of recognition before the instant passed. Then Sir Gabriel came in, tonight very beautifully dressed as he was escorting Maud to the playhouse, this being her last evening in London before she returned to her home in Chelsea, and the mood was broken. Nursemaids appeared; the child was taken away; a footman came in, stoked the fire, then brought a tray of refreshment. John and Joe were left alone to talk.

"Sir John tells me that the peachers could find no link between Mrs. Bussell and the attack on Aidan. Is that right?"

"Absolutely, Sir. None of the rough boyos were employed, that's for sure. None's that's known, that is. Also, Mrs. Bussell had no large sums of money about her: banks are reluctant to give information but the name Sir John Fielding carries great weight."

"So where does that leave us?"

"Where indeed? At the moment it seems impossible to tie the first murder in with her."

The Apothecary slapped his fingers to his forehead. "And we are mad even to try to do so. Now that she is dead it is obvious that another hand was behind it all."

"Yes," said Joe. "Yes." And he sat silently.

"What are you thinking?" asked John.

"I don't know yet, Sir. But there might be a web here. Supposing, just supposing, mind, that Mrs.

Bussell had her lover murdered, and then somebody else murdered her out of spite."

" 'Zounds! Are you serious?"

"It's as good a theory as any other."

"Then where does Montague fit in?"

"Whoever took her out, took him as well for good measure."

John sipped his wine. "It makes a certain kind of terrible sense."

"I think it's the answer, Sir." Joe puffed on his pipe and looked at the Apothecary through the swirls of blue smoke.

"So, let me think it through. Ariadne hires two assassins and kills Aidan. Someone, probably a member of his family, finds out and wreaks a Jacobean revenge."

"I don't know about the last bit, Sir," said Joe earnestly, "but the rest sounds right to me."

"Then it's back to the family, every last one of 'em."

"Including the recently wed Lieutenant."

"Certainly including him. By his own admittance he had few prospects until he married a pretty little heiress."

"How has the dead man's property been devolved?"

"I could be wrong but I think Evalina has the Bloomsbury Square house, Jocasta Foxfire Hall, which she intends to share with Millicent. Louisa I'm not sure about."

"She won't be left poor in any event."

"Joe, the dashing Lieutenant called into my shop earlier today, before the death of poor wretched Bussell, and said that he was being accused of hiring assassins to do away with Aidan Fenchurch."

Jago's face temporarily vanished in wreaths of smoke. "Um. Interesting."

"Do you think he did it to draw suspicion away from himself?"

"It's possible."

"But even if he did kill Fenchurch, for whom his family had no liking, why should he kill the Bussells? What grudge could he possibly have had against them?"

"None that we know of. No, I think I'm right. The late Ariadne arranged for Aidan to be killed. The other two deaths were acts of revenge for that first crime."

"But you yourself said that there was nothing tangible to associate her with Fenchurch's murder. So perhaps there is just one single person behind it all."

"There's only one thing certain about the whole affair," said Joe thoughtfully.

"And that is?"

"That it is going to be well nigh impossible to solve," answered the clerk, and puffed ferociously upon his pipe.

Churches are open to all and sundry and, with this in the mind, the Apothecary had written to Serafina de Vignolles asking her, if her social calendar so permitted, to attend the funeral of Ariadne Bussell and remark anything of interest that should take place there. So he was more than pleased when the day after the sad event a letter came by special messenger. It read as follows.

'My Dear Friend,

Even though the Deceased was A Person of Obnoxious Ilk, the Occasion of her Burial was Indeed Sad. The Two Hulking Sons, as full of Sentiment as they are Devoid of Wit, seemed Wrung to their Veritable Withers by the Loss of Two Parents in So Short a Space of Time and Howled like Hounds at the Gravemouth . . . '

Reading this, John Rawlings did not know whether to laugh or cry.

' . . . and Drank Themselves to Surly Stupor at the Wake. Madam Boscawen was Present, as were Several of The Onslows. The Fenchurchs presented a Formidable Front, Grim Faced and Silent. Miss Evalina Fainted with a Shriek, calling Out "Father How Could You?" as Mrs. Bussell's Coffin was Lowered. Other than for the Usual Muted Disputes which Always Occur at Interments, there was Nothing of Particular Interest to Report. However, it Did Appear to Me that the Grief of the Two Sons was So Acute as to be Almost Unreal. Was it A Charade? I asked Myself. Or are They too Stupid to Enact such a Thing? Good Hunting in Your Search for the Villain.

I Have the Honour to Remain, Sir, Your Loyal Friend,

S. de Vignolles.'

John put the letter down, then sat in silent thought. Serafina had responded so quickly that he doubted if any present at the funeral had as yet returned to London, with the possible exception of Lieutenant Mendoza, whose army duties would not allow him freedom to roam. Yet he had no idea where the Lieutenant and his pretty wife were housed permanently, then remembered that they were staying with her sister in Curzon Street.

On the previous evening Joe had made one of his famous lists, setting out whom both of them should visit. At the top of the Apothecary's had been the name of Jocasta Rayner. So, John thought, a call to the new development of Mayfair would seem the most sensible course of action. He drew out his watch and saw that it was still very early. None the less he felt an enormous need to take action of some kind, even if it was only to find out that everyone remained out of town. Calling out to Irish Tom to bring round the coach, John went upstairs to say goodbye to his wife and daughter.

"You look worried," said Emilia.

"It's this damnable case of bludgeoning and poisoning. Joe thinks there are two different hands behind it."

"The first murder triggering off the other two?"

"Precisely. Then there's Jocasta's sinister note. 'There is a poisoner in our midst'."

"Um," said Emilia thoughtfully. "I don't trust that."

"Why?"

"Because why say it? She can't name a member of her family — unless she is very spiteful — so what is she trying to achieve?" She did not stop for an answer. "She is deflecting suspicion from herself in my view. She's up to no good, mark my words."

"You are very acute, Madam, for a woman who has just given birth."

"For a woman who has just grown very bored," she replied. "John, today I am going to get up. I feel I have gazed too long on this bedroom. Rose is allowed downstairs so why shouldn't I go too?"

"No reason," he said, and kissed her. "If I told you to rest you would only grow irritable. I long ago realised that I am just clay in your hands. Act as you will, Wife."

She laughed and threw a pillow at him. "Don't worry, Husband. I have every intention of so doing. Good day to you."

"Good day," he answered, and went downstairs to his awaiting carriage.

He could have walked to Curzon Street, in fact would have enjoyed doing so, but time was of the essence as Nicholas had already gone ahead to open the shop. Therefore John arrived at his destination shortly before nine o'clock. In the event, Tom was forced to draw up in a side street, where the Apothecary disembarked and proceeded the rest of the short distance on foot. So it was that as he was approaching Jocasta Rayner's house, the front door opened and Lieutenant Mendoza stepped out without seeing him.

John was just about to call a greeting when the Lieutenant ran towards a hackney coach that was just dropping off a lady passenger. Having gallantly helped her out, the military man said quite distinctly, "Liquorpond Road, Holbourn, if you please."

Every hackle rose as John was seized with the sudden conviction that another twist in the strange tale of Aidan Fenchurch and his associates was about to reveal itself. Running as fast as he could, the Apothecary hastened back to where Tom was edging his way through the carts and chairs.

"A change of plan," he called up to the Irishman. "To Liquorpond Road."

"Same number as the other day, Sir?"

"I don't know at the moment but I wouldn't be at all surprised."

And sure enough, just as they entered the end of the street they saw the Lieutenant's conveyance draw up outside Mrs. Trewellan's house and the young man run up the steps. John got out of the coach with a jump and hurried up the road, hoping to catch any conversation that might take place.

Mrs. Trewellan, still resembling a big black bed, came to the door in the wake of the servant who answered it. Flattened behind a pillar, the Apothecary peeped round just in time to see her smile rapturously.

The tiny little voice was full of joy as it said, "Oh, my darling."

"I've missed you so much," answered the Lieutenant, and with their arms wrapped tightly round each other, the couple went into the house and closed the door.

CHAPTER
TWELVE

"What the hell," said John Rawlings crossly, "do I do now?"

"Well, you can't call in on 'em, that's for sure," Irish Tom answered cheerfully, sinking a great mouthful of ale. "Not without some mighty good excuse."

They were sitting in the taproom of The Three Cups, master and servant in discussion in a most democratic manner of which Sir Gabriel Kent would have thoroughly disapproved.

John drank a swig almost as large as Tom's, then shook his head and sighed. "The most interesting development since Jocasta's note and there's nothing I can do about it."

"How about a letter?" said the coachman. "Could you not forge something and say you were delivering it on behalf of someone? You've got to get in there, Sir. Why, even now they could be rolling in bed together merry as fleas on an old dog's chin."

"Even if they are," the Apothecary answered gloomily, "I can't walk into a lady's boudoir uninvited. Dear God, the fellow must be mad, Tom. That little Louisa's a pretty doll, and a rich one into the bargain. What the devil's he playing at?"

"Perhaps he likes 'em big," said the Irishman with relish. "I mean to say, she's been a pretty woman in her day, but that day is long past. As for her voice, sure t'would be enough to frighten the little people themselves. Hey, Sir, do you think they are the murderers? Carrying on and plotting the whole thing behind the scenes?"

"I don't know what I think any more."

"But they could be," said Tom, warming to his theme. "She could secretly have hated Mr. Fenchurch, as you say the Lieutenant did. So the two fellows who attack him are him — the army man — and Spotty. She poisons the rest."

"A good theory but unfortunately Mendoza was in the process of eloping when Aidan was killed."

The Irishman looked downcast. "Oh well." He cheered up. "Why couldn't I visit and say I was presenting her with a bottle of perfume with your compliments?"

"I could do that myself but I don't happen to have any perfume about me."

"True enough, but I could race back to the shop and get some."

John looked doubtful. "By the time you returned, the Lieutenant would probably have gone."

Irish Tom spread his hands. "Then we're finished, Sir. I've no more ideas."

John looked thoughtful. "I suppose I could call and ask if she has details of Montague Bussell's funeral."

"But why should she?"

"No reason at all. But at least it's an excuse. Come on, Tom, let's do it. Down your ale and get me there before I lose heart."

It was only a quick journey to Liquorpond Street but even in that short space of time the Apothecary questioned whether he was doing the right thing in going. Yet the puzzle was so intriguing he felt he would have a seizure if he did not solve it. For what could a handsome newly-married man with a gorgeous and rich young bride be doing making amorous advances to Mrs. Trewellan, who, when all was said, might well appeal to the likes of Aidan Fenchurch but certainly not to the younger generation. Uneasy with such thoughts, the Apothecary reached his hand up to pull the street door-bell, then withdrew it again, then finally gave a short purposeful tug before he could change his mind.

A maid appeared. "Yes, Sir?"

"Mrs. Trewellan, if you please. My card." The Apothecary produced one and thrust it under the girl's nose.

She read it with some difficulty. "I believe Madam is resting, Sir."

John's mind cut capers at the images the words conjured up. "Then may I wait? The matter is somewhat urgent."

"Mr. Sperling is here, Sir. He's home early from his business."

The Apothecary assumed an expression of delighted surprise. "Oh, how excellent. He and I are very friendly."

The girl looked as if she did not believe him but none the less ushered him into a small parlour where Sperling, his spots on fire, sat, looking decidedly unwell. John bowed beautifully.

"My dear Sir, what a pleasure to see you again. I trust I find you in good health."

Sperling rolled a somewhat yellowish eye. "No, Sir, you do not. I was sent home by my employers because the sight of my skin offends them. See here, how foul it grows."

And he pointed with a slightly shaky finger at one of the more hideous eruptions. John produced a pair of magnifying spectacles from an inner pocket and, putting them on, bent close to Sperling's face.

"May I?" The young man nodded and the Apothecary examined in silence. "Morphew," he said eventually.

"What?"

"You have a severe form of the skin complaint known as morphew. But surely you have been told that before."

"I have consulted the family physician, yes, but he prescribed some blasted product that turned my face bright green. Mr. Rawlings, I told you t'other day of my financial position. I have to work to help this household. So I hold a wretched post in a shipping office, clerking. Anyway, my work fellows despise me and are only too happy to deride my wretched condition. My verdant face was a subject of so much hilarity that I was forced to stop using the ointment."

"And you tried nothing else?"

"No, I gave up. Which I suppose was rather feeble of me."

"Yes, I'm afraid it was. I am going to prescribe a special mixture of my own. It consists of an infusion of Scurvy-Grass, of which you must take several doses a day, and the juice of Sheep's Rampion which you must apply externally, again several times a day. This is a powerful combination and should cure you within two months. It may leave a few scars but better that than weeping sores."

Sperling looked slightly doubtful. "You are an apothecary, aren't you?"

John felt sufficiently sorry for him not to become irritated. "Yes. Now, Sir, would you like to call into my shop later this morning and we can have the medicaments ready for you? It is in Shug Lane, Piccadilly." And he handed the young man a card.

Sperling read it and looked a little shame-faced. "I'm sorry I sounded doubtful. It is just that I had it in my mind that you were some kind of Runner."

John smiled. "I suppose I am in a way. I have worked with Sir John Fielding on several occasions. As you know, he is blind. Because of this he likes to have around him sighted people he can trust. I happen to be one of them and I consider it a great honour."

"Indeed." Sperling rang a bell. "Will you join me in a sherry? I allow myself this luxury when I am not working."

"Just one," John answered. "I unfortunately have a great deal to do today."

Sperling nodded, gave the order to the maid, then smiled at the Apothecary rather sadly. "You called to see Mama?"

"Yes. I wondered if she had any information regarding the funeral of Montague Bussell."

The young man managed to look doleful and excited simultaneously. "I say, what a business. Is it true that he died in Bow Street?"

"Yes."

"What was he doing there?"

"Apparently he wanted to make a statement of some kind but never got that far. Whoever had poisoned him had done so shortly before he arrived, and he started to cast and have laxes, then died."

Sperling clapped his hand over his mouth and widened his eyes. "'Zounds, what a disaster."

"It was indeed."

"Do you know I almost felt sorry for those two brutes at their mother's funeral. To lose two parents to the poisoner's juice within a matter of days must make them not only sad but uneasy."

"Why do you say that?"

"Because they could be next."

The girl returned with a decanter and two glasses, then left the room again.

"That had never occurred to me," said John.

"What?"

"That this might be a vendetta against the Bussell family. But if it were, where would that place the killing of Aidan Fenchurch?"

Sperling shook his head. "I don't know. Could have been a street robbery all along."

John groaned aloud. "What a terrible affair this is. As soon as one settles into a theory another one comes along to displace it."

Sperling looked sympathetic. "It must be awful for you."

The Apothecary decided to change the subject before too much was said. "Is your mother within? I need to have the briefest of words with her."

The young man pulled a face. "She has a visitor at present. I don't know how long they will be."

So he knew that Mendoza was in the house, John thought. But whatever excuse could the amorous woman have made?

"A little early for a call," he ventured.

"But you came now," Sperling replied pleasantly.

God's wounds, thought the Apothecary, wondering where to turn next. But his dilemma was solved for him by a further clank of the doorbell.

"Another early caller," he said.

"Yes," answered Sperling and burst into violent laughter which seemed to the Apothecary to be quite inappropriate.

The maid appeared. "Mrs. Mendoza, Sir."

John nearly fell clean out of his chair. So here was a can of worms. It would appear that the beautiful Louisa had discovered her husband's infidelity and was on his trail. He shot a glance at Sperling who had gone very white beneath his pimples.

Seized by the horrid idea that the young man was going to send her away again, the Apothecary decided to intervene.

"Ah, dear Louisa," he said, shooting to his feet. "Such a delightful girl. It will be a pleasure to have a glass of sherry with her."

Sperling looked stricken. "Yes," he said in a strained voice. "Mary, show her in."

A second later there was a flouncing of skirts in the doorway and there stood the little beauty, radiant in deep blue and white, her red hair unpowdered and a mass of flying curls, a saucy concoction of feathers atop the lot.

"Charming," said John, bowing and kissing her hand. "Mrs. Mendoza, we meet again."

She looked blank, then recognition came. "Weren't you at Father's funeral?"

"Indeed I was, Madam. I am investigating his death on behalf of the Public Office, Bow Street, and have become quite friendly with your family in the meantime. I am an apothecary by trade and was able to treat your sisters for shock and depression."

"How kind of you," Louisa said absently. She turned to her host. "Sperling, is my husband here? He flew out of the house in a veritable whirlwind but one of the servants thought he heard him direct a hackney to Liquorpond Street."

Sperling gulped. "I think he must have been mistaken. The Lieutenant's not here."

Louisa frowned. "Oh, how strange. Well then, I'm sorry to have disturbed you."

"Have a sherry," said John, quite overstepping the bounds of polite behaviour in his desperation to keep her there.

Both she and Sperling looked utterly astonished but at least he had the good grace to mutter, "Yes, please do."

John made much of drawing his watch from his pocket and staring at it.

"I wonder how much longer Mrs. Trewellan's visitor will be," he said loudly. "I really cannot leave my apprentice alone in the shop for another half hour."

Louisa, who had taken both a seat and a glass, looked startled. "Your mother has a caller?" she asked Sperling.

"Er, yes. But he . . . she . . . shouldn't be much longer. Hark . . ." he announced theatrically, ". . . I think I hear them going now."

And there was indeed the sound of footsteps in the hall. "Ha, ha," said John, looking quite insane as he once more shot to his feet and grabbed his hat. "I must be off. Indeed I must. Thank you, thank you, my friend. Madam, it has been a pleasure."

And he flew through the door and into the hallway, startling the maid who was just showing the visitor out.

"I must leave," the Apothecary told the terrified girl. "A matter of the uttermost urgency."

And he grabbed the inner knob and hurled himself into the street.

The Lieutenant was already several strides ahead of him and John took to his heels in order to catch him up. At the sound of pounding feet, Mendoza whirled round.

"Mr. Rawlings!" he exclaimed in utter astonishment. "What the devil are you doing here?"

"I might well ask the same of you," the Apothecary replied grimly.

A look of intense fury crossed the military man's handsome Latin features. "Exactly what do you mean by that?"

"I mean that I find it odd you should be whiling away an hour or two with a mature widowed lady while your pretty young wife is forced to come looking for you."

"I don't like your inference, Sir."

"You must draw from it what you will."

Lieutenant Mendoza appeared to explode with wrath. His face went red, his eyes bulged, a bead of sweat burst onto his forehead. "How dare you accuse me? You know nothing of the matter whatsoever. You should keep your nose out of other people's affairs, you interfering little prick."

"I do not think it is your place to insult me," said John haughtily.

"Place be damned," shouted the Lieutenant, and crashed a hard-knuckled fist onto the Apothecary's chin, swearing violently as he did so.

"Oh dear Lord," groaned John with an air of resignation, as he slowly slithered to the ground, saw a wonderful flurry of stars, and then lost consciousness.

CHAPTER
THIRTEEN

He awoke to find that he had been propped up against some railings and that Sperling and Louisa, together with Samuel Swann of all unlikely people, were administering to him in a somewhat ineffectual manner. With a groan of pain, the Apothecary reached into his pocket, found his bottle of salts, took an extremely hearty sniff and thus revived himself.

"My dear friend," said Samuel loudly, clapping John on the shoulder and making him wince. "What happened to you? Were you set upon by footpads?"

The Apothecary gingerly fingered his chin. "No. I was crunched on the jaw by one extremely angry young man."

"The blackguard. Who is he? I'll knock his damnable block off."

John was just about to open his mouth to say 'Mendoza' when Louisa's charming little face came into his line of vision and he thought better of it. However Sperling, looking agitated beyond belief, caught the Apothecary's eye then rapidly glanced away again as he guessed the truth.

Samuel was snorting like an angry horse. "It's too bad, so it is. Hare and hounds, but a man can no longer safely walk the streets of his home city without fear of attack. We need more Runners, and that's a fact."

John grimaced as he started to heave himself to his feet. "Stop sounding so middle-aged and give me a hand up, will you? What are you doing here anyway?"

The Goldsmith looked mysterious, then winked slowly. "Private business," he said.

If it hadn't been so painful John would have laughed. It was crystal clear that Samuel had made good his plan to call on the Blind Beak and offer his services, and that Sir John had found him something relatively unimportant to do.

Sperling spoke. "You'd best come back into the house, Mr. Rawlings. I'm sure Mama will be ready to receive you by now."

"Yes, I'm sure she will," John answered with meaning. "Anyway, thank you all the same but my coachman should be somewhere near by and I really must get back to my shop. I will be perfectly all right, particularly if Mr. Swann would care to accompany me."

Groggy though he was, the Apothecary managed to convey a note of mystery into the last few words which set Samuel sniffing the air like a hound catching a scent, an endearing characteristic of his which never failed to amuse John.

"I passed your coach on the way but the driver wasn't there," he said earnestly, then looked contrite as if he had betrayed a secret.

"He'll be close by," John assured him. With a heave the Apothecary managed to get on his feet.

203

Louisa looked anxious. "Are you sure you're all right, Mr. Rawlings?"

"Perfectly." But for all that he was glad of Samuel's strong arm as they made their farewells and walked slowly back to the deserted coach. As they approached, Irish Tom came panting up.

"I saw the affray and gave the villain chase, Sir. He wouldn't stop and fight me like a man but for all that I gave him a good trounce over the arse with me whip. Foreign devil."

John smiled bleakly. "Thanks, Tom."

"'Twas nothing, Sir. There's nothing I like better than a good mill and I'd have had one if the coward hadn't run like the hound of hell was in hot pursuit of him."

"I think it was more likely his wife," said John.

Tom looked very wise and nodded several times. "Ah now, that would explain it, so it would."

"What on earth has been going on?" asked Samuel, as the coach made its way through the crowded streets towards Shug Lane.

"What hasn't," answered John, and caught his friend up with all the latest developments as the journey proceeded.

The Goldsmith looked aghast. "You mean to say that the man who hit you is having an affair of the heart with that full-blown friend of the late Mr. Fenchurch?"

"How colourfully put. But yes, is the answer. That is unless they have some other sort of connection." He looked thoughtful.

"What could that be, though?"

"I have no idea. But as this case has more strands than any I have ever come across before, nothing at all would surprise me."

Nicholas, pale but determined, had managed to cope with a rush of custom, all entering the shop together on the way home from a rout, while dealing with his personal anxiety as to the whereabouts of his Master, who appeared to have vanished without trace. And when John had finally come staggering out of his coach and made his way straight to the compounding room, looking far from well, he had risen to the occasion even more admirably. Without instruction a potion had been mixed, a cooling bandage soaked in lavender water, and tea had been prepared and poured. Gratefully accepting the Muscovite's ministrations, John had thought to himself that here was a young man more than ready to take over a shop of his own.

"Well," said Samuel, clearly thrilled to be in the thick of it, "what would you like me to do?"

"Did Sir John give you any particular instructions?"

"Merely to assist you. He told me to tell you that Jago is visiting Miss Evalina and Miss Millicent today and will confer with you later on. So, that message conveyed, I am yours to command." He laughed merrily.

"Perhaps you could start by taking a letter to Bow Street. I must inform Sir John of this morning's events."

"Of course I will. Tell me, is this fellow Mendoza a bit of a rum cove?"

"He pretends to be very honest; confided that it was his original intention to ruin Louisa until he lost his heart to her."

"I see."

"But this latest turn of events puzzles me immeasurably. The choice between the dead man's mistress and his exquisite daughter is too ludicrous to be taken seriously."

Samuel nodded. "None the less, the Lieutenant did call at her house and something did take place this morning, even if it was only a conversation."

The Apothecary had been writing while they spoke and now sealed his letter with a blob of wax which had warmed in one of the compounding room's pans.

"There we are. And Samuel . . ."

"Yes?"

". . . find out what you can about poor Bussell's funeral. I feel I should attend."

"If you are going, then so shall I," said Samuel stoutly.

John looked at him fondly. "What would I do without you?" he said, and meant it.

"I do realise that I am of some help to you in these investigations," the Goldsmith answered happily.

"Yes indeed," lied John, and watched his friend go purposefully from the shop.

The two men were much amazed to see that Emilia, dressed in a loose robe admittedly but still up and about with brushed hair and painted face, awaited them in the library.

"I've been lying still too long," she said as John bent over her chair to kiss her. "So, my dear, I have decided to join you for dinner."

"How did you know I was coming?" asked Samuel, somewhat amazed.

"Irish Tom told me." She looked at her husband narrowly. "He said that you were involved in some kind of fracas. Are you all right?"

He nodded. "A little the worse for wear but nothing serious, I assure you."

"What happened?"

He told her and Emilia sat silently, nodding occasionally. "There's bad blood in that family, John."

"Which one? The Fenchurchs or the Bussells?"

"Both. Their deeds are dark and murderous."

"Like a terrible, tragic play?"

"Indeed. And I have a feeling that it is not over yet."

"What do you mean?"

Emilia shivered. "I'm not sure. But these black acts of revenge are far from played out. In Jacobean tragedies do not the pieces end with bodies all over the stage?"

"Good God!" said Samuel, clutching his throat. "Who do you think is going to be next?"

"Sperling Trewellan believes the brothers Bussell are in danger. Which reminds me, he called into the shop this afternoon and bought some medicaments for his morphew. He was very solicitous for my welfare and thought I should have gone straight home."

"And so you should," Samuel replied firmly. "What would you have done if I hadn't happened to have been passing by?"

"What were you doing on that route anyway?"

"I was actually on my way to Bloomsbury Square with a letter for Mrs. Rayner from Sir John. I believe he wishes to speak to her about the Poisoner note."

John nodded. "I don't think you would have found her there. Apparently she has returned to her house in Curzon Street." He paused. "Do you still have the letter?"

"Yes."

"Then let's deliver it. Tonight. In person. After we have dined." The Apothecary suddenly looked apologetic and turned to Emilia. "If that is agreeable to you, sweetheart."

She nodded. "It is no trouble. I intend to retire to bed once we have eaten."

There was a knock on the door and a maid appeared. "May I bring the baby in, Ma'am?"

"Of course. Let's spend half an hour with the little thing."

And so they did, playing and cuddling and talking to her.

Sitting on John's lap, she gave him that windy smile of hers and he smiled back. "There, she smiled at me," he exclaimed.

"Naturally," said Emilia, and winked at Sam.

But he knew, quite definitely, that his daughter not only understood every word they were saying but had given him her secret sign of approval.

As soon as they knocked at the door they were allowed to enter the house and, further, it was only a moment or two before Jocasta Rayner came into the room to which they had been shown. Tonight, clad in merciless black from head to toe, she looked amazing. Thin to starvation point, the bones on her face gave her a sculpted look that was not quite of this world. John noticed with sadness that the eyes — he had never seen them looking quite so big — were filled with tears which had not brimmed. Samuel, standing up and clutching his hat, gulped audibly at the stark vision which had just entered the room. Jocasta gave him the briefest of glances and turned back to John.

"I trust you have forgiven me," she said.

"For what?" he asked, surprised.

"For intruding on you as I did the other night."

"Oh that. I have already forgotten it. Now, Madam, you have heard of poor Bussell's death?" She nodded. "Then let us not waste any time. Who was it you meant when you wrote 'There is a poisoner in our midst'?"

Jocasta paused momentarily, just long enough to give the game away. "Montague Bussell," she said.

"Really?" asked John. He indicated the chair behind him. "May I sit down?"

"Of course. How rude of me. These terrible times make one forget oneself completely." She rang a bell. "You'll take some refreshment, of course."

Without waiting for a reply she settled herself into a chair, keeping her face averted. By the time she turned back to John her features were completely under control and her eyes had lost that vast luminosity.

"Yes?" she said.

"Could you explain that a little further," John asked, as icily polite as she was being herself.

"About Montague?" The Apothecary nodded. "Well, I saw him, after my father's funeral."

"Doing what?"

"He was pouring something into Ariadne's glass."

"I see. Can you give a little more detail."

"Certainly. The two glasses were side by side on a tray. Montague was leaning over and I saw him pour something into one of them. Then he picked them up, quite carefully, and handed her the one with something in it."

"Why did you not raise the alarm? At the very least you could have knocked it from his hand and pretended it was an accident."

Jocasta twisted her head away. "It was very difficult. I didn't know what to do. Anyway, she had already taken a mouthful of it. I . . ."

But fortune was on her side. A footman entered and stood bowing before her. Jocasta took a deep breath.

"Ah, Jennings," she said. "Brandy and port, both white and red."

The man bowed and retired, as did the last of Jocasta's deep breath.

"And that is all I have to say," she concluded.

"I see," said John. He steepled his fingers, feeling a thousand years old, wondering what the devil he should do next. But yet again he was to be thwarted. The

210

servant reappeared, bearing a tray, and the Apothecary realised that it must have been standing immediately outside, even the number of glasses taken care of while he and Samuel had made their entrance.

"Excellent," stated Jocasta heartily. "Now gentlemen, how may I serve you?"

She dismissed the servant and set about pouring, rather relieved to have something to do, it seemed to John. He decided to have one more go at her.

"Well, now . . ." he started, but too late. Samuel had joined the throng.

"A delightful home you have here, Mrs. Rayner. Is this one of Mr. Adam's designs?"

She flashed Sam a look that would go down in the halls of fame. Intense gratitude together with just a flicker of interest, John thought.

"Yes, it is. Do you know his work at all?"

"Well, yes, now you come to mention it . . ."

They were off, conversing freely and fast about an architect of whom John knew little. He decided to sit back and let them talk, waiting his moment to return to the exchange. But it did not come and half an hour and two brandies later, he was still waiting. Eventually, the Apothecary decided that he must taken action. He made much of looking at his watch.

"Ah, I see that it is growing late, Samuel. We will have to think about moving on." He turned to his hostess. "So, in your opinion, is the case now closed?"

She choked on her port. "Oh, excuse me please. I thought we had done with sad talk for tonight." She dabbed at her lips with a handkerchief. "Yes, Mr.

Rawlings, I do. I believe that it is all over. I think Montague poisoned Ariadne and then poisoned himself. He was on his way to Bow Street to come clean about the whole thing but, unfortunately, his frame was weaker than he thought and he died before he could confess."

"I see," said John. He stood up. "A very interesting theory. I shall report it to Sir John tomorrow morning. You will be around should he wish to interview you further?"

For the first time Jocasta looked put out. "Of course. I have no intention of returning to the country. Except, of course, for Montague's funeral."

"Quite so."

Samuel, who had been happily imbibing, gulped down the remains of his glass and also stood up.

"Well," said John, "it has been truly delightful in your company."

"Oh yes," Samuel repeated with enthusiasm, "it has been a marvellous occasion."

Jocasta flashed him a smile of great sincerity. "Thank you for saying so. I do hope that you will call again one day."

"I most certainly will," Samuel answered with relish, and kissed her hand.

Afterwards, out in the street, he stood back to let a cart go by. "I say, John, what a charming woman. Don't you think so?"

"I think," John answered carefully, "that she is one who could do with a great deal of watching."

CHAPTER
FOURTEEN

It had been a working day just like any other. John had compounded and infused, laboured in the shop, gallantly lied to a lady that she looked scarcely a day over thirty, and generally got on with all the things he usually did in order to make the time pass quickly so that he could get back to Emilia and Rose. But at four o'clock everything had changed and after that there had been no let up until he had finally fallen through his front door, exhausted, tired and hungry but too far gone to do anything about it.

It had started when a messenger had come in from Bow Street; a tall good-looking young man whom John hadn't seen before.

"Mr. Rawlings?"

"Yes, the very same."

"Sir John says could you come, Sir. A body has been found and he thinks you should see it."

"Very well," John had answered, and removed the long apron he wore in the shop.

They had driven to Bow Street at quite a reasonable trot and there been picked up by Joe Jago, his customary grin for once removed.

"Who is it?" John asked when they were once more on their way.

"The last person in the world you would have expected to see."

But further than that Joe had refused to go and led John towards the body which lay, guarded by a solitary constable, in a stony silence. They were in St. James's Park, about a mile, no more, from Buckingham House.

She was lying face down, her green and black striped dress raised a little to show legs thicker and less attractive than John would have imagined. He still had difficulty in recognising her but as they drew nearer the constable raised her and turned her to face her visitors. John drew in a breath. For there, lolling in the constable's arms, was Evalina Fenchurch, her face twisted into a paroxysm, her lips drawn back in a ghastly smile.

John felt himself recoil, horrified by what he was looking at, and realised that even the implacable Joe was tense.

"No poison here," said John, almost to himself.

"No Sir," Joe replied tersely. "Taken out exactly as her father was."

"Beaten to death," John answered, and then added, "What a terrible way to go."

Joe approached the body and, after a second's hesitation, put out his hand and felt the skin. "Only just cold," he said.

"How long would you say?"

"About an hour, give or take fifteen minutes."

"So she came to the park alone and there met her end. Is it possible it could have been an accident?"

"Anything's possible, Sir."

"But you don't think so."

"No, frankly, I don't. I truly don't believe that a woman comes to this remote part of the park and there, by no fault of her own, just happens to get in the way of a lunatic with murder on his mind. Do you?"

"Put like that, quite definitely not."

"Then, Sir, I must ask you to examine the body. If you don't care to, then Sir John will call in somebody else. But being as how you've been in on this one straight from the top, I'd ask you to continue to help him."

And with that Joe Jago walked briskly away, pulled a pipe from his pocket, and started to smoke very rapidly indeed. Alone with Evalina, John began with the worst, forcing down an overwhelming urge to shout as he did so. With fingers that trembled as he moved them, the Apothecary started with the face.

She had died giving a smile, that much was obvious. But now the smile had become frozen in time and would remain like that despite the moulding of her features. The red mark, hidden by her hair as it was, still stuck out, livid in the afternoon air. While her eyes, as yet unclosed, had that extraordinary blank look that comes upon the dead as soon as life has departed. But it was to none of those that John's attention was led. Instead, he looked at the neck, at the way that it hung in relation to her body. That it was broken was clear to see. Poor Evalina had been beaten, first one way then another, until life and hope had been knocked clean out of her.

Even though the rest of the body was fairly straightforward, John, having got the face over, took his time. Over his head the afternoon sun began to lose heat and then, finally, started to go downwards through the sky. But still he worked on and it was a good half hour before he finally let the victim go and got to his feet, brushing as best he could at the detritus and mess which clung to his legs, in particular his knees.

"There. I've done," he said.

Joe Jago turned round and John could see at once that he was in a far more cheerful mood. "Ah, so you have, Sir."

"She can be taken away now."

"Right, Sir."

And Joe signalled to a group of men standing by with what looked like a cart but in fact was a vehicle for removing the dead to the mortuary.

"Come along, lads. The Apothecary says she can be removed."

But still, even after he had attended to her, John found the last sight of Evalina, lifted high before being placed upon the cart, one arm still hanging down and swimming lightly on the breeze, extremely distressing, and had to force himself to stand and watch her go.

"All done, Sir?" said Joe in a cheery voice.

"Yes, all done."

"Then I suggest we go back to Bow Street. Sir John wishes to discuss the matter with you and call out more

216

men if necessary. It is time we had an end to it and that's a fact."

"Yes," said John, but he saw again in his mind's eye that arm of Evalina's swaying on the evening breeze, listless and lonely, the last time she would ever wave at anyone.

In Bow Street, however, all was action. The Blind Beak was obviously riled and was allowing himself to be seen so. In his office he sat, dealing with correspondence being read out to him by a man that John had never noticed before. They both looked up as John and Joe knocked and the Magistrate bellowed, "Come in, come in, whoever you are," though not before he had guessed who was visiting him. "Mr. Rawlings?" he continued in a similar vein, then paused momentarily and went 'Humph'.

"Yes, Sir?"

"Take a seat over there, would you. I'll be damned if I'll waste a moment, so the niceties will have to hang fire."

He gestured to a distant seat and went back to listening, something he did with an almost acute observation. After exactly half an hour, during which time both John and Joe had dropped off to sleep, he stood up, said, "Thank you Mr. Dodds. Now, gentlemen," and led the way outwards. Joe and John hastily pulled themselves together and followed.

Marching up the stairs just as if he were sighted, the Blind Beak took a seat in his salon and sent for tea.

Then and only then did he turn to his guests. "Well, gentlemen, how did she die?"

Realising that it was his turn to lead off, John launched into a vivid picture, sparing the Blind Beak nothing, telling him everything he possibly could wish to know.

"So she died with a smile," said the Magistrate, and it was a mere statement of fact and in no way a reflection of the way things were.

Joe cleared his throat. "Mr. Rawlings did a very good job, Sir. I must say that I was proud to be seen working with him."

"So you should, Sir. Anyway, gentlemen, what's your verdict?"

John and Joe stared at one another in astonishment. It was fairly obvious that the Blind Beak was going for the kill.

"What exactly do you mean, Sir?"

"I mean, how many murderers do we have on our hands?"

"Two, Sir," said Joe, neat as you please.

"Yes," answered Sir John. "Yes, yes, yes. How much longer was I going to have to wait to hear it?"

"No longer than it took me to say it," Joe replied sharply, and John hoped and prayed that he was not going to see one of their famous and almost legendary fallings out. However, all was calm and the Magistrate merely replied, "Just so."

There was a momentary silence before John said, "So now that that has been agreed, where next?"

"We must make an arrest," answered the Blind Beak.

"But who?"

"The Bussell brothers for a start."

"And second?"

"I'm not so sure," said the Magistrate thoughtfully. "Several of those horses are beginning to act most strange." He sat up with interest as the tea tray came in. "Well, gentlemen, when we have refreshed ourselves I suggest we go to see Mrs. Jocasta. She probably hasn't even heard the news yet." He took a bite from a buttered crumpet.

"The news of her sister's death?"

"That, and the fact that she is now legally and definitely head of the family."

As is so often the way of things, Mrs. Rayner was out. And, to complicate matters even further, nobody seemed sure of where she was or what time she would be back. In the words of the Public Office, they had drawn a blank. However, this was not going to put off Sir John Fielding. Determined that his men should be allowed to hunt, he made his way to Belgrave Square and there, sitting very tall and somehow casting a spell of respect, the search began.

Within twenty minutes of their starting, Miss Milicent came back, her face to fall with alarm when she saw that six men had systematically started to look through their things, two men to each room. To break it up a bit Joe and John were not working together, but had started on their own in different rooms.

"Oh gracious," the poor soul blurted out, "what a to-do. I don't know what Evalina will say when she returns."

"I think you had best come with me, Madam," the Blind Beak had said solemnly, and had led her into a small sitting room and closed the door. From behind, the pair had heard his voice, though none around them had been able to identify a word. After he had finished speaking there had been silence, and then a terrible moan. Then had come the sound of the door being wrenched open and for one brief second Millicent had appeared. Then she had fainted, quite suddenly and without further ado, and that had been that. She had been carried into a room that had already been searched and there laid to rest on a bed, only a maid keeping her company. John could not help but worry what would happen when she regained consciousness.

Meanwhile the search had continued, everyone working to the best of their ability in almost total silence. Then it had been broken by a cry.

"I've found something, Sir."

The footsteps had run along the landing, down the stairs, and into the room where the Blind Beak sat alone.

"And what is it, Rudge?"

"This, Sir. A book, Sir." Then the door had closed and there had once more been the sound of muted voices from within.

After a while it had opened again. "Work on, lads," called the Blind Beak. "See if any of you can manage to come up with anything to equal this."

But nobody had and eventually the Blind Beak had called them into the little room in which he still sat. "Gentlemen," he said, "there has been a major discovery by Runner Rudge. I think it best that, in view of its importance, we leave now and that we don't come back. Apparently Miss Millicent has returned to consciousness but is lying still. So all is as well as it will ever get."

A voice spoke up. "May we all be present at the reading, Sir?"

"Yes," said the Blind Beak, and for the first time that day he sounded glad to be alive. "You will all be there if you so desire."

There was a cheer and suddenly, just for a second, John knew what it was like to be a member of a close-knit team.

But the mood had slightly died down by the time they returned to the Public Office and went upstairs. In short, the feeling of elation had gone but there was an enormous, tired satisfaction that they had come out of the day with something to show for it.

Sir John passed Joe the book and, having carefully put on his spectacles, the clerk started to read.

"I hardly know how to contain myself," *it started*. "Today L. — I don't know what I should call him but I shall choose the name Lancelot for his disguise — is coming and I feel sure that he loves me and is going to tell me so. Imagine my delight after all these years . . ."

221

Again, John saw that arm swinging so limply from the body as it was carried away, and he felt his heart plummet.

". . . in knowing that somebody cares."

Joe looked up. "All of it, Sir?"
The Magistrate looked up. "All of it, Joe."

"*The next entry is for a week later.* It is as I dreamed — and more — because he cares and has told me of his feelings. He has asked me to go into the garden and he says that he will come to me. He didn't come though. *Anyway, the next bit is dated several days later.*"

The wine and beer which they had ordered came in at this point and there was a natural break. Finally though, when everybody was reseated, Joe started to read again, his voice the only sound in that small close room.

"A week later. I was walking in the town with my youngest sister and there I met L. I was covered with confusion but my sister believed it to be the cause I had mislaid my gloves."

So the sad tale went on, one of serious love on her part; on his, who could tell? Though John suspected that Evalina was drawn into the affair almost against her will, then, when all came to fruition, fell more madly in love than she had ever done anything before in her life. Joe read on and on and finally came towards the conclusion.

"Today was the day of Ariadne Bussell's funeral. Oh, what a sad occasion."

So she had clearly not suspected Ariadne of murdering her father, John thought.

"I was there and, obviously, so was L. He did not speak to me, as I supposed would happen. Still, I had hoped. But this night — thank God Foxfire Hall is as big as it is — he came to me and what I had known, or rather prayed, would occur, finally took place. I am married now in the eyes of God and thank the Lord that what will be, will be."

Joe made a small coughing sound. He had reached the last page and was preparing to stop but yet found himself strangely moved by the thought of the large ugly creature so very deeply in love.

"L. wants me to meet him later today. I shall be off soon. How I love writing — ."

"And what date does that entry have, Joe?"
"Why, Sir, it is today. Good gracious. This is the last thing she wrote — ever."
"Yes, I think we can be pretty certain about that. Anyway, continue."

"*There's hardly anything more.* — writing this account of everything that passes between us. Lord be praised, but I am so happy. *That's it, Sir.*"

"Yes, that's it. Any ideas, gentlemen, who this extraordinary fellow might be? Lancelot, as she insisted on calling him."

Without even wanting to, John found himself speaking up. "One of the Bussells," he said.

"Very much as I thought," answered the Magistrate. "Tomorrow we shall issue a warrant for the arrest of the pair of them. Till then, there is nothing further we can do."

John got to his feet. "Then may I take my leave? Exhaustion is truly setting in."

"Certainly," said the Blind Beak. He lowered his voice. "And, Mr. Rawlings, may I take this rare opportunity of thanking you most sincerely."

"Thank you, Sir," said John, and despite the lateness of the evening left Bow Street in a warm glow of pleasure.

He crawled into bed extremely late and immediately had a dream about Evalina and L. In it, Lancelot kept his face hidden by a mask but Evalina was transformed by youth, strangely beautiful despite the devil's mark on her cheek. It was John's mission to tell them something of vital importance and he ran behind them down long, vast corridors, calling to them to wait for him, to stop for a moment so that he could deliver his message. But, in the way of dreams, they took no notice and ran ahead, chattering and laughing like children.

The dream changed course and now he was outside, back in the park. Yet the body lying on the ground was not that of Evalina at all but of another woman. She lay, face down, hair fluttering in the breeze. And then Joe Jago lifted the woman in his arms and John found himself staring into the face of Emilia. Emilia, his wife, mother of his child, lay there, cold and dead.

The Apothecary woke with a scream to find that it was already past his time for rising. He put his head back on the pillow and closed his eyes and the next thing he knew was when a maid came in with his washing water and a message that it was half-past eight.

"God!" said John, leaping out of bed in a flurry. "Oh heavens, I shall be late for work."

"Your wife, Mrs. Rawlings, says that for once it doesn't matter and that as soon as you are respectable you are to go and see her."

"Tell her I'll be five minutes at the most," said John, and suddenly gave a loud and curiously tuneful whistle which he continued until he joined Emilia and Rose, who were both out of bed and ready to socialise with him.

The dream still hung over him, horribly so, and it was a relief to see that she was up and moving round the room, not hearing him for a moment. But when she did and spun round, Emilia gave him the most beautiful smile. He crossed over to her and pulled her into his arms, then gave her a deep and loving kiss. And they were still like this, kissing and hugging, when Dorcas came in.

"Oh, beg pardon, Madam. I didn't know you had company."

"Oh Dorcas, don't be silly. It's my husband."

"I can see that, Madam."

And she would have gone out like that, slightly sad and miserable, had not John picked her up and carried her round the room, where she, with much giggling, rushed out again to adjust herself before the housekeeper caught her.

So it was that the two of them went to Rose Rawlings, who had fallen asleep again on the big bed, and wondered at her beauty and said words of praise, before the father and husband reluctantly went downstairs to start the working day.

Without the presence of Mrs. Alleyn and Sir Gabriel, both of whom had returned to their respective country addresses, the house seemed empty and quiet. John sat alone, stolidly eating breakfast but not really tasting anything, as memories of the dream came back to taunt him. And try as he would he could not shake the vile thing off throughout the rest of that day, when flashes of it came back to him. Still, he put a brave face on it and was preparing to close the shop when Joe Jago called.

"Sorry to be so late, Sir, but just thought I'd better tell you that the lads have flown the nest."

John stared at him blankly, the words not meaning anything.

"They've gone, Sir. Justin and Greville. The Runners went to their house but they weren't there and no message as to when they'd be back either."

"So where are their late father's remains?"

"In the earth. No sooner had the Coroner released the body than he was buried. Here, in London. Nobody present except the two boys. So that's a funeral you won't be attending."

"No," John answered, and sighed deeply, "I won't, will I."

CHAPTER
FIFTEEN

Two days passed and there was no action, except that on the second day the coroner's court met and pronounced that Evalina Fenchurch had been murdered but that her body would be released for burial. So another sorry victim of the vicious killer of the Fenchurchs would be laid to rest. John was just wondering where the committal to earth was going to take place, when a letter arrived for him early that morning. In a fearful mood, he opened it and saw that it was from Jocasta.

"My dear Mr. Rawlings,
    It is with Much Misery that I Write to Inform You of the Events that are Scheduled to Take Place in Three Days Time. My Sister is to Be Laid to Rest beside the Frame of My Father in St. Mary's Church, Stoke d'Abernon. We, As a Family, Would very Much Like You to be There and Hope that You Will Find a Way to Join Us."

It went on with the usual signature, and John, immediately flying up to the bedroom with the letter in his hand, found his wife and daughter both awake and cuddling.

"Here's a thing," he said, and passed her the note to read.

"Well," Emilia said, "it's the very excuse I wanted."

"What do you mean?"

"That I am going to get up and go with you — and Rose of course. We shall drive down tomorrow and stay with Serafina, who is beside herself to see the child. Oh John, please don't argue. It is absolutely no use. I intend to go and there's an end to it."

"But darling . . ."

"There is no good you starting, Husband. I intend to rise and to prove that I am capable of it, I shall come and have breakfast with you."

And before he could stop her, she pulled on the bell so hard that the cover came away in her hand. He had been about to tell her that he could not possibly go, that owing to all the circumstances he was staying behind in London, but Emilia had that look about her that meant only one thing. He was going and that was the end of that. With a sigh of reluctance, John went downstairs to finish his meal and pen a swift letter to Serafina telling her that they would all three of them be coming, in addition to two servants, the very next day.

It became obvious that Emilia had been up all day as soon as he got home that evening. The big trunks had been set out in the bedroom and she was up and very busy. However she did listen to his pleas and retired to bed as soon as she had dined. Therefore John was quite alone, sitting down in the library and reading the newspaper, when there came a clamouring of the street doorbell. Moving a little nearer, John listened.

After a few moments, a servant came. "It's Mr. Jago, Sir."

"Really? I wonder what he wants so late. Show him in, Peters."

A minute or so later, Jago's face appeared in the doorway. "Mr. Rawlings, my dear, I do hope that I haven't caught you too late."

"Not at all. Come in."

It was obvious from his grin and breath that he was slightly the worse for drink but nothing that John had not coped with in the past.

"My dear fellow, take a seat. What would you like?"

"I'll have a brandy, my friend. But what about you? You're not drinking anything."

"I'll join you, if I may. I hadn't realised how the time was getting on," said John.

Jago waited until a tray of drinks had been brought in and then launched into why he was there.

"It's the Governor, Sir. He was very angry that those Bussell boys have slipped the net. Course he looked for 'em in London, but they weren't there either. Said we couldn't have people flouting the law and that was all there was to it."

"Has he calmed down?"

"Not greatly. As a matter of fact I've just come from his office now. Lady Fielding — Elizabeth to you — has told him not to be such a silly arse and I think he's finally bowing to the inevitable."

Jago finished his glass and held it out for a refill.

"That makes a change," said John, pouring him a stiff measure and a smaller one for himself.

"That is what I thought. Anyway, I said, 'Blessing on you, Beak, for getting off your high horse and giving us all a breather'."

Joe Jago convulsed with laughter and so did John, though slightly less so.

"I says to him, 'Beak you've outrun us all, so here's to you'."

It was getting very repetitive and John saw tears behind Joe's eyes but whether from too much laughing or whether from some other, deeper, cause, he did not know. He hesitated before saying anything and this brought about the usual result. Joe, with an enormous snort, applied the handkerchief to both eyes and nose, gave a huge Harumph, and then laughed all over again. John sat in silence and waited for the next turn. But none was forthcoming and Joe now sat, grinning a little, sipping on his third brandy.

Eventually, John said, "I wonder if there are two murderers, really. Or if it is a ruse to unsettle all of us."

Joe looked instantly sober, in that alarming way of his. "Oh yes, at least two, I think. There's a great deal going on. It's all very well for the Magistrate to suspect the two young Bussells, but there's a lot involved in this. A lot."

"What do you think about Lieutentant Mendoza?"

Joe turned to look at John and the Apothecary saw that now he was absolutely sober. "A strange young cove, if you ask me. What was all that business with Mrs. Trewellan?"

John spread his hands. "I can only presume that they are lovers. But I've heard no more of it. So, for the moment, that matter has been dropped."

Joe put his glass down and once more stared into the fire. "There's an awful lot of weird goings on in this case, Sir. First, there's Mr. Fenchurch. Then, no sooner have we recovered from that, then there's Mrs. Bussell. Followed a few days later by Mr. Bussell and Evalina. Then Sir John orders the arrest of the brothers Bussell and, lo and behold, they have gone. This is to say nothing of Mrs. Rayner's first husband, who died of poisoning, and Mrs. Trewellan who is having an affair with a handsome young man at least twenty years her junior. It's a very rum state of affairs if you ask me."

"But we're not asking you, we're asking Sir John," said the Apothecary with a laugh.

But the clerk was away, staring into the flames, not hearing what had been said to him. It was, John decided, the very moment to have a stiff drink himself, then to join him in silent contemplation.

The next morning, relatively early, they set off for West Clandon. Into the carriage swept Emilia Rawlings, and her baby was handed to her a moment later. Then followed Dorcas, in her best travelling outfit, and finally in went John. The luggage, which had been stacked on board for the last thirty minutes, was then checked over on a list prepared by Emilia but read out by John. Then finally they were off, with much waving and one or two whistles from the staff.

"Now, now young ladies," said Axford, the head man, but the girls merely bobbed at him and said, "Yes, Sir," then continued to whirl about and giggle.

The carriage meanwhile had disappeared into Gerrard Street and though one or two ran down the length of Nassau Street to give it a final wave, it shortly vanished from view and they ran back into the house.

Irish Tom was heading straight for the Hercules Pillars where he had planned his first stop before they left London completely behind them. In this way, travelling slowly and making sure that the horses had an hour's rest at certain prescribed points, they reached West Clandon as night began to fall and made their way up the drive.

"What a gorgeous house," said Emilia, close to John's ear.

He looked at her and saw that she was as entranced with the building as he had been when he had first come across it. Forgetting all about Dorcas, John bent down and kissed her, then licked her ear for good measure. She smiled up at him and the smile seemed to say volumes.

Whooping round her knees, Serafina's two children had come to say hello, though a nurse hovered nearby to make sure they did not make a nuisance of themselves. However, this eventuality need not have been bothered with. They were entranced by Rose, they adored Rose, they insisted at once that should anything ever befall Rose's parents they would be the next in line to adopt her. They walked round with her, they talked to her, they hugged and kissed her. And she? She gave them that steadfast gaze of hers, then that slow smile that others thought was an attack of wind.

Eventually, though, everybody left for their rooms and there came that glorious moment when the house was being prepared for dinner and delicious smells, albeit faint, were wafting on the currents of air.

"What a heavenly place," said Emilia, taking off her hat and flinging it on the bed. "Oh John, it's divine." And she threw herself backwards and kicked her legs aloft. In a minute he was beside her, doing likewise. Thus they kicked wildly, then drew stiller, then — not having shared a room since Rose had been born — they toyed and played for half an hour, then reluctantly drew apart and started to get ready for dinner, telling each other repeatedly that it was only another week or three before they could be united in absolutely every way.

"By which time we should have all the perpetrators of these horrid murders behind bars," said Emilia.

The mood changed and they grew quieter, thinking of all the terrible things that had been done recently. And they were still like this, not bad-tempered but contemplative, when they went down to dinner.

"My dear friends," said Louis, who had been wandering the estate when they had arrived and so had not seen them, "how good of you to call on us. I hope that we shall have the pleasure of your company for several days at least."

"Certainly. We are here to attend the funeral of Miss Evalina Fenchurch, which is to take place the day after tomorrow. So I expect we shall take in the weekend before we depart. Emilia . . ."

234

But she was already off on a tour of the house with Serafina and the men were left alone. Louis, seeing this, at once drew in a chair and motioned his old companion to do likewise.

"Tell me, my dear friend, who is doing these awful crimes?"

"I would imagine the Bussells. But they opened the most damnable void when they did so, because they were hit back doubly, but by whom I have no idea. Then, in revenge, they killed Evalina. What a terrible tragedy it all is."

Louis spread his hands. "Isn't it just? The wiping out of innocents. And where will it all end? Is there to be another murder — or two, perhaps — for this reprehensible crime?"

John shook his head. "I don't know." Then he braced himself. "No, of course there won't. Sir John is quite prepared to make an arrest as soon as the Bussells return. With them locked away there won't be any more trouble."

But he wished he felt the jaunty note that he had in his voice. However, their conversation was at an end. Emilia and Serafina had rejoined them and they must make light of it, for the moment anyway.

They had finished everything and were sitting back replete, Emilia just showing the first signs of being up late and starting to yawn. It was then that Serafina, unaware that the conversation had already touched on the matter, asked a difficult question.

"Well, has Sir John found the fellow responsible?"

"No," said John, "not yet."

"What?" said Serafina.

"I meant what I said. He imagines the Bussells to be responsible for some of the deaths. A person as yet unknown, for the others."

"But this is preposterous. There is a criminal mind out there which, even now, is glorying in what it has done."

"But how can you know that?" interrupted Louis.

"Because of the facts."

They were off, determinedly going at one another in an attempt to prove the other wrong. Very covertly, John and Emilia exchanged a secret look, then grinned. Meanwhile, the other two continued to argue boisterously, each determined to see the other go down. Eventually, though, a certain air of resignation crept into Louis's tone and he suddenly said, "You are quite right, of course."

Serafina stopped with her mouth open. "What's that you say?"

"I said, 'you're quite right'."

She rapidly rethought her reply and came up with, "Strangely, I was just going to say the same to you."

"Were you now?"

There was definitely a catch in his voice which indicated a laugh and, after looking at one another once again, Emilia and John tittered. The stage was set for Serafina and awaited her grand exit, stage right. She made it.

"Excuse me Emilia, gentlemen. I must go and see to my affairs. If you will forgive me for a few moments."

And with that she swept out. There was a rush of good humour in her absence and John said, "Ah well, we live and learn." To which both Emilia and Louis said simultaneously, "What do you mean by that?"

But the tension had been broken and they all fell to laughing and joking until one of the servants entered and said something beneath his breath to the host.

"What did you say?"

"I said, Sir, that the old dame is in the kitchen. The one who professes to read the lines on your hand. You said next time she called that we were to show her in."

Louis looked puzzled, then his brow cleared. "Oh yes, I remember her. What a good thing she happened to come tonight. Please send her to us."

She was very small, admittedly, but this could have been caused by the fact that she was bent practically in half, some accident of long ago or, perhaps, some cramping complaint of the spine. Whichever, she shambled over to the table, and started to thank John but, when corrected, turned to Louis with great dignity. A hood hid most of her face and she kept a hand constantly at the ready, its purpose to pull the lining of the embracing garment should it slip back in any way. Her voice came from far away but seemed to have a strange French accent.

She bent over Louis and started to mutter in his ear but he turned her away towards Emilia.

"Hello, young lady," she murmured. "Cross my palm with silver."

John leaned a little closer, determined to catch what was being said, though it wasn't always easy.

Emilia rubbed a silver coin, the largest she had, over the grimy hand. The woman spoke.

"You're afraid of summat . . . there's a child, but she will survive you . . ."

"Of course she will. But surely there are going to be more?"

"I don't know . . . look for the woman with two faces . . . look for when the sun is red . . . look for . . ."

Her voice dropped to its lowest ebb and he strained, then gave up. Then, when he was turning away, losing interest, just about to suggest another drink to Louis, there came a tugging at his sleeve.

"Hello, young Sir. Cross my palm with silver, then."

He could never afterwards tell why he was so attracted, what it was about her that seemed to weave this compulsive spell, why he needed to have his fortune read by her so urgently. But whatever it was, the charm had an almost inescapable symmetry. He bent low over the figure.

"Go on then, what do you see?"

"I see sadness and I see joy. But first there is gladness. Gladness that your case is solved, happiness that nobody has to go to Tyburn. But then comes sadness. Sadness that you are again alone. Sadness for the young one. Sadness that she has no mother."

"I don't want to hear any more of this," John whispered, furious with her for all that she was implying. Yet he knew, deep in his heart, that he wanted to know, wanted more than anything else in the world.

The old woman turned away from him and suddenly it was over. She had slumped to one side as if exhausted and was asking permission of Louis to withdraw. And he, completely unaware of the effect she had had on her audience, was giving it. John shot a quick look at Emilia and saw that she had either ignored the woman or else been unable to hear her properly, for she was as bright and happy as ever and giving everyone, and that included her husband, a radiant smile.

The woman limped out, a bent mysterious figure, and after a few moments Serafina came back in. Normally she would have chided her guests, asked them if they had missed her when she had been away so long, but on this occasion she seemed strangely quiet. However, she did turn on Emilia a deep and brilliant stare which could have meant anything.

"Why are you looking at me like that?" asked John's wife, suddenly nervous.

"My dear," said Serafina, "am I? Forgive me. It is just that I am concerned for you and am absolutely determined that nothing shall spoil your fun. If that silly old woman . . ."

But Emilia was already exploding with laughter. "My dearest, I could scarce hear a word the old besom muttered. Something about a woman with two faces and a setting sun. I mean, has one ever heard such nonsense."

And she gave a highly pitched laugh that John recognised at once as being utterly false.

He turned to her. "She didn't really frighten you, did she?"

"No, of course not. The silly old thing scarce knew what she was saying. I won't hear her name mentioned again and there's an end to it."

But later on that night, when John crawled into bed beside his wife and luxuriated in feeling the warmth of her flesh and the sheer delight of knowing that she was next to him, he mentioned it again.

"Do you know, I've realised who that old woman was?"

"Um?" said Emilia, right on the verge of sleep.

"It was Serafina of course. Just for one moment, when she thought I wasn't looking, I caught a glimpse of her face."

There was silence from beside him.

"It was Serafina herself," chuckled John, and wondered if his lie would ever be discovered and, if so, how.

The day after that was a day of complete relaxation, when the sun shone and it was wonderful to be young and alive. But the day after that was grim, as if they knew from the very beginning that it was going to be momentous and dark. Drawing back the curtains, up before the housemaid had come into the room, John felt a momentary thrall of gloom.

"'Zounds, but it is depressing out there."

"Whatever's the matter?" said Emilia, giving a great yawn.

"It's a day that befits a funeral. Leaden skies, pouring rain, servants wrapped in oilskins. I'd much rather get back into bed and forget the whole thing."

"Why don't you?" asked Emilia, holding open the sheets invitingly.

"Very well, put like that I see that I would be accused of growing old if I refuse."

And he hastened in, closed his eyes, and attempted to resist all her efforts at keeping him awake, until at last she proved too much and he woke up properly and gave her several enormous kisses. They were still enjoying this tremendously when there came a knock on the door which started to open. Drawing apart, the pair of them feigned sleep once more.

It was a little girl whose job it was to light the fire and draw the curtains. John and Emilia remained very still until she had gone, when they burst into laughter. But after that he rose and crossed to the window again.

"It's a day to lay a great-aunt to rest," he said, then thought about what he had said and pulled a melancholy face.

Shortly afterwards Dorcas brought in a red-faced and protesting Rose, obviously annoyed at not getting her feed when she had first asked for it, and after that everything became quiet and peaceful as the little thing snuggled to her mother. During this time John dressed in sombre black, the only white thing about him his shirt. And so it was that a very colourless young man, clad in dark hues, descended to breakfast and found himself alone.

Picking up a day old newspaper and starting to read, John took little notice when the front door bell pealed loudly and somebody was admitted. He continued to study but a raised voice in the hall caught his attention.

"... dashed nuisance, I'm aware of that. But I believe an old friend of mine is staying here."

A murmured reply.

"Rawlings, actually. John Rawlings."

John put the paper down and rose to his feet just as the door opened. He caught the eye of the servant hovering there and gave a broad grin. "Yes, it's all right," he said. "It has to be Samuel Swann."

"Very good, Sir. Shall I . . . ?"

But there was no time for an answer. Samuel had seen him and bounded up enthusiastically, holding out his hand to shake and bowing simultaneously, an odd sight.

"My dear old friend, how very jolly. I travelled up last night, don't you know. Stayed at The Onslow Arms. Thought I'd get a man with a trap here first thing." He lowered his voice to a confidential whisper. "I knew you'd be around. Nick Raven told me."

Another of Sir John's little wheezes, John thought. Aloud he said, "Delighted to see you, old chap. I've no idea where our host and hostess are but do please join me for breakfast."

"Well," Samuel's honest countenance beamed, most unsuitable for a funeral John couldn't help but think, "I'll try."

In the event, despite numerous protests made about already having eaten, Samuel had a positively huge breakfast, unlike John who ate little, always settling for the side of discretion when it came to funerals. This done, they talked a while before their hostess bustled in, already full of apologies for the lateness of her arrival. She stopped short on seeing Samuel, then hurried forward to kiss him on both cheeks.

"My dearest friend, how lovely to see you. But what has kept you away so long? We have so often invited you to dine. But you must be starving, come let me fill your plate."

This time good sense did prevail as Samuel declared robustly that he had already eaten enough for two people and that he could not manage one item more. And he would not be shifted despite numerous protests, so that in the end the Comtesse was forced to eat alone. However, she had little and was just suggesting that they should leave the table when the door flung open and Emilia, radiant as ever and only just a little plumper, stood there, arrayed from head to foot in deepest black, pretty as a picture.

Immediately, John felt the lunge of his heartstrings, which he knew had been caused by his being cast out of Emilia's bed. Roll on the time when I can have her back, he thought, and was just letting his mind run off down a naughty avenue, when Irish Tom came for instructions and he was drawn back.

"I think, Sir, that we ought to be setting off soon," the coachman announced. "It took us a long time last time, if you understand what I am saying. And I presume that today will be even worse. So, how many is it to be?"

"Just the three?"

"Well, we'll all lump in somehow," responded the Irishman cheerfully, and left the room with a ten minutes warning.

"You'll not come?" said John to Serafina.

"I think I'll be in the way. Let me keep the house warm for you."

Samuel touched the side of his nose as if he had very important information to impart but dared not say a word. "Best," was all Serafina could get out of him.

"Where's Louis?" asked the Apothecary.

"Out riding. He always goes off early, whatever the weather." She lowered her voice. "And before you get excited and wonder if I suspect anything the answer is quite definitely, no. I neither worry what he does or where he goes or who he sees. And in this way he is entirely faithful to me."

And she gave a light laugh before kissing all three of them on the cheek and waving them farewell as they set off in the direction of the village of Stoke d'Abernon.

As it transpired, Irish Tom had left so much time that they arrived an hour early and went immediately into the village hostelry. Even before they stepped inside, John knew that he must be careful, that there was someone within whom he must avoid. Plucking his hat down well over his eyes and sending Emilia and Sam ahead, he sidled in and heard their voices in another bar. The brothers Bussell were there ahead of him.

244

Samuel, a face they had not seen, went to the girl to place their order, while Irish Tom, much to his annoyance, came into the same room as his master and mistress and settled in a far corner. Sitting quietly, with his back to the door, John's flesh positively crept when another voice, conversing softly enough in all truth but perfectly recognisable for all that, started to speak behind him. Instantly gesturing to Emilia and Samuel, who had started with a "'Zounds and 'zoonters but the ale is damnably cheap . . ." then realised that something was up, John listened.

". . . the whole thing is turning into a damnable bore."

"But we've had this out so many times. What's to be done?"

"I've no idea. Short of you dying then coming back as your own twin brother, I cannot think of a solitary thing."

"But you know that isn't possible."

"I'm aware, I'm aware. But you must admit . . ."

"Seriously, Sperling, what am I to do? I never reckoned on falling for the girl."

"Search me. I've no idea."

The two men relapsed into a morose silence. Neither Samuel nor Emilia said a word. The Apothecary winked an eye at her and gestured for her to speak.

"It's simply awful weather," she began gamely.

"Terrible," answered Samuel heartily. "I thought this morning when I woke up that I hadn't seen such a dreadful day for ages."

"And who knows when it will let up," she continued.

"Who knows?" Samuel answered, and sighed heavily over his ale.

There was a total silence and then the sound of the pushing back of chairs.

"I think we'd better be on our way," said Sperling.

"Yes, I reckon we had."

"Where is Mother?"

"She's in the coach with Louisa," the other man replied, then added, "God love her, she knows nothing of this."

"Well, she'll have to know soon. There's no way forward else."

There was a huge sigh, nor far short of a sob. "I reckon she should be told today. I can't face the future."

"It's not just you, my friend. It's all of us, remember."

"Yes, I know."

They started to walk towards the door; John could tell by the sound of their footsteps. And then he heard another noise. Unaware that they were in there, somebody else had come into the bar.

"Well, well, well," said a voice, not jolly but most certainly not aggressive, yet whose very ring sent a chill down John's spine. "If it ain't the military man and his little friend."

"I'll have you stand aside, Sir. We're on our way to a funeral," said Sperling.

"As are we, my friend."

"Same one, no doubt."

"No doubt."

The four men stood silently for a moment and then there was a further shifting of feet and suddenly the main door opened and closed again.

And into that silence, presumably bored with his own company and of sitting by himself, Irish Tom called out, "Well, Mr. Rawlings, it's time we were off" — and suddenly the bar was empty.

CHAPTER
SIXTEEN

There was no one outside, no one at all. In the second since Tom had called out, the entire yard in which the hostelry stood had emptied, only an old pig and some disconsolate hens scratching for company.

"Well," said John, "was that all a coincidence, or what?"

"I'm not so sure," said Samuel, scratching his chin and looking portentous. "It seemed very odd to me."

"But how could they have known," put in Emilia. "Firstly, that it was John Rawlings — would the name mean anything to them? — and secondly, that you are under such strict instruction to watch for them." She stuck her chin out, a gesture which John found strangely endearing.

"Well, I'm going to finish my drink," he said. "There's no point in standing out here and freezing to death."

"Hear, hear," replied Samuel. "Good plan."

They all three turned and went back into The Onslow Arms, passing Tom, looking puzzled and not quite understanding, in the doorway.

Ten minutes later and they were on their way, the coach going at an excellent speed through the sprawl of houses but lowering its pace to a respectful crawl as soon as they came in sight of the church. John, as was his way, chose a place at the back but sent Emilia and Samuel further into the main body of the building. There were a few people there ahead of them but nobody that he recognised and he was just wondering when the main party would turn up when in walked the two Bussell boys. Seated as he was, the Apothecary found himself in an excellent position to observe them.

There was no doubt that Justin had been upset quite recently; telltale marks round his eyes and a slight pinkness of the nose said so clearly. His brother, a little shorter than he but a deal stockier, said nothing to him, but just stood looking around. He saw John, knew that he knew him from somewhere, but clearly failed to make the connection. Therefore he gave a terse bow of the head and left it at that. Meanwhile other members of the funeral party were arriving and taking their seats which, after a moment or two, Justin and Greville, clearly disappointed that nobody of any importance was there, did also.

Now John was left as he liked, quite alone to study everyone. But this state of affairs did not continue. With a suddenness that was almost crude, the coffin arrived, followed by a trail of people in various states of collapse. First to walk behind was Jocasta Rayner, thin to starvation point, but straight and tall for all that. Next came Millicent, in a flood of weeping, supported on either side by Lieutenant and Louisa Mendoza, who each had a hand beneath an elbow and literally guided her to her designated pew. Almost finally, looking somewhat flustered but nevertheless making as good a show as she could, came Mrs. Trewellan with Sperling. Last of all some rather dismal-looking cousins.

The parson, who was terribly old and looked fit to drop, started the service in a quavery voice which, untypically, he kept very quiet. John, for once wishing that he had decided to sit nearer to the front, very soon gave up trying to listen and instead concentrated on those who were present, wishing that something like an answer would come to him.

The most immediate problem was that of Lieutenant Mendoza, who was now sitting beside his wife and Mrs. Trewellan, a lady on either side. That young Sperling knew about the relationship was obvious, particularly after the overheard conversation. But where did it get any of them? And what did any of it mean? And what, if anything at all, did it have to do with the matter in hand? The Apothecary felt the whole thing was getting too much for him and without thinking where he was, plunged his head into his hands.

He was summoned back to reality by the sounds of somebody breaking down — and not far away at that! Horrible sobs were coming from somewhere close by and the Apothecary allowed himself the luxury of turning slightly so that he could get a better view. On his right, and not far away, Justin Bussell was slowly beginning to disintegrate, raked by heaving cries that, for the time being at least, were quiet but getting progressively louder. John caught brother Greville's eye and recoiled from the black look he was given.

There were not many sitting near the back but those that were were becoming more and more uneasy at the sound. In fact most of them had given up on the country parson and were staring quite openly at Justin, who was by now totally out of control. It was then that Greville acted, suddenly and without warning. Rising to his feet, he put one hand under Justin's arm and escorted him towards the door, not hesitating for one second in his determined flight. Acting on an impulse and nothing further, John followed.

They had gone round the corner by the time he got outside, but the Apothecary could hear Greville quite distinctly.

"Listen, you fool, stop your damnable caterwauling or you'll have half the church out here. Christ, but I've never heard such a wailing. Anybody would think to listen to you that you had some feeling for the old bitch."

There was no reply, just a faint glugging sound as if the owner were trying desperately to settle his breath.

"I said shut up, just in case you didn't hear me."

Again there was no reply but the breathing was starting to sound more settled.

"For the last time, will you be silent."

This time there was a response, and its very swiftness startled the Apothecary witless. Without hesitation there was the noise of a flying fist and John Rawlings heard, quite definitely, the crunch of skin upon skin and the exhalation of air as one of the brothers went flying and crunched upon his back. Then he heard the other one take off, at speed and with a quite definite purpose.

Slowly he peered round the graves and saw that Greville lay flat out beside a tombstone, his hat flown away and blood coming from his nose. Very swiftly John went to check that he was breathing, saw that he was, and with that crept back into the church, saying to himself that there were moments when even an apothecary's vow could be forgiven him.

The wake, held at Foxfire Hall, was to John just like the one that had taken place a mere three weeks ago. Everybody who was anybody was there, even Justin Bussell. However, of Greville there was no sign, and somebody offered the idea that the poor chap had gone down with a frightening megrim which had come upon him in church. As nobody bothered to contradict this, this became the accepted version of why he was missing, and people were heard wishing him better via his brother, which rounded the whole thing off very neatly.

John found himself once more with the forthright neighbours.

"My dear Sir, how very nice to see you again. Though I suppose one shouldn't use the word nice in these depressing circumstances. Oh dear, I don't know what to think," said the wife in a breathless rush.

"Is it true," said the man, cutting straight to the point, "that Evalina has been done away with?"

"Do you mean murdered, Sir?"

"Yes, I do, damme. Well, is it?"

There was no reason why he shouldn't be told, so the Apothecary came directly out with it. "Yes, it's true enough. She was walking in the park and apparently met up with some ne'er-do-wells. Anyway, they attacked her and left her dead."

"And robbed?"

"No," said the Apothecary slowly, "she wasn't robbed, not that I'm aware of."

"Oh, you'd have been told if she had. So, another one, eh?"

"Yes."

"Um." The husband looked suddenly foxy. "Had she gone to meet anyone, do you know?"

"Why do you ask? Do you know something I don't?"

"Matter of fact, I do." The man touched the side of his nose and winked an eye. "Won't say any more at present but I definitely have some information about poor Evalina. No looks at all. But money always attracts, don't it?"

"Yes, I suppose it does."

"Oh Henry, you're always speaking out of turn," said the wife, loving every minute.

"Nonsense, my dear. No the truth is, old fellow, she was having an affair with . . ."

But silence was being called for and the neighbour, alongside everyone else in the room, was shutting his mouth out of respect.

Jocasta spoke up. "My friends and family, thank you again for your support. I cannot tell you how much it means to me. Your help and love are worth more than money can buy at this time. I thank you with all my heart."

She then stood stiffly to one side while an old uncle began to ramble on about Evalina, a boring and dry-as-dust childhood adventure with very little point to it. John ceased to listen and began to look round the room, then caught the eye of the neighbour and withdrew, following the meaningful direction of the man's gaze, into a corner recess. There was no one about, only some glasses of claret that had been left standing on the table.

"Very dull story, what?"

"Very. Do go on."

The neighbour scratched his head. "Where was I?"

"You were just saying that Evalina had a bad attack of love. In fact you were on the point of telling me the identity of her lover."

"Oh, what a point to leave off, dear boy. How very remiss of me. Well, it was . . ."

Here the poor fellow's voice broke off and he stared aghast at the table of drinks. Very slowly and very deliberately an arm, an arm wreathed in veiling so it was utterly impossible to tell the sex of its owner, was emptying the contents of a small vial into one of the glasses. John felt utterly frozen as he watched, unable to shout or utter, merely to look. Then he was released from his catalepsy.

Another arm went out to pick up the glass and it was half way to its owner's lips before the Apothecary could make a move. Then he shouted, "Don't", and at the same time sprang forward and tipped the contents onto the floor. The glass went flying and a very surprised Justin Bussell stared at him open-mouthed. But it was

254

not too late. With an athletic move he hadn't really expected to make again, John swung over the table and pursued someone he couldn't even see but knew was ahead of him.

He chased through the crowd, still standing in reverential silence while the old chap mumbled on, and tore through the gathered onlookers. But he knew that with each passing second he was losing time. The man — or woman — he was after had hidden themselves amongst the people and was probably, even now, watching him as he fled frantically through the very heart of them.

". . . and Evalina, dear little soul, was saying, 'That's my booboo, Papa . . . '" the old man's voice continued.

John drew to a halt, knowing that the other person had won the day, for the time being at least. With a smile on his lips he picked up a cup of claret, and raised it. "To Evalina," he said, then downed the wine in one draught.

The chase had ruined the moment. By the time John had made his way back to the pair of gossips, Emilia and Samuel had joined him, and somehow the vital information became lost in the whirligig of introductions and pleasantries that were exchanged. And though he caught the old man's eye and they exchanged a look, nothing further was said. Indeed, the conversation was mostly about the hunt for the missing person and who it could possibly have been.

Justin, looking more than restored, in other words bordering on the state of being drunk, explained that it was somebody who wished him ill and that his very life had been saved by the gallant Mr. Rawlings. John, meanwhile, made light of the whole affair and said that it was a person playing a practical joke. An explanation that did not go down well with the other people who had come to see Evalina Fenchurch laid to rest. Anway, the matter was eventually allowed to drop, except for Justin who continued to thank John long after he had been quietly put in a corner, where he finally fell asleep and snored very loudly.

"So," said Emilia, "I think it is time we were leaving."

"High time," answered her husband, and sent a servant for his cloak and those of his party.

It was as they were going that Jocasta drew him to one side.

"Mr. Rawlings, what did happen earlier?"

"Nothing of any importance, Ma'am."

"Please don't insult my intelligence. Tell me exactly what you saw and what you did about it."

"I saw an arm pour something into Justin Bussell's glass. The next thing was that he had retrieved it and was about to drink. Everything made me suspect the action and give chase. But I did not find the offender. It was probably as I said — a practical joke."

She pulled a very serious face. "I don't think so."

"What do you mean? That the poisoner was here?"

"It would have been much easier than you realise."

"Why?"

"Because this is an old house, Sir. A house of many mysteries. One of which is a secret passage used by the priests when it became illegal to see them."

256

Despite the fact that Emilia and Samuel were standing at the doorway, looking thoroughly out of favour with him, John felt his interest quicken.

"Really? I would love to see it."

"Come back tonight."

"I can't."

"Then come tomorrow. Towards evening. I don't think it will be safe for you until then."

And before she could say another word, Jocasta had turned on her heel and gone.

They rode back through the late afternoon in a desperate quiet. The weather of earlier that day seemed to have penetrated inside the smart equipage that housed the three of them, and even Irish Tom was silent as the grave. Everywhere was the hushed stillness of that hour of the day and Emilia, as much to protect herself from things seen and unseen, fell uncomfortably asleep, her head jolting to and fro as the coach proceeded on. Seeing his hostess unconscious, Samuel leant forward.

"John?"

"Yes," the Apothecary answered tersely, his mind racing ahead down a million tracks towards a dimly spotted light in the distance.

"What was it you saw again?"

"How many more times? I saw somebody pour something into Justin's glass. I gave chase but there was nobody there. That's all I have to say."

He sounded more terse than he meant and saw Samuel's face turn away. "I see. Sorry."

For once John did not do his best to pacify but instead attempted to lapse back into his silent reverie. But the mood was broken. Whatever thought he had been giving chase to had vanished. Irritably he stared out of the window.

A mist had started to come up, a mist that spread its tendrils over and under the coach in a kind of sea, a mist that John found it impossible to see through. Slowly he realised that Tom was driving more and more deliberately until, finally, he drew to a halt. John opened a window.

"Everything all right, Tom?"

"Can't see a damned thing, Sir. I don't know where in hell we are."

"Oh." John turned to Samuel but saw that he, too, was now feigning sleep. "Wait a minute, I'll get out."

"Give us a minute, Sir. Then I'll be with you."

There were the faint sounds of a man making water, followed by a curse and a groan as Tom fell over something. Reckoning that it would be safe to join him, John stepped from the coach with care and stood very still.

"Tom," he called softly. Then louder, "Tom."

Nothing moved in the silence, nothing whatsoever. Then, suddenly, it was upon him. There was a rushing, as of wings, then a crunch. John had just time to say, "What . . .", and the rest went dark.

CHAPTER
SEVENTEEN

Slowly, slowly he was regaining consciousness but because he was more comfortable, because he had no wish to come back suddenly and cruelly, John sat for a while, his eyes closed, listening to the sound of utter silence. He was alone, of that he was certain. For no other human could make so little sound. Yet, small questions were already beginning to nag at parts of his brain. Where were Irish Tom and Samuel? And even more importantly, in fact a great deal more importantly, where was Emilia? Where, in short, was everybody else that had been with him when the coach had slowed down completely and then come to a halt? Very gingerly and very slowly, John Rawlings opened first one eye, then the other.

The answer as to where Tom had ventured to was immediately apparent. Lying across from him on the other side of the room was the Irishman, face down but just now showing signs of life. Very slowly, the Apothecary fiddled in his coat and there, hidden in an inner pocket but still viable to the touch, was his bottle of salts. With an enormous amount of difficulty he managed to pull it to the front and get it out. Then he sniffed and sniffed until his head cleared and with a little more effort, sat up. He had been dropped semi-upright by a wall and now he found his knees, weak though they were, and dragged himself into a kneeling position.

He looked round and confirmed that he and Tom were the only two living creatures in the room, except for some mice — or worse — which scuttled in a corner. Still too weak to try standing, John crawled to where the coachman lay and applied copious amounts of his smelling salts to his nostrils.

"What? What the hell?" said the Irishman, coming round.

"Shush. We're alone but I've no idea for how long or why. Where are the others? Do you know?"

"No, Sir, I don't. I've no idea. Last thing I remember was relieving myself. Then all thunder came at me."

"That must have been when I climbed out of the coach to look for you. Tom, where the devil are we?"

"I don't know, Sir. I truly do not."

They sat in silence for a moment, listening for any sound around them. Very distantly they could hear a faint whirring but what was the cause of it, neither had any idea. Other than for that, the scuttling in the corner was all they could hear.

"I'm going to have a look round," whispered John.

"Careful, Sir. You don't know who's about."

"The only other thing is to sit and wait and I don't feel quite up to that."

"Be very careful, then."

With this warning the Apothecary had to be content as he slowly got to his feet, weaving slightly as he went,

260

crossed the room and pulled the door open a fraction. After quite a while spent peering through the crack, he opened it a little further and stood back, waiting. Nothing happened. Whoever had been put on guard duty had clearly got other fish to fry.

Walking more easily, John returned to Tom's side. "What's on the other side of there? Do you know?"

"I think there's a staircase going up with a door at the top. I seem to recall coming round for a moment or two just before we were thrown into this hellhole."

"Good. As soon as you're a bit better we're going to run for it."

"No, you go, Sir. Don't wait for me. I'll be fine."

"Nonsense. We'll rest here for half an hour and that should see you restored. Here, have another sniff of these."

They waited in the dubious light, watching it grow dimmer and dimmer, awaiting the arrival of their captor. But still there was nobody and soon Tom started to move his legs around.

"I'm as ready now as I'll ever be."

"Right. Here's the plan. We climb the stairs, assault the man at the top — I'll take him because I think I'm stronger — then we go home, wherever that might be."

Tom pulled a face. "Search me. I've no idea."

"Good. Then come on — and to hell with it."

They opened the door and climbed the staircase in total silence, making their way step by step. Tom dislodged a bit of brick which fell to the bottom making a small clatter as it went. But still there was nothing.

Then at the very last minute there came sounds. Footsteps, only one set, were coming towards them. John motioned the coachman to remain exactly where he was, standing one step behind him on the narrow stairs. There was the sound of a key fumbling in the lock and then the door began to swing open. Suddenly rearing up, the Apothecary fetched their captor the most terrific blow over the back of his neck, a blow that splintered and crunched momentarily before the man began to fall down the stairs. Then he grabbed the coachman and they stepped outside.

They were in a spruce courtyard, quite well-maintained, with a stable of a dozen or so horses in loose boxes. There was nobody about but not far away they could hear somebody singing to himself as he worked. Ahead of them, yet seeming a million miles away, was the path to their freedom: an archway through which carriages passed on their way in and out of the establishment. "Don't run till we're through it," murmured John.

And a second later was glad that he had made that remark. A stubby figure carrying a pail was coming towards them through the arch, whistling to himself as he walked.

"Good evening," the figure said.

"Good evening," John replied crisply, while Irish Tom muttered a greeting.

They continued on their way, walking nonchalantly, then slowly disappeared through the arch. John waited a moment, turning his head slowly. From behind came a muffled shout and a cry. He grabbed Irish Tom.

"This is it. We leg it as fast as we can. I've no idea where we are but just pray we hit a track soon."

With that he was off, Tom, heavier built, springing as fast as he could in the background. They crossed a bridge and went through some woods, though fairly open-plan, as if they were farmed. Then they crossed a meadow, still running, though both were starting to feel the strain. Eventually, they drew to a halt, gasping great lungfulls of air, unable to take another step. There was total silence, as if nobody else were alive but them.

John looked at Tom. "We've made it — I think."

Tom motioned him to be quiet, then stood like that for several minutes. Eventually he nodded. "We're safe, Sir. But where the devil are we?"

"God knows."

They started to walk on, just following their feet — and then the strangest thing happened. They rounded a corner, or rather a bend in the track which had started about a quarter of a mile back, then both suddenly stopped. Before them in the distance burned several lights in what looked like a large dwelling. The strangest frisson ran through John even as he saw the place but he said nothing, denying to himself that he could possibly be right. But as he drew ever closer, he became more and more convinced that he was not wrong. He turned to Irish Tom.

"Does that house look familiar to you?"

"It certainly does, Sir."

John quickened his pace. "I'd swear that it's Scottlea Park."

"So would I, Sir."

They both stopped together and peered through the fitful moonlight. Then they saw it. John's coach, his wedding present from Sir Gabriel, lay outside, slightly silvered by the beams. With a whoop the two men embraced one another, then broke into the final run for home.

It was after midnight and yet everyone in the house was still awake. Louis had summoned the law — a glovemaker from West Clandon who had not been at all pleased at being awoken from his sleep. He stated he could do nothing until the morning and returned, grumpily, to his couch. Nothing daunted, the Frenchman had organised his own search party — a team of twenty-five men altogether — and had sent those out to comb the area. But now all were returned and a good jar of brandy being served in the kitchens to those who had taken part.

It seemed that Samuel, too, had eventually stepped out of the coach and looked around, though by this time all had become quiet. His search had grown a little wider, then he had returned, in a panic, to Emilia. It had been half an hour before they decided to drive home, though at a snail's pace, calling and calling, stopping every few minutes to scrutinise. Yet nothing had been revealed and eventually they had picked up speed and returned to Scottlea Park, where Emilia had hurried upstairs and fed her baby. But now the question was, where were John and Irish Tom — and who had taken them into captivity?

"It is fairly obvious to me," said Louis dryly.

"You mean the Bussell brothers?"

"Certainly."

"I'm not so sure about that. Justin was still asleep on the sofa when we left the house."

"Then it was Greville working alone," Louis answered certainly.

"You're most likely right. He's a vicious bastard."

And John recounted his story of Justin breaking down in church and the punch that had said it all. Louis looked reflective.

"Who was Evalina's secret lover, do you think?"

"My money is on Justin. I think it started off as a dare — something of that nature, anyway — and ended up as a great deal more. Probably not love, as we know it, but certainly a sort of admiration. He was definitely knocked out by her death."

Emilia spoke up. "Oh John, I do wish you would stop putting yourself at risk. How I worry when things like this happen."

It came so suddenly that it almost sent him flying. Black hair, mocking eyes, the scar that ran down one side of her face, making her so ugly and so attractive at the same time. The words that Emilia had spoken were repeated in his head, but this time he was saying it to her, to Elizabeth di Lorenzi, he was begging her to be careful.

"What?" he said after a moment or two, staring at his wife.

"Oh never mind," answered Emilia angrily, and rose to her feet. "If you'll forgive me Serafina, Louis, I am well weary. I shall make my way to bed."

Immediately John was full of apologies. "I'm sorry if I . . ."

She cut across him. "Goodnight, everyone." And that said, she marched out.

Serafina took her cue from Emilia. "I, too, am tired. Will you forgive me?"

Suddenly there was nobody left in the gracious living room but the three men, who sat for a moment looking from one to the other.

"John, forgive me for not giving chase immediately. I was very nearly asleep," said Samuel apologetically.

"My dear old chap . . ." said the Apothecary, and then he spoke at some length about friendship. But his brain had cut off from his lips and his mind had gone westwards, reminded of Elizabeth, wondering if he would ever see her again, if the extraordinary grip she had over him would ever release him from its hold.

He slept late next morning, so late indeed that there was no smell of breakfast in the air. Further, there was no one about upstairs to enquire as to the whereabouts of his family. Consequently, John washed and dressed and hurried downstairs to where he knew the servants would be.

The revelation was the day itself, which was as bright blue and shiny as the previous had been dull and misty. Everywhere the Apothecary looked there seemed to be glorious vistas of burgeoning green beckoning to him, speaking of the mysteries of the year's cycles, of the fact that spring had stepped forth and settled on the land. Suddenly full of excitement, he longed to get himself out and face his captors, who last night had seemed so mysterious and strange. Full of determination, he turned away from the window and bumped straight into a manservant who was walking along with a bucket of coal.

"Ah, life!" said the Apothecary, somewhat to the man's consternation. "Tell me, where is everybody?"

"They're all out, about their business, Sir. The two ladies and the children have gone to East Clandon to see Mrs. Boscawen, who has only been widowed a year. Monsieur le Comte and Mr. Swann have disappeared off somewhere, but I'm afraid I have no further information."

"Did they leave any message for me?"

"No, Sir, they didn't."

Much annoyed, John said airily, "Be kind enough to tell them that I have arisen and gone off on my own. I do not know what time I shall be back."

This said, he donned his hat and coat and, walking round to the stables, borrowed a fast dark horse he had spotted amongst the group of other, lazier, animals. It eyed him as much as he eyed it but there was to be no argument. John mounted it and cantered off in the direction of the Bussells' estate. As he went he calculated the miles he was doing, and everything worked out. Unless he had come from an entirely different direction, a fact he did not think possible because of the terrain, it was indeed the Bussells — or one of them — who had held him captive on the previous night.

Raising his whip to his hat in salute, John passed through the lodge gates and came up to the front door in good array. Here he dismounted.

"Is Mr. Bussell at home?" He deliberately did not say which one.

"No, Sir. Mr. Bussell is out."

"But it is the other one I wish to see."

This flummoxed the footman, who stood opening and closing his mouth while he thought. Eventually he said, "I shall go and see, Sir. If you would be so good."

He allowed John to enter and perch on the corner of a couch, fixing him with a look that did not bode well if he should so much as move a muscle. Then the man walked off in a dignified manner and slowly ascended the stairs.

Wandering in from an entirely different direction came the bleary figure of Justin, ill-shaven and dressed in a night-rail. He pulled up short when he saw John, then sat down on the other end of the couch.

"Hello," was all he said.

"Hello to you," John replied, as charmingly as he could muster.

"And you are?"

"Rawlings. John Rawlings. We have met several times but you swore I saved your life yesterday. Of course I didn't but it seemed as good a way as any of making you remember me." He pulled a long face. "Obviously with few results."

Justin, to give him his due, looked terribly embarrassed. "Look, I do apologise. It all comes back to me now. I do indeed recall you. We certainly have met before. I didn't see the arm but I clearly recollect the way that you smashed the glass from my hand." He suddenly looked suspicious. "I suppose there was an arm. You didn't make the whole thing up to draw attention to yourself?"

"No, I didn't. Listen, you must have got some idea. Who was it?"

Justin looked at him for the first time, his face terribly unkempt but completely sincere. "I have no idea. That's just the devil of it. I truly don't know."

John remained silent, turning ideas over and over in his mind. Finally he said, "I was hoping that you weren't going to say that. That you had some notion who it might be."

Justin shook his head, then stood up. "I can't help you. I'm sorry but I've got to go and get dressed. Your appearance has reminded me that there's still a life out there."

John also rose. "Thank you for your time. I must . . ."

They were interrupted by a loud banging of the front door and the next minute Greville had come in. "Are you up?" he was calling, then he saw John and his entire manner changed.

"Oh," he said.

John gave his third best bow. "How dee do?"

There was no answering bow back but at least he said, "Very well," before he went on with, "I trust I find you in good order."

"Excellent, my thanks."

"I see. And how is dear Serafina?"

So that was going to be it. He had decided on trivial chitchat as his means of communication.

"Very well, heaven be praised."

Greville gave John rather an odd stare.

"I actually called to see if Justin would care to come riding with me," John continued smoothly.

Justin looked as flabbergasted by this remark as did Greville, but boldly said yes.

His brother turned on him a look. "But surely you're not ready."

Justin fingered his chin nervously, then said, "No, perhaps you're right. Perhaps I'm not."

John tried to bluff it out. "Oh, come as you are. Just throw on a riding coat."

Greville was clearly used to having his own way. "I think another time, Mr . . . My brother was very poorly at the funeral yesterday and quite honestly cannot take any rough exercise at the moment."

The Apothecary decided that enough was enough. "Very well. But soon, I insist."

Greville opened his mouth to refuse but Justin's voice cut across. "Yes, Mr. Rawlings, I shall be ready. In fact I will ride over to your place one morning shortly. Shall we say ten o'clock?"

"Yes, let's," John answered, and with that, and with only the briefest adieu, bade them farewell.

There was nothing for it but to make for the hamlet of Stoke d'Abernon and Foxfire Hall, the great house which lay a couple of miles beyond it. However, various internal rumblings had already told the Apothecary about his missing meal and a call at The Onslow Arms became imperative. Therefore, one hour later and past three o'clock, he set out for his destination, determined that he must not stay long nor would he venture back through the woods.

The way, which yesterday had been so evil, today seemed blessed. John cantered through the trees unchecked and arrived at the mansion, standing proud and dominant, just over an hour later. He was immediately ushered in and was told to await Mrs. Rayner in the small parlour. Indeed, he was glancing through a copy of a newspaper, several days old, when a sudden noise in the doorway startled him. Looking up, John saw that Millicent was standing there, hovering uncertainly. John immediately rose to his feet.

"Miss Millicent, how are you? Is everything well with you?"

She flashed her eyes at him gratefully. "Oh my dear Mr. Rawlings, how very kind of you to ask. Yes, I'm as well as can be expected with all the losses we have had to endure recently. Really, I don't know how to get over it. First Aidan, then the two Bussells, bless them. They were such jolly people, you know. Always made everything seem so much brighter, somehow. Then, of course, like a bolt from the blue, Evalina. I mean to say, Mr. Rawlings, where and when is it all going to end? Who is the next in line, I ask myself? Surely not Jocasta? — oh surely, surely not."

"Miss Millicent, you must keep a grip on yourself. It is almost certainly over now."

"But is it?" she said, advancing close to him, her little dark eyes positively rolling with anxiety. "Is it, I say?"

"Yes, it is. Now sit down and be calm, I beg of you."

She was beginning to breathe very irregularly but John managed to get her to take a seat and lower her head, from which position she gallantly fought to bring her panting under control. Meanwhile, he knelt in front of her, patting her hands and making soothing sounds, all of which were quite useless but made him feel a great deal better. Eventually, Miss Millicent raised her head.

"Mr. Rawlings, you are a life saver in every way. I don't know what I should have done without you. I had been working myself up into quite a state."

She gave a little tremulous laugh and his heart warmed to her. Impulsively he kissed her hand and then rather regretted it, for she giggled madly, went red as a beet, then gave him a coquettish smile. John stood up rather hurriedly.

"Now, where is Mrs. Rayner? She has promised to show me . . ."

He had almost betrayed the reason for his visit and cut himself off in mid-sentence.

"Yes?" asked Millicent, suddenly very girlish and eager.

"Some of the family portraits," John improvised rapidly. "Are you familiar with them, Miss Millicent?"

"Oh, just Millicent please. I feel that we know one another well enough by now." She, too, got to her feet and John was terribly aware of how tiny she was. "Shall I start showing them to you? Jocasta can catch us up if she so desires."

He paused, not quite certain what to do. "Well, if you think . . ."

But his dilemma was about to end, and less painfully than he had feared. There was the sound of footsteps — several pairs of them if he was not mistaken — making their way towards the parlour.

"Cooee," Millicent called out.

"Where are you?"

"Here."

And the next minute Jocasta appeared framed in the doorway with Samuel, of all the people in the world, right behind her. Millicent was clearly aghast.

"Oh, Jocasta," was all she managed to say.

The Apothecary was equally thunderstruck but far better at concealing it. He gave the most elaborate bow while he tried to think what to say. Meanwhile, his friend spoke up.

"Well, John, we do keep running in to one another in the oddest places." He gave a bow in Millicent's direction. "How do you do, Ma'am? Well, I trust."

"Very well, I thank you," she answered coldly. She turned to Jocasta. "I was just about to show Mr. Rawlings the family portraits, dearest. Would that be in order?"

Jocasta gave her a sweet, sad smile. "Oh course. But why don't Mr. Swann and I come with you." She turned to the Apothecary. "Mr. Rawlings, you are rather early. I apologise but I wasn't expecting you quite so soon."

He gave her the most charming smile he could muster but his feeling of irritation with Samuel, which had started on the previous evening and had only just gone away, returned with a vengeance.

"This way, Mr. Rawlings," chirruped Millicent, and led the way as if she hadn't a care in the world, across the mighty Great Hall and up to the Long Gallery, which ran the entire length of the west wing. Jocasta and Samuel, meanwhile, positively dawdled behind them.

Instantly the Apothecary's eyes were drawn to a picture which hung, dominating the others, at the far end. So much so that his feet were drawn there despite the fact that Millicent was already starting to speak about some of the earlier portraits.

"My God," he said, beneath his breath, and stood away from it, regarding it in awe.

It was of a woman, her face closed and shuttered, her expression secretive. Her hair, what little he could see of it beneath a Tudor headdress, was dark, dark as the eyes which seemed to regard the Apothecary with a knowing look. Yet knowing was perhaps the wrong word. It was a look that unconsciously shared a secret, as if he was aware of the darkest workings of her mind, while she, it was obvious to John at least, knew everything in the world that there was to know about him. By the very fact that he had come to look at her portrait, he felt himself drawn into a secret that he could not explain.

In the far corner of the portrait crouched a monkey, its little face sad and wizened. Yet when the Apothecary stared into its features he saw that it had a look of the woman about it. He gazed and gazed, realising that

274

Millicent had come to join him and was standing at his side.

"That's a portrait of a cousin of ours, all of the family I mean."

"Oh yes?" said John, continuing to stare.

"Yes. Lucinda, Lady Tewkesbury, her name is. They say that she betrayed her husband."

"Oh yes?" John repeated, suddenly very interested.

"Oh yes indeed. He was one of old blood — his ancestors came over with William the Conqueror — and she had no titled blood at all. Yet he fell madly in love with her and after his second wife died took this one for third. She gave birth to one son, the son who was our common ancestor, but nobody could be sure that the boy was his."

"Go on."

"Well, she had fallen in love in her turn."

"With whom?"

"With Roger de Courtenay, a noble from the North of England who came visiting."

John turned to look at her and saw that her little fingers were working the cuff of her sleeve.

"Tell me about it."

"Well, I don't know that much. All I'm aware of is that she and Roger disappeared one night . . ."

"What, literally?"

"Yes. One moment they were here, probably in the Long Gallery. The next they were gone. Well, that's what we are told anyway."

"But what happened?" asked the Apothecary, suddenly irritated to have got so far and no further.

"I truly don't know."

He leant forward, as if being closer to the portrait would give him the answer, and there was a sudden whirring sound. John turned just in time to see Miss Millicent's nervous eyes, then suddenly hurtled forward through the panelling into a strange, black room that lay beyond. For the second time in that twenty-four hours, the Apothecary found himself alone in the darkness.

CHAPTER
EIGHTEEN

This time, however, he was wide awake, and as he got used to the light realised that he was in a large room, so large that it was not easy to see the far corners. From somewhere — at present he had no idea where — a great deal of light was being let in. But to find its source was not his top priority. Instead John turned and beat loudly on the panelling, shouting at the top of his voice.

"Millicent, Millicent, are you there? Let me out, there's a good girl."

He strained his ears but there was no answering sound, in fact no sound at all except for a faint scuffling. "Oh 'zounds and 'zoonters and damnation," he said aloud. "What the devil's happened to her?"

There were two possible solutions, neither of which appealed to him. One was that she was lying unconscious, the other that she had taken to her heels and fled to wherever Jocasta and Samuel were at that particular moment. Both of which involved time.

He turned back to the panelling and set up a mighty pounding which got something in the room behind him jumping. Cursing wrathfully, the Apothecary gave up and decided that the best thing he could do was get out of his present situation as quickly as possible. This meant starting with a proper examination of the place in which he found himself.

It was a very large room, partially furnished with decaying bits, long since left to moulder into obscurity. The source of light was, he discovered, a chimney breast, a good-sized opening at the top allowing daylight in — and more. Birds' nests lay in the hearth, together with twigs and other detritus which had fallen down the chimney over the years. But just as he was going to pass the fireplace by something made him pause and come back to it. Recently, within the last month or so, somebody had lit a fire in part of it. The smell, though faint, was still in the air. Thoroughly intrigued, the Apothecary conducted a hasty search of the room, then made for the door, which opened at once to his touch.

He was standing in a corridor which ran to both right and left, albeit narrow and carved from stone. Never having had a good sense of direction the Apothecary stood for several minutes, wondering which way to go, and eventually decided on left. But after a few moments of making his way, he turned back. Neither right nor left were going to be any good until he found some sort of light to guide him.

Back in the room there was very little of use; a drinking cup, a rotting cushion, a piece of a rug being about the only things. Then, as he passed the mantelpiece, instinctively he searched once more. And there, tucked in amongst the cobwebs and invisible to the naked eye, was a small piece of candle, about ten minutes' burning time in all.

He went down the corridor as far as he could, then struck a tinder and tried to ignite the thing. All the time he was praying that it would work and eventually, after what seemed like hours of struggling, a measly flame caught and lit the way. John marched on to the left, knowing that he had little light left to him. And then he heard it. Very faintly, somewhere a dog was barking.

He started to follow the sound, though he had no choice but to do so, praying that he would reach the end of the corridor before the flame went out. Meanwhile, the barking was getting louder and louder until, at last, he reached the top of some rough hewn steps. As carefully as he could, John made his way down, listening for the sound of the dog. It was only a fraction away from him he could tell, yet where was the damnable thing? Then as suddenly as if it had been there all along, which, of course, it had except that he had been unaware of it, light flooded in. The candle blew out as with one last heave John pushed at the door which swung back with a groan. He had reached civilisation once more.

Twenty minutes later he was seated in the grandeur of the big salon, imbibing brandy with his tea to help him recover from the shock. Poor Millicent had fainted clean away at his disappearance, and though now conscious was only able to take a little boiled water to clear her head. Samuel, who had been on the point of departing, had stayed on to help with the search.

"The extraordinary thing is, John, that none of us could find the wretched mechanism, try as we would.

279

Nor could we hear you. It had apparently gone dead as the tomb."

Warmed by the brandy, cheered by their genuine relief that he had got out safely, John asked a question.

"Do you mean to say that that is the first you have known about the concealed place in the Long Gallery?"

Jocasta spoke. "Oh yes. Completely and utterly. The passage I wanted to show you runs off the Great Hall. It is a series of corridors, two of which lead out, the others are dead ends. It was used at one time to hide the priests during religious persecution. We call it the Valley of Shadows. I don't know why, really."

"Then there is more than one secret passage in this house?"

"There are probably half a dozen if we could but find them all. Anyway, when you have gathered your strength, we'll go and look for that other one. See if we can discover it."

John nodded, turning over in his mind the fact that someone had lit a fire in that hidden grate. "Millicent was telling me a story about the woman under whose picture I vanished. Something about her disappearing with her lover there."

Jocasta gave another smile of sadness. "Poor Millicent, if she can get anything confused she will. Lucinda Tewkesbury died, you know."

"Yes, I'm sure she did. But what happened to her in the years between?"

"She ran off with Roger de Courtenay but her husband gave chase and killed him. Then he took her back, meek as you please. Nine months later she presented him with a son."

"I see. And which one was the child's father?"

"Nobody knows for sure. In fact I don't suppose Lucinda was certain either." Jocasta laughed and looked at Samuel, who coloured and stared rapidly away. "Well, if you're ready, Mr. Rawlings. Shall we go and see what Lucinda has to say to us now?"

"Certainly. Your turn to be locked in, Sam."

But he wasn't feeling in any mood for laughing as he entered the Long Gallery for the second time that afternoon and once again stood beneath the portrait.

"I was just here when it happened," he said.

"What were you doing?"

"Nothing really. Just staring at your ancestor, wishing she could speak and tell me her secrets."

This said, John pressed the place where he had been leaning, or rather where he thought the place to be. But this time there was no click, nor did the panel swing away. In fact nothing happened at all. Faintly embarrassed, John tried again. Once more, nothing happened.

"Here, let me try," said Samuel, and came over and stood where the Apothecary had just done. He leant forward and pressed but nothing happened. He turned to John. "Are you sure you were here?"

"Of course I was there. Ask Millicent."

"Oh no," said Jocasta rapidly. "She really is too poorly. Let her rest, do."

John vaguely wondered if the sad little woman was heading for the beginning of the end of her courses, but did not allow himself to dwell on the matter. Far more pressing was the discovery of the button that would release the panel. Yet try as he would the mechanism remained concealed and eventually he and Samuel were forced to turn away, defeated.

"Well," said Jocasta, "I don't know what to say."

"It's perfectly true," replied John. "How else could I have got outside?"

"Well, I believe you," answered Samuel stoutly, instantly restoring himself in his friend's affections.

"Good chap."

And there was a moment's heavy silence before Jocasta said brightly, "Would you like to see the Valley of Shadows?"

"Yes, very much," answered John, but his brain was heavy with the mystery of the Long Gallery and what it was that was precluding him from finding the mechanism.

Yet, despite this, he was still overwhelmed by the Valley of Shadows. It was so much bigger than he had thought, almost as if another house existed beside the big one. Entranced, John watched as Jocasta pressed the middle of a piece of Tudor panelling and saw the lower panel creak back, then was forced to bend double in order to gain entry. This time, in order to be on the safe side, he allowed Jocasta the privilege of going first.

A maze of corridors, lit by her candletree, stretched before him on either side. Though all quite narrow he saw that they included a staircase which, no doubt, went down to the cellar.

"Amazing," said Samuel.

"Very useful," Jocasta answered pointedly, "for those having to hide in a hurry. Or for gentlemen serving tea and baccy, if you know what I mean." She turned to John. "Do you wish to see more or shall we save it for another day?"

"I think, if you don't mind, that I'll call an end to it. I've a mind to have one more go at the upstairs cipher before I take my leave."

"Certainly. I feel I can hardly refuse you."

Laughing they trooped out of the cavern and back into the Great Hall, though all the time John had the uneasy feeling that they were being observed. However, despite various covert attempts at looking round, he could see nothing.

The portrait stood, as enigmatic as ever, its message as strong and as powerful as when he had first seen it. But again the panel resisted any attempt at being opened, so much so that John began to believe that he had not experienced what he knew perfectly well had happened. This time, though, he made light of it.

"Oh well, the lady is definitely annoyed with me. So, if you will forgive, Madam, I really think I must take my leave."

He turned to Samuel, fully expecting him to comply, and was astonished to see that his friend was frowning.

"Samuel?"

"I believe old chap, if it's all the same to you, that I'll follow on later. Mrs. Rayner has promised to show me some miniatures which I would rather like to see."

Very surprised, the Apothecary found himself bowing and making his way out on his own. But he was glad that there was still sufficient daylight to give him a clear run through the woods before the shadows grew even longer.

Back at Scottlea Park there was such an air of tranquillity that John immediately became suspicious. It seemed to him that everything was perfection. His daughter had just been fed and was now ready to play with him; his wife, whose hair was being dressed by a maid, blew him kisses; Louis winked his eye and offered him a glass of claret. And over all triumphed Serafina, gliding round the house, as tall and elegant as ever. Everything was set for a perfect evening and so it turned out to be.

Not one word was spoken in complaint; the food was divine; and afterwards the others lay back against cushions and listened to Serafina effortlessly play Scarlatti at his most demanding.

"Superb," said John, when she had finally finished, and applauded with the others.

But the efforts of the day and memories of the strange affair in the Long Gallery had not been far away, and soon he had started to yawn with genuine fatigue. At this, Serafina had risen from the harpsichord and suggested that they have one final drink before retiring.

"For surely you are off tomorrow," she had said.

The truth had hit John hard. While he had been away entertaining himself in secret and getting thoroughly lost, Emilia had been packing. He turned to his wife and she nodded.

"Oh darling, and I left all the arranging to you," he said remorsefully.

She smiled. "Not for the first time."

"And not for the last. Oh these men, these men!" said Serafina, but she was smiling as well and John felt more at ease than he had for a long time.

Yet the minute he got into bed all his old tension returned. He only had to close his eyes and he relived those times he had endured when he had been locked behind the portrait. He sat bolt upright, eyes wide open.

"Why the devil did I say locked?" he asked the room aloud.

"Um? What?" said Emilia, already deep down in sleep.

"Nothing, darling."

But he knew then what had been at the back of his consciousness ever since he had stepped through the hidden door and out into the glade. He had been locked in that terrible room, he was certain of it.

CHAPTER
NINETEEN

The next morning was too confused for any clear thoughts to emerge and it wasn't until later, after Irish Tom had drawn the equipage away from the delightful villa in which dwelt Serafina and her family, and had his party well on the road to London, that they began to crystallise in John's mind. The first thing was that he had been locked into that mysterious room by a person unknown. The second thing was — and here John paused in order to get his thoughts in order — the openness with which Jocasta Rayner had displayed her lack of grief. Because, though she had wept openly at the loss of a father, she had done little more than shed a tear at the departure of her sister.

And his brought him, much against his will, to Samuel. Had his friend intervened in the matter? Had he offered a shoulder to lean against? John sat grimly, chewing over the facts and making something of a face as he did so.

"John, whatever are you thinking about? What is it that gives you such a horrid mouth? Why, you look as if you've swallowed a packet of pins."

The Apothecary returned to earth with a crash, his thoughts flying in all directions. "What? Oh, sorry. I was miles away."

He was looking directly into Emilia's eyes which at this precise moment were very far from angelic.

"Boo!" John added, and smiled.

She did not smile back, and he felt his heart sink. In fact he was just preparing an elaborate excuse when Emilia suddenly snatched his hand and gazed into it. Worried, John said nothing. Eventually, his wife came out with, "I wonder what she could really see, that old woman."

Suddenly, it was all clear to him. "Oh, you mean Serafina. When she dressed up."

Emilia gave him a deep look. "I don't think so. I thought she was genuine. An old beggar woman who haunted their kitchens."

A thread of that evening's strangeness came back to pluck at John's heartstrings but he pushed it away angrily.

"No, it was Serafina. Why, she was laughing when she came back in."

"That was more than likely about something else. I'm telling you John, that old woman was genuine."

Remembering the oddness of the entire event the Apothecary saw off his desire to convince Emilia that it was Serafina all along and, instead, remained silent. After a while Emilia dropped his hand and herself sat saying nothing. John decided that the best way he could regain his thoughts was by feigning sleep. So, pulling his hat well down over his eyes, he closed them. Instantly he was back in that room, picking his way round that huge grate, surprise and bewilderment coming with the thought that somebody had recently lit a fire there. But who had it been? Surely Millicent was too cautious a person to have thought of doing such a thing. And yet ... Slowly and carefully the Apothecary forced the image of her face into his mind. He remembered her look of astonishment, followed by something else. Her eyes had seemed so nervous temporarily, just as he vanished from view. Had Miss Millicent been guilty? Or was she as astonished as he was by the whole incredible scene?

John let his thoughts rove on, returning briefly to the problem of Jocasta. Had her lack of guilt been entirely because she was happy with Samuel or had there been another, darker, purpose? Had ...

He opened his eyes suddenly as the coach dropped speed and realised that he was in London, or what passed for London, driving through the leafy lanes of St. George's Fields, prior to turning off for Westminster Bridge. Guiltily, John turned to his wife and Dorcas but saw that they and the baby were all three fast asleep. Leaving them where they were, he stared out of the window, once more immersed in deep thought.

An hour later they were within doors, the women waking in a flap, only Rose Rawlings regarding them all with a discerning eye.

"Oh my dear," said Emilia, "what a to-do."

"Nonsense," replied her husband forthrightly. "I'll take Rose for a little walk and when I get back you and Dorcas will have organised everything."

So saying, he had Rose in her bassinette and out of the house almost before a voice could be raised in objection. Anyway he was longing to get out and about having been stuck in the coach for nearly a day. Thus, father and daughter, leaving the house quite quickly, turned into Gerrard Street, then into Macclesfield Street, to get to St. Ann's, Soho, where he thought to show her the place in which he had been married. But just as the church was coming into view so, too, came a figure. A figure which as it drew closer revealed itself as Lieutenant Mendoza.

"I see we meet again," said the Apothecary, stepping directly into the Lieutenant's path and giving the curtest of bows.

"Sir, I owe you an apology," came the reply.

"You do indeed."

"I thought you were one of the common herd and put my hands about you. I was mistaken and I humbly ask forgiveness."

"What has brought this about if I might ask?"

"I saw the error of my ways," the Lieutenant answered humbly.

And something else beside, the Apothecary thought. Someone has spoken to him. But who? Aloud he said nothing, waiting for the Lieutenant to come to the point.

"And whose is this delightful child?" Mendoza continued, holding out a hand to Rose, who grabbed a finger and held on tight.

"Mine," said John, and surprised himself at the terrific surge of pleasure that saying such a thing could bring about.

"I should have guessed. She will be a great person," the Lieutenant continued. He straightened up. "Shall we sit in the church for a while?"

"Why not?" answered John, but within he was almost bursting, certain that the military man had been coming to see him with the express intention of unburdening himself.

They made their way inside and sat down in a deserted pew near to the front. Looking round, John saw that several people were busy about the place but nobody had taken any particular notice of them and they were going to be left alone. "You'd best tell me why you wanted to see me," he said.

The Lieutenant gazed at him. "I don't know where to begin."

"Everyone says that. So why not start at the real beginning."

Mendoza looked blank. "I'm sorry. I don't quite follow."

"Oh, you follow well enough. Tell me about the woman you're in love with."

"Louisa? Oh, she's adorable, she's an . . ."

"No. I mean the other woman in your life."

The angry look was beginning to come back in the Lieutenant's face. "What other woman?"

"Mrs. Trewellan," John said quietly.

"Ah, therein lies a big confession."

"I guessed as much. Tell me everything."

"Well, what does one say? How does one put it?"

"I'm hoping you'll show me."

The Lieutenant shrugged his shoulders and sighed. "You know, of course, that she has kept our relationship entirely hidden from the world."

The Apothecary looked wise.

"Which, of course, has given rise to certain questions," Mendoza continued.

"Has it?" asked John, more than a little surprised. He frowned, not seeing at all where any of this was leading.

"I was born just a fortnight before her eighteenth birthday."

"To whom?" asked John, totally perplexed.

"Well, to her, of course," said Lieutenant Mendoza. "Mrs. Trewellan is my mother."

There was a profound silence into which Rose farted loudly.

"Good God!" exclaimed the Apothecary. "And there was me thinking . . . Are you telling me that . . . ?" But his voice died away and John Rawlings hung down his head. "I feel my mental powers are on a parallel with that noise my daughter has just made."

After a second's silence, the military man suddenly put his head back and gave a laugh, though with rather a bitter undertone.

"I must never tell my poor mama," he said, "and neither must you."

The Apothecary couldn't raise a smile. He sat, head bowed, taking in what should have been obvious from the start. That Mrs. Trewellan and the Lieutenant were mother and son was so glaringly clear that now he knew the fact he couldn't think how he had missed it. But still it remained that he had and, worse, had been caught in the act. John could not remember a more embarrassing moment in his entire life.

Meanwhile, Lieutenant Mendoza sat laughing dryly to himself, though still with little humour.

Rapidly John thought over everything the young man had told him, fitting the story in with the new information. It all made sense, of course. The boy brought up by his uncle, his real father dying at the age of nineteen, the redoubtable Mrs. Trewellan not mentioned, but then neither had there been any pretence. Who the Lieutenant's actual mother was simply hadn't been discussed.

Still, the Apothecary felt deeply ashamed of himself. "Look, I'm terribly sorry to have made such a foolish mistake," he said.

"Nonsense, nonsense." The Lieutenant was brushing the whole matter away with his hand. "I suppose it was easy enough. None the less, I would like to have been thought a little more selective. Not . . ." he added hastily, ". . . that there is anything wrong with my dear mama, but I would have considered her fractionally old."

"Oh yes, oh yes," the Apothecary agreed. "Far too old."

It was only then that he realised how everything he was saying was making the situation worse. With an enormous effort of will, he changed the subject.

"Tell me," he said pleasantly, "what is it you actually wanted to see me about?"

The Lieutenant's smile vanished and he suddenly looked wary. "Someone suggested to me that I should talk to you."

"Someone who?"

"Ah, that would be telling. I promised to keep their secret. No, it is just with all these murders going on that I felt I should apologise."

"Only that?"

"That, together with a belief that you and I should see ourselves on the same side."

"Which is?"

"That we're tired of this carnage and believe that it should come to an end."

John had the inescapable feeling that the conversation was going round in circles. "Look," he said, "how much do you know about Foxfire Hall?"

Lieutenant Mondoza positively stared. "Very little," he answered. "Why?"

"No reason really, except that I believe our murderer has a certain knowledge of the place."

The Lieutenant gave him an odd glance. "Oh? Why is that?"

The Apothecary decided on the side of discretion. "Just one or two things I have seen that is all. So, just to remind me, why did your mother turn Aidan Fenchurch down?"

"Because of Sperling. He hated Aidan with a burning, childish hatred, probably caused by jealousy as much as anything. Anyway, she told Aidan that he would have to wait until Sperling was off her hands, then she would reconsider."

"But it never came to that."

"No," said the Lieutenant, with something that resembled genuine sadness in his voice. "it never came to it."

John paused, wondering quite what he should say next, and at that moment Rose woke up and started to cry. It really was, the Apothecary thought on a whimsy, as if they were working together on this case. He turned to Lieutenant Mendoza and gave his second best bow.

"My dear Sir, I see where my duty calls me. It has been a pleasure to catch up with you. Forgive me but my daughter insists that we go."

With that he bowed again and they parted company. Strangely, as soon as the Lieutenant was out of sight, Rose stopped crying and the journey home was conducted in harmony. That is until John went through the front door. Almost immediately a footman hovered by his elbow.

"Sir, Mr. Jago is here to see you. I have shown him into the library."

"Excellent," said John airily, and without further ado handed the bassinette to the footman and walked to his guest at double speed.

Joe was standing by the window, the very droop of his shoulders telling a newcomer that all was not well in his world. However, hearing John come in he braced up and turned with a smile to greet his host.

"My dear Sir, how are you? Have there been adventures since we last met?"

"I should say so. Why don't you sit down and let me tell you about them?"

"I would like that very much, Mr. Rawlings."

He took a chair opposite that of the Apothecary and the next half hour was filled with tales of adventure, of secret passages, and of mysterious capturings and escapes. Added to which, of course, was the information that the Bussells had returned home.

"I reckon they were just jinking about in London when we couldn't find them. They are walking round their place quite openly. They've no idea they're wanted men."

Joe frowned. "Damnation. The Flying Runners have set off for Winchester and the rest are hard stretched in London. Still, we'll have to try and get someone down there to arrest them." He paused, his blue eyes strained. "And are you any nearer to the murderer, Sir?"

Reluctantly the Apothecary shook his head. "I fear not. Though, saying that, I think that Justin is Lancelot."

For the first time Joe looked surprised. "Surely not, an oafish creature like that."

"She was desperate for affection. Besides, who knows what his motives truly were."

"Very true, Sir. Anyway, our news ain't good. Do you want to hear it?"

"Of course."

"Well, the Governor's very far from pleased. He says that every time there is a principal suspect they are promptly removed from the scene. Says it's almost like tit for tat."

"Tit for tat," repeated John thoughtfully. "You know, he has a point there."

"Aye, he has. But the question remains. Who is doing it?"

"You know there could be several people involved in this."

"Oh, we came to that conclusion some while ago. One from each side as it were."

"Or more than one," murmured John, so quietly that Joe did not hear, or did not appear to do so.

"Anyway, we've not achieved any kind of solution and Sir John is wondering who will be next."

"You're not serious?"

"Yes, I am, Sir. Deadly serious."

"Surely he should take action."

"But what?" Joe held up a capable hand in front of his face. "Let us see who is still at large. First of all, there's Mrs. Jocasta. Then there's the Lieutenant, his missus, his mistress . . ."

John interrupted with a brief laugh. "That's all been explained to me. Mrs. Trewellan is his mother."

"His mother, did you say?"

"I certainly did."

And as briefly as possible, yet leaving nothing out, John repeated all that had been told him.

"I see. Well, it makes more sense, if you see what I mean."

"It definitely does. Anyway, you were saying."

Joe began to count off the people left. "Lieutenant Mendoza, his wife, Mrs. Trewellan, Mr. Sperling. That's that lot. Miss Millicent; too timid in my view. Mrs. Rayner, of course. Then, on the other side, the two Bussell brothers. That's it, unless you can think of anyone else."

"No, I can't say that I can."

"Then, Sir, our murderers are hidden amongst them."

"I wonder if there is another person," said John thoughtfully.

"Who, Sir?"

"Do you remember Mrs. Rayner's husband, one Horatio. Wasn't he poisoned accidentally?"

"Yes."

"Don't you think that that is something of a coincidence?"

Joe looked thoughtful, pursing his lips. "Well, I suppose it could bear looking in to."

"I wonder if there is any point now. But it might be worth our while to establish who was in the house on that occasion."

"Yes, it might indeed," answered Joe. "I shall put a Runner on to that. Mark you, there are bound to be the usual memory lapses after such an age."

"I wonder."

"I wonder too," repeated the clerk meaningfully. His light eyes met the Apothecary's and they gave each other a glance that spoke volumes though neither of them said a word.

Eventually John broke the silence. "I've got to get back to the country, haven't I? Our killer — or should it be killers — is waiting there."

Joe's ragged face grew very still. "I reckon so, Sir. Yes, I do."

"But this time I must go alone. I won't catch them otherwise."

The clerk hardly moved, then he said, "I'd rather that the Runners were with you."

"No, Joe, I insist on this. You mustn't do anything to stop me."

"That I can't do, Sir."

The Apothecary pulled a face. "You could take my place when it comes to telling Emilia that I'm off again."

Joe Jago allowed himself a humourless grin, then said, "I don't envy you that, Sir. Truly I don't."

"None the less, it must be done."

Joe cleared his throat. "Might I suggest, Sir, that this time you don't stay with the Comte and Comtesse. In fact the quieter you can keep your visit, the wiser it might be. Put up at the inn if possible. That way you can go in and out as you desire."

John shivered. "You realise that at least one of the killers is mad, don't you?"

The clerk shook his head, almost sadly. "Yes, I know. The question is, who is he — or she?"

"I can hazard a guess."

"A guess is no good, Sir. You have to be certain."

The light was starting to fade and noises of the household preparing for the hours of darkness suddenly began to filter in. Joe sighed deeply.

"Let me come with you, Sir."

The answer was on John's lips before he had time to think properly. "No, you must stay with the Blind Beak. I can take care of myself."

But after Joe had gone and he sat in the semi-darkness, preparing himself for what he thought was going to be his worst conversation to date with

Emilia, John caught himself wondering if, in fact, he really could.

That was how she found him, sitting in the gloaming, staring out of the window at what was left to see of the fast-retreating garden.

"John?"

He didn't say anything but put out his hand and caught her wrist. "Emilia. I'm glad it's you."

Very gently she released his hold and went to sit down opposite him, but, once there, she took hold of his hand again.

"What's the matter?"

He sighed. "Joe's been."

"Yes, I know." She was silent for a few moments, then added, "What did he say?"

"Not much." John sighed again.

"Whatever it was has clearly affected you deeply."

"Yes, you can conclude that. Emilia . . ."

"What's the matter? Why do you sound so sad?"

"Oh, just because. Emilia, he and I discussed the situation and I have to go back. Back to West Clandon, that is."

"I see," she said very quietly — but she did not remove her hand.

In the years ahead of him John would never forget that moment, how she said 'I see' but still held him handfast.

"Don't you mind?" he asked, his voice low.

"I mind very much, very much indeed, but there is nothing I can do that will stop you."

"You could shout and scream."

Her fingers tensed beneath his. "That is not my way, John. You ought to know that."

"Yes, I know it." He raised her hand to his lips. "I love you, Emilia," he said.

"And I love you. More than you will ever know."

He stood up and raised her to face him. Then he kissed her, full on the mouth and very deep.

Emilia held herself back, at first, but suddenly gave in, overwhelmed by what they both were feeling. Then they left the library and made their way upstairs, to where the great bed lay waiting for them in all its ivory-clad splendour.

CHAPTER
TWENTY

He rose just after dawn and was met at the front door by Irish Tom. The two men said nothing, their minds set on what they had to do, and it wasn't until they had left London well behind them and were on their way to Surrey that Tom spoke for the first time.

"You said to Guildford, didn't you, Sir?"

"Yes, I want to hire a horse from a livery stable and make my way quietly to The Onslow Arms."

"And me, Sir?"

"I want you to go back to London and support your mistress."

"But I had hoped . . ."

"I'm sorry, Tom. Those are my orders."

The Irishman promptly plunged into gloom and did not speak again until the town of Guildford had been finally reached, and then it was with a bad grace that he toured the outskirts looking for a livery stable. Eventually, though, one was found and John put his head out of the window.

"Drop me here. I'd rather go incognito."

"I don't understand you, Sir. I truly don't."

"Well, humour me then," John answered shortly. He disembarked. "Now, Tom, I'll be in touch as soon as this matter is resolved."

The coachman raised his brows but said nothing.

"So wait for me to call you."

"If you ever do," the Irishman muttered just below his breath.

John ignored him. "Until next week then."

"Humph," Tom answered, and climbing back onto the box, turned the coach and vanished from sight without a backward glance.

A half hour later and John's business was all done. He had hired a horse for a week, in return for a healthy deposit, and was just preparing to take her to West Clandon. His usual choice of dark uncertain horses had been thwarted and he had had to settle for the fastest the Livery had to offer, not at all up to standard in his book but, he told himself, beggars cannot be choosers. In the event, though, the mare, name of Herring, did her best and they clattered into the inn yard just as light was beginning to fade. Leading Herring round to the stables, John went inside to book a room.

It seemed that luck was with him for there was no sign of recognition on the landlord's part and he was given a small but serviceable room on the first floor without anyone saying a word about having seen him before. So, reasonably confident that they regarded him as a complete stranger, John wandered down at about six o'clock. Making for the taproom, the Apothecary disappeared into a corner with a newspaper, his purpose to be as inconspicuous as possible. Opening the paper up wide, John listened to the various voices.

There was the usual hum of sound, out of which one in particular rose to meet his ears. It was Justin Bussell, drunk as usual, and complaining in a whining sort of way to anyone who would listen, which did not appear to be very many.

". . . it wasn't love . . ." he was saying, "more a fondness. Yes, a fondness, that describes it. Utterly."

"Who was this?" somebody asked.

"Oh, I can't reveal her identity," said Justin morosely. "Let me just say that that she lives about ten miles hence." There was the sound of him supping which turned into a snorting kind of sob. "What do I mean, lives? I should say lived."

This story was obviously old news to his audience, who could be heard shifting their feet and making to move away. John sat behind his paper wondering whether to interrupt or let Justin drone on. But it would appear that his followers had gone somewhere else to get a free drink, for now there was the sound of subdued weeping accompanied by regular swigs of ale, but no 'oohs' and 'aahs'. The Apothecary decided that the time had come. Folding up his newspaper and leaving it, he rose from his chair and walked round the edge of the bar.

Justin certainly presented a pathetic sight. His shoulders were hunched over his tankard, his face was blotched and weary, in fact he seemed smaller, almost as if he had shrunk. Mustering as sympathetic an expression as he could, John approached.

It was perfectly obvious from Justin's response that he didn't even realise that the Apothecary had returned to town and come back again. He looked up, startled, as John greeted him, then gave him a tremulous smile.

"I'm so sorry I haven't come riding yet," he said. "You must forgive me."

The Apothecary thought on his feet. "How about tomorrow?" he said. "I could come and call for you."

Justin nodded listlessly. "Yes, yes, that will do fine." A small sob escaped. "You must forgive me, my friend, I am a little disturbed by recent events."

John looked kind. "I don't know how you bore it. First your mother, then your father. It was more than human flesh and blood could tolerate."

Justin regarded him properly for the first time and John could see that there had been a great deterioration. In the short month that had elapsed, he had indeed lost weight, and his eyes, once so confident and dismissive, had sunken back in his head and had heavy circles beneath.

Had this really been Evalina's Lancelot? Had she loved him? And had he put out a hand to strike her down, as she smiled at him in her death dream? John stood silently, staring, saying not a word, waiting for Justin to make some sort of reply. Eventually, the other man spoke.

"Of course there have been other things as well."

"Of course," John replied soothingly.

"Too many deaths," said Justin.

He looked on the point of tears again and John hesitated, wondering what to do next. Then, instinctively, he touched the other man's arm and simply said his name. It was enough. Justin wept bitterly.

Somehow John managed to catch the landlord's eye and mouth the fact that Justin needed to be removed to a private parlour. But, unfortunately, there was no such thing, The Onslow Arms being but a small place, six guests at the most. However, the snug only had one man in it and he was fast asleep. So, clasping John's arm, that is where Justin was taken, and once there, sobbed despairingly.

The other man woke and shuffled out, giving the two men an extremely odd look as he did so. But at least they had the place to themselves. The Apothecary sat silently, waiting for Justin to quieten down, which, eventually, he did.

"I'm so sorry," he burbled, blowing his nose and wiping his eyes.

"My dear Sir," said John calmly. "Take your time. I have all the evening."

A bleary eye appeared round a corner of the spotted handkerchief, followed by a loud gulp. "I shall be perfectly recovered in a moment."

John nodded but said nothing, sipping his wine and lighting a pipe, the very picture of someone totally self-controlled. But within he was utterly alert, positive that never again would he get Justin in such a weak state of mind. Certain that if any kind of confession was going to come, it was now or never.

Justin gave another tortured swallow then removed the handkerchief, giving his eyes a final wipe. "My very dear Sir," he said, his voice low, "how can you forgive me?"

"Nothing to forgive," John answered cheerfully. "We all get depressed from time to time."

"Yes, but this was unusual."

"Very. Don't forget that I know you, Sir. Know your ways. I'm sure that to find you like this is a rarity."

Justin nodded, starting to recover. "Yes, it is indeed."

John recognising that the other man was beginning to sober up, said silkily, "But you're short of a drink, my friend. Here, have some claret. I'll order another bottle."

Justin hesitated, then answered, "Why not?"

The Apothecary hastily poured a large glass and proposed a toast.

"To us, Sir. Who's like us? And to the devil with anyone who thinks he is," and threw back his glass rapidly.

Justin followed and said, "Damme, that's better."

John poured him another. "And now I'll drink to you, Sir. A brave fellow if ever there was one." He emptied his glass once more.

Over the rim he studied Justin carefully. The face was hardly at its best, but for all that it had the puffiness and slow blurring of features that only a life of dissipation could bring about. John wondered how old he was and came up with thirty, realising with a start that was his own age, at least for another few weeks. Suddenly and from nowhere he felt desperately sorry for the man, wondering what he, John, would have been like if he had been left to rot in the gutter alongside his

306

begging mother, had Sir Gabriel Kent's carriage gone on its way.

Justin, meanwhile, was still struggling to control himself, his lips quivering occasionally, his face a study in melancholy. The Apothecary decided that if he left it any longer the moment would pass and be gone. Clearing his throat, he asked, "Tell me, Justin, how well did you know Evalina Fenchurch?"

The young man shot him an involuntary look, his eyes startled, though a second later he dropped them to his lap.

"I knew her reasonably well," he answered eventually.

"Wasn't her death appalling?" John continued implacably.

"Horrible," said Justin, and his voice shook.

"They say it was a robbery but I can assure you that nothing was taken from her."

"Oh." A pause, then, "How do you know?"

"Because I was summoned to examine the body."

Justin swallowed hard. "Oh, I didn't realise that."

"Not many people do."

"Is it true that . . ." Justin broke off abruptly.

"That she died smiling? Yes, perfectly true."

"Oh God!" said the wretched young man, and plunged his face into his hands.

John was on his feet and beside him in a second. "Why don't you tell me about it?" he said, one hand on Justin's shoulder.

A hail of sobs and, "I can't. I mustn't."

"Who says so?"

"Greville, of course. Who do you think?"

"Greville," repeated the Apothecary softly, and drew in his breath.

"The bastard, the bastard," said Justin vehemently. He looked at John helplessly and at last broke his silence. "He made me send her a message to go to the park. Then, at the last minute, even while she was approaching, he told me his plan. She smiled at me, smiled for me. I ran away. I couldn't have laid a hand on her. And that's where he misjudged me, completely and utterly." He relapsed into sobs.

"And her father?" John asked quietly.

Justin gave him a terrible look, a look that spoke for itself. In it the Apothecary read guilt and remorse in almost equal quantities. It was at that moment that he made up his mind.

"Look, go home now and get yourself in hand. Then, tomorrow morning, at six o'clock and not a second later, I want you to meet me outside the lodge, a little further down the road. Bring with you a bag containing a change of clothes, three shirts and anything you treasure. That's all. Do you understand?"

"Yes."

"Excellent. Now, good night. I'll see you in the morning."

The last glimpse the Apothecary had of Justin was shambling out into the courtyard, still weeping. Fortunately the horse he mounted knew its way home blindfold; in fact had done this journey many times before.

"Till the morning," the Apothecary called from the doorway.

But Justin did not return his greeting and trotted off into the night.

Why John should sleep lightly after all the day's activities was only something to be guessed at, but the fact was that he did not lapse into unconsciousness till gone one o'clock. So it was that he felt as if he had just closed his eyes when the girl banged on his door at five. In fact, the Apothecary shouted that he was up, then pulled the blankets up round his ears and slept once more.

When he next woke it was twenty to six. Uttering an oath, John leapt out of his bed and into his clothes in almost one movement. Shoving a brush through his hair he hastened down to the yard to find nobody about at all. Extra time was taken with saddling Herring, his hands slipping over the unfamiliar fastenings, but eventually he was ready and led the horse round to the mounting block. It was by now a quarter past six.

John literally thundered to his destination, driving Herring as fast as the wretched beast would go. But even as he drew near, he could see that the lodge and the gates beside them, to say nothing of the stretch of road leading up, were deserted. Drawing his watch from an inner pocket and cursing once more, John drew to a halt and waited.

Nobody came. A thin column of smoke rose from the lodge's chimney but other than for that there was no sign of life at all.

"Oh hell!" said the Apothecary, then drew off the road at the sound of approaching hooves.

But it was no one of importance, merely a passing post girl. Rather a pretty one at that, John noticed. She smiled and wished him good morning, and he bowed from the saddle and did the same, forgetting, just for a moment, that he was a married man. He watched her as she turned into the lodge, then decided that as soon as she had gone, he would do likewise.

The girl reappeared and made off at speed up the drive. After a few moments, John left his place and followed her slowly to the imposing front door. A surly-looking individual answered, just the sort to be employed by the Bussells, John thought.

"Is Mr. Justin available?" he asked pleasantly.

The footman made something of a face. "No, Sir. It is only six-thirty, Sir."

Horrible snot, thought the Apothecary. "We had an arrangement to go for an early ride," he continued in the same affable tone.

"Well, Sir, I can assure you that Mr. Justin is still in his bed and will probably remain there most of the morning."

"And what about Mr. Greville? Is he around?"

"Mr. Greville is away, Sir."

"Oh, I see," the Apothecary answered, slightly non-plussed.

"Will that be all, Sir? Who shall I say called?"

"Might I come in and leave a note?"

"Well, er . . ."

310

"I'm sure it will be in order," John said, and was through the door before the footman could say another word.

As luck would have it, the servant limped slightly and the Apothecary made much of entering noisily and banging about before the man was upon him again. However, there was no responding stir from upstairs.

"Would you like paper and pen, Sir?" the footman asked, and turned to call another servant.

It was all the Apothecary needed. Moving rapidly he was halfway up the stairs before the footman, shouting, "Stop it at once! Stop it I say!" had his foot upon the bottom step. Sprinting like a hare, the Apothecary sped down a corridor.

To his horror the room which he entered was the very room in which Ariadne had breathed her last. Blinds down, furniture shrouded in white, John could almost see her lying still upon the bed. Recoiling, he sped out and down a further passage which led off to his left, realising as he went that the upstairs was built in a semi-circle.

The footman had come up the stairs and was not far away, if his footsteps were anything to go by. Frantically, John dived into the very next room he came upon, and stood silently behind the door. Then his eye was caught by the reflection in the mirror which hung there. For Justin was also in the room, sitting motionless in an armchair. Slowly, slowly the Apothecary turned, his stomach heaving as he did so.

Justin was absolutely still, the room was totally quiet, nothing moved except for the hammering of John's heart. For Justin only had half his head left, the other half sprayed across the room with the violence of the gunshot wound that had ended it all. Despite the wave of nausea which swept him, the Apothecary slowly made his way round the chair.

The gun had slipped to the floor but the fingers still curled into its shape. The eye that was left was open and John, despite the shaking of his hand, closed it. Then he noticed that on the table beside the corpse lay a scrawled note. Still with shaking hands, he picked it up and read it.

It said, very simply, 'Evalina forgive me. We will meet again.'

Struck to the heart, the Apothecary turned to the window and stared out over the parkland as the footman, panting and cursing in the doorway, suddenly became silent at the sight that awaited him.

CHAPTER
TWENTY-ONE

Without a word, John turned and walked from the room, the footman making no attempt to stop him. Blindly, he descended the stairs, crossed the echoing emptiness of the hall, and left the house, looking to neither right nor left. What he had seen had struck him so hard that the Apothecary was in a state of shock.

"Are you all right, Sir?" asked the hostler, handing over the hired horse.

John muttered assurances as the man assisted him into the saddle, then, having taken one last long mournful look over his shoulder, he plodded off over the cobbles. But once away he urged Herring into a canter and thus sped off into the hinterland, as if, by riding fast, he could forget the last thirty minutes and the sight of Justin Bussell with half his head missing, spattered over the wall beside his chair.

He rode furiously on, trying to keep his mind clear, but thoughts came like daggers. First he considered that one of the murderers was now quite obvious. Justin and Greville, acting as a team, had removed Aidan Fenchurch from the world, then Evalina. But his thoughts sheered away from that last idea. He could see Justin, bribed or threatened into inveigling the poor wretched woman into the park, frozen in horror as the first blow was struck. Then turning, running, unable to betray his brother but unable to live with his conscience either. And with what an end indeed!

It slowly impinged on John's consciousness that the horse was starting to labour beneath him and he reluctantly pulled Herring to a halt. Puffing and blowing, the horse stood gasping as John slipped from the saddle and looked round, gazing from this high point at hills and fields and vast expanses of cloud and sky. There had never been such a fine wild morning, he thought; such a day for sending the great white masses scudding across the heavens. Just for a moment the Apothecary felt exultant to be alive, then notions of death came crowding in and he sat down on a tree stump and plunged his head into his hands.

The murderer — or should he say murderers? — of the Fenchurch family were now totally clear. But who had killed Ariadne and Montague? Who of that doom-laden bunch of people had raised a hand against them?

John ran through the suspects. There was Jocasta Rayner; Mrs. Trewellan and her two sons, the elder of whom had fooled him completely into believing that he was the widow woman's lover. Then there was Louisa, beautiful and vivacious, and Cousin Millicent, almost her opposite in every way. Which of them was it?

The Apothecary sat in silence, listening to the horse, which had regained its breath and was now placidly cropping the turf. Then eventually John put his foot in the stirrup and started to descend the hill on the far side, wondering as he did so what further events could possibly befall him on this most fated of days.

At the bottom of the hill lay a village and in it a tavern. Glancing at his watch, John saw that it was past eleven and that he had been up several hours without his customary large breakfast. Determinedly turning Herring in the direction of the tavern which, on closer inspection, was smarter than the Apothecary had imagined, he tethered his horse near a water trough and went inside. Much to his surprise the place heaved with custom, people jostling elbows at the counter to get served. Wondering why such a small place in such a remote village should be so in demand, John waited patiently at the bar.

His question about popularity was answered almost straight away. Listening to a couple talking next to him, he learned that the Guildford stage had cast a wheel, thundering through the very village in which he now found himself, and those gathered in the hostelry were waiting for a repair.

Having secured himself a tankard of ale — breakfast was out of the question in view of the rush of custom — John made his way into a corner, complete with chair, and was just about to take a mouthful when a familiar voice greeted his ears.

"Is there anyone here with a trap? I want to get to Foxfire Hall actually."

There was a mumbled answer from a yokel, the message of which John couldn't hear.

"Oh jolly good," came the reply. "I can wait an hour or so. Will you come to the door?"

Again the mumble, presumably agreeing. Taking a good swig, John stood up, grinning, though slightly puzzled for all that. "Samuel, over here," he shouted.

The effect on his friend was extraordinary. The Goldsmith choked on his drink, then contrived to look embarrassed, guilty, and definitely as if he had something to hide. "John," he said eventually.

"My dear boy," said the Apothecary, instantly noting Samuel's reaction. "How very nice to see you."

"And you. And you," the other man answered unenthusiastically.

It was on the tip of John's tongue to ask what Samuel was doing but he resisted, realising that the Goldsmith was obviously under some kind of strain.

"No, I'll stand if you don't mind. Caught the stage in London and have been up on the roof. Bit cramped." Samuel laughed hollowly.

"Yes," said John thoughtfully. He changed the subject. "What's the name of this place?"

"Damned if I know. It wasn't one of the stops. It's just that we cast a wheel on some evil rut in the track. Now we're having to wait."

There was truth in the story but there was more to it than that, John thought. Then he remembered that whenever one was faced with a mystery it was always a good move to *cherchez la femme*. "Off to see Mrs. Rayner?" he asked innocently.

The effect on Samuel was quite amazing to see. First he went white, then two high spots of colour appeared in his cheeks. All this while desperately trying to

316

assume an air of extreme nonchalance, sipping his glass of wine and laughing over-heartily.

"Damnable thing is, I left a pair of gloves — oh, and a hat — when I was last there. Thought I'd call in and retrieve them."

John was flabbergasted, first that his friend should use such a feeble excuse and, second, that he should use it to him whom he had known most of his life. Guessing that the Goldsmith was yet again in love, he nodded encouragingly.

"I see. How wretched for you."

Samuel looked at him suspiciously. "Yes, indeed," he said slowly.

The Apothecary thought rapidly. Should he challenge his friend or remain silent, he wondered. He stole another look at Samuel's face and decided that to say anything at this delicate stage might bring about a rift between them. He therefore composed his features and said, "Sam, I have something to tell you."

"What?"

"Justin Bussell is dead. By his own hand. He left a note apologising to Evalina and begging her forgiveness."

The relief on Samuel's face was rapidly overtaken by a look of immense wonderment. "So we know who the killer is."

"It's not quite as simple as that," John answered. "First of all it would appear that Greville was the leader, Justin merely followed. But, secondly, it is obvious that the boys did not kill their own parents, unless there are deeds so dark here that one can hardly bear to think of them. No, we have solved one set of murders but as to the others, the field remains open I fear."

Samuel put down his glass and assumed such a serious expression that John had to fight to control a fit of laughter. "I see," the Goldsmith said meaningfully. "But who?"

The Apothecary bit his lip. "Could be anyone," he said, his voice slightly muffled.

"Well, my money's on Mendoza. A slimy bit of work if ever I saw one."

"I doubt it," John answered, and launched into the story that the Lieutenant had told him a few nights previously.

Samuel, clearly glad that the conversational topic had changed, sat in silence, listening, then eventually said, "So Mrs. Trewellan is his mother."

"So it would seem."

"Well, that certainly puts a different slant on things. Though still he could be . . ."

John shook his head. "No, I don't think so. It doesn't feel right somehow."

Samuel considered. "Perhaps, it's someone entirely different. Perhaps it's an old enemy of the Bussells. Nobody connected with the Fenchurchs at all."

Realising that he was skating on thin ice, John gave a small smile. "Yes, Sam, it could well be so."

And there he rested his argument, talking generalities until the man with the trap came back, when the two men thankfully parted company, each going about their business.

As he rode back through the blustery afternoon, John reflected on friendship and thought how close he and Samuel had drawn to falling out.

"And all over a woman," the Apothecary realised — and at that a train of ideas started that would not leave him alone until he had run them through his brain and come to rather a startling conclusion.

CHAPTER
TWENTY-TWO

There was only one thing for it, John thought, as The Onslow Arms came into view. He must get back to London and put his new idea to Sir John Fielding. And the more he considered the matter, the greater the urgency to return became. Going into the inn he paid his bill, changed into his travelling clothes and rode poor Herring back to her livery stables in Guildford, where he thanked the owner politely and dispensed with her services. Then, having been told that there was a stage from Portsmouth making a stop at The Angel in quarter of an hour, John ran through the dusk and squeezed onto the roof, where he sat, shivering and uncomfortable all the way to London, where he was put down at The Bald Stag in Southwark.

Pulling his watch from his pocket, John stared at it. It was after midnight and too late to wake the household in Nassau Street. Yawning and tired and scarcely able to move a muscle, the Apothecary booked himself a room in the hostelry and went straight to sleep.

He awoke much refreshed and immediately thought of the idea that had come to him yesterday. Whichever way he looked at it, it still made sense, and John determined to go to Bow Street as soon as he had

320

breakfasted. This he did with tremendous appetite, realising that it had been a full twenty-four hours since he had last eaten. Finally replete, he paid his dues and hired a hackney coach to take him to Bow Street.

The court was not yet in session, Sir John and Joe sitting downstairs in the room they used as a study, dealing with correspondence. They both looked up as John entered and Jago rose to his feet.

"Mr. Rawlings! What a surprise. We thought you were in West Clandon, Sir."

"So I was till yesterday afternoon. But pray don't let me interrupt you. I'll wait outside until you've finished."

Sir John chuckled deep. "My friend, you would not have come here unless you believed the matter urgent. Indeed, I make out from your voice that you are quivering to tell us something of vital importance. So please, be seated and do so."

There was a third chair before the desk and as the Apothecary sat down he thought for a minute of all the times he and Sir John had shared in the past, some of them in this very room. Then he felt Joe's eyes on him, giving him a look so kindly, so well-intentioned, that his heart lifted in his chest.

"Well, gentlemen . . ." he said.

Thirty minutes later it was done. John had told them everything. He had also put to them his idea as to the identity of the murderer of Ariadne and Montague Bussell, an idea which they received in total silence.

". . . so you see, Sir," he concluded, "that willing though I am to return to West Clandon, I truly feel I could do with a little help."

Sir John Fielding was very quiet, his hands folded over his stomach, his powerful features set and stern. Eventually he said, "I'm thinking," then became silent once more. Joe, meanwhile, fixed John with his light blue eyes, one of which he slowly winked. He mouthed, "He's not pleased," but obviously not quietly enough.

"No, I am not," said Sir John, raising his head. "I am not pleased because the whole idea confounds my theories. But never let it be said that I have grown small-minded. You are right, Mr. Rawlings, I feel it in my gut. So, go to. Back to West Clandon with you and make your claims. But you'll have to wait a few days. The Brave Fellows are away on a case at present and are not expected back for some time."

"I'm afraid I do not trust the person concerned. I think they might strike again, Sir."

"Yes," said the Beak, nodding slowly. "You may well have a point there. But what can I do? It is too dangerous for you to venture there alone."

The Apothecary smiled crookedly. "Yes, I had rather thought so. That is why I came back."

"I see." There was another protracted silence, then Sir John said, "You and Jago could go, however."

At this, Joe winked again and held up a large, knobbly thumb but did not risk saying a word.

"I imagine you two are grinning at one another," said the Blind Beak, and rumbled his laugh. "Very well, be

322

off with the pair of you. I shall have to do without my eyes for a day or two. Oh, and Jago . . ."

"Yes, Sir?"

"This time I want Greville Bussell brought in."

Joe Jago stood up and bowed in the Magistrate's direction. "Thank you, Sir. I've been anxious for a bit of adventure."

"So I've noticed. Now, go. Straight there and two quiet arrests if you please. I don't want any bloodshed."

"None the less, Sir, I shall take the opportunity of being fully armed."

"And you Mr. Rawlings? Are you armed?"

"Indeed I am, Sir," said the Apothecary, and patted his pocket.

An hour later and it was done. Joe had slipped home to Seven Dials to pack a bag while John had waited for him in Will's Coffee House. For some reason that he could not explain, not even to himself, he had not gone to Nassau Street nor, indeed, Shug Lane. He felt very strongly that a rush back, to be followed by another rush away again, would disrupt the entire household, even upset the implacable Nicholas. Yet there was another reason, another reason that John refused to admit. The simple truth was that he didn't want to, that he wanted to stay anonymous and ready for the difficult task that lay before him.

A hackney to The Borough where John and Joe hired a flying coach in company with a mother and daughter who chattered all the way to Guildford, where they all disembarked.

"Do look us up when you are next in town, Sir."

"I certainly will, Madam."

Then with much bowing and general goodwill, they parted company.

The expression on the face of the livery stables' owner was beyond belief.

"I thought you'd finished with my poor beast, Sir."

John contrived his honest expression. "Would you believe that no sooner was I back in London than I received a message to return? So, if I may hire a horse once more and another for my friend."

"Of course, Sir."

It was not, the Apothecary considered, the best of stables. Poor Herring, looking rather weary, was led out, accompanied by a grey gelding named Finn, who plodded over the cobbles, head down. However, once mounted, the horse had a new lease of life and went away to West Clandon on the double, John fighting to keep up. Consequently, the pair clattered into the courtyard of The Onslow Arms in good time to dine, which they did in a small parlour reserved for the handful of guests. Fortunately there was no one in it beside themselves. They were completely alone to discuss tactics.

"You know, Sir," said Joe thoughtfully, "we've done this a bit too quick."

"What do you mean?"

"Well, whoever we arrest first, one of us must escort them back to London. That leaves the other one on their own again."

324

John looked thoughtful. "Yes, I see what you mean." He was silent for a few moments, then said, "Oh well, we'll just have to take a chance."

"Ah Sir, there's many a man as said that before he went to his death."

The Apothecary burst out laughing. "You're damn cheerful company I must say. Anyway, shall we get Greville tonight?"

Joe fingered his chin. "No, tomorrow morning — early. Let's catch the bastard while he's abed."

John shivered involuntarily, remembering the sight he had seen when last he called at Merrow Place early. "I wonder what's happened to Justin's body," he said slowly.

"Well, it will have been removed, that's for sure."

"Should we arrest a man before his brother's funeral?"

"We not only should, we will," Joe replied forcefully. "That bastard. Think of Evalina. My God, her avenging is long overdue."

"You're right, of course. So tomorrow morning it is."

"I'll drink to that," said Joe, and clinked glasses with the Apothecary.

The next morning he woke abruptly. It was a grey dawn, promising rain, not light enough for a body to be stirring, but Jago was already up, half-dressed, and standing at the washbasin. He looked round and grinned as John bade him the best of the day.

"Ready to catch your fox?" he asked.

"Good and ready," said the Apothecary, sitting up. He yawned and ran his head through his hair which, as usual, was in need of cutting.

"I won't be long," Joe added, turning away and applying a dangerous looking razor to his chin. "I told the girl to bring some more hot water."

"Good." John consulted his watch. "Great God! It's only five o'clock."

"I said we'd get our man early."

"And early it is. We'll probably miss breakfast."

"Breakfast," said Joe Jago firmly, "can wait."

Somewhat against his better judgement, John found himself in the stable yard some thirty minutes later, struggling to saddle up Herring.

"Here, let me," said Joe. And yet again revealed another facet of his amazing personality by getting the animal ready in a matter of minutes, all the time talking in a soft voice, using cant mixed in with English.

"You are truly incredible," said John admiringly.

"Something I learned from my father," answered Joe. And the Apothecary realised that never before had he mentioned a member of his family or, for that matter, discussed anything personal.

John felt he dared to ask a question. "Did your father come from London?"

"No, Sir," answered Joe, and there he dropped the matter. "Well, we'd best get on our way. I've a feeling about this."

"What sort of feeling?"

"I don't know yet. But I've most certainly got one."

They trotted out of the stable yard, John leading the way, and after ten minutes came to the gates of Merrow Place, which were firmly closed. Joe descended rapidly and knocked at the door of the gatekeeper's lodge.

"Open up at once," he shouted. "I'm here on behalf of the Public Office, Bow Street, and here I stay until you let me in."

A grizzled head appeared at a first floor window. "The master said . . ." it began.

Joe went perfectly white with anger and John realised that the man had been more affected by Evalina's murder than he was admitting. He recalled the turned back and the furious pipe puffing, the infinitesimal pause before Jago had touched the dead woman.

"Now are you going to admit us or do I break your door down?" the clerk was bellowing.

The head muttered, "All right, all right," and withdrew.

"I will not be denied entry," said Joe furiously, more to himself than anyone else. And so he continued, muttering beneath his breath, until eventually the lodgekeeper appeared and the gates were swung open.

"So I should think," the clerk said as he went through.

He cantered up the drive like a man possessed, John struggling to keep up, but reined in and proceeded quietly for the last few minutes.

"Is this where you and Irish Tom were kept prisoner?" he hissed over his shoulder at the Apothecary.

"Yes."

"You're certain?"

"Positive. Look at the stables." Joe followed the lines of John's pointing finger. "There's the archway. I'd remember it anywhere after an experience like that."

"I'm sure you would," said Joe grimly.

He dismounted and went to the front door, his anger only just under control, and there set up a thunderous knocking and bell pulling, fit to waken the dead, a thought that brought no comfort to John.

"Open up in the name of the law," Jago shouted.

There was the sound of many bolts being pulled back and eventually the oily face of the same servant that had admitted John on that fateful morning — had it really only been two days ago? — appeared.

"Yes?" he said.

Joe produced a card from an inner pocket and thrust it under the footman's nose. "I demand to come in now and see your master," he said shortly.

The footman was very cool, John had to grant him that. Taking his time, he produced a pair of spectacles and perched them on his nose, then he slowly and laboriously read the card.

"Joseph R. Jago, clerk to Sir John Fielding, the Public Office, Bow Street, London," he read laboriously. Then he licked his lips. "I see. You want the master, do you?"

"Yes, I do."

The servant's eyes flickered over John. "I think I know you, Sir."

"This is my assistant, John Rawlings," Joe continued in the same harsh tones. "He goes where I go."

"You've been here before, Sir." The footman was addressing John direct. "On the day Master Justin died. I wanted to speak to you but you just left the house."

"Well you may speak to me now," John answered. "May we come in, please?"

"Yes," the man answered. "You may."

And he opened the front door wide and allowed them into the vast echoing wastes of the hall.

"The master is still abed," the man continued. "If you will wait in here, gentlemen."

He crossed the hall and ushered them into another huge room. Then he closed the door quietly behind them.

Not only were the curtains drawn but the shutters closed across the four huge windows which formed almost the whole of one wall. Just for a moment John and Joe were blinded, unable to see anything, then they slowly began to make out shapes. Furniture with white sheets over loomed like ghosts. Distantly, John noticed a sofa and several chairs, all closed beneath their pale drapes.

"Are we meant to sit down or what?" he asked Joe.

Then a voice spoke out of the darkness. "No, gentlemen, you are meant to remain standing."

They froze, rooted to the spot, and John, narrowing his eyes, made out a dim shape sitting behind the desk. A shape which had remained so still that until this moment he had not even seen it.

"So, my dears, you thought you'd catch old Uncle Greville unawares, did you? Thought that by turning up here at this ungodly hour you'd find him napping. Well,

329

my friends, your every move has been watched. I knew last night that you had returned to West Clandon, Mr. Rawlings, and that you had a henchman with you. So I reckoned that, being a creature of habit, you'd come for me almost as soon as it was light. Only you didn't expect a reception committee, did you?"

Greville paused for breath and Joe Jago spoke into the brief silence.

"Mr. Greville Bussell, I have here a warrant for your arrest. I would suggest . . ."

"Suggest be damned," replied the other man harshly. "I'll tell you what I'm going to do. I'm going to shoot the pair of you, then I'm taking off abroad for a long tour. By the time I come back your mysterious disappearance will be something that people tell their children about when they want them to go to bed."

And in the darkness John heard a pistol cock. He had never been so frightened in his life and he spoke wildly, determined to get a little more time.

"It was you who killed Aidan Fenchurch and Evalina, wasn't it? Why, for God's sake?"

"Aidan had given my mother the runaround for enough miserable years. I was sick to the back teeth of him. As for the woman, she was in revenge for the deaths of my parents."

Just for a moment there was the suspicion of a catch in his voice and the Apothecary caught himself thinking that perhaps there was some feeling in Greville after all.

"Why did you take me prisoner?" John asked. "What did you hope to gain by that?"

330

"You were getting too damned close on my trail, you bastard. I sensed it at the funeral. You would have vanished, you and your coachman, if you hadn't managed to escape."

"But what about Justin," John went on, "surely he didn't want to do those things?"

"Justin was softer than I am, poor fool. But he went for Aidan right enough. We'd both had enough of my mother's complaints. It was a pleasure to take him out."

"It might have been for you. But Justin paid the penalty," John said softly.

"Enough talking, goodbye my friends," Greville answered.

And with that a pistol fired, twice, in the half- light. The figure behind the desk rose to its feet, staggered a few steps towards them, then fell back with a groan. Despite everything, John's training came to the fore and he rushed forward.

"Careful," said Joe Jago's voice behind him, and the Apothecary, reluctantly, slowed down.

Walking past him, Jago knelt down beside the body while John, at last, hurried to the window and let in some much-needed light.

There lay Greville, shot through the head and the heart, steeped in his own blood.

John stared at Joe and thought he had never seen his face more ragged, his expression sterner.

"So die all of his sort," Joe said shortly and, blowing the end of his smoking pistol, put it away in his pocket.

CHAPTER
TWENTY-THREE

The temptation to leg it through the window was almost overwhelming but Joe gathered his dignity round him like a cloak.

"I am an officer of the law and the man resisted arrest," he announced. "That is what happened."

John, kneeling over the body, grinned wryly. "Yes, I suppose it did. Joe, how did you shoot him? He had the gun in his hand."

"Let it just be said that I was quicker than he was."

"But I never realised you were such an excellent shot."

A humourless smile crossed Joe's features. "Another hobby of mine. Now enough. I am going back to the hostelry to have some breakfast and a large brandy. Will you accompany me or do you intend to stay here and answer questions?"

"I'll come with you."

As luck would have it the hall was empty, the servants obviously at work in another part of the building. None the less, Joe Jago insisted on leaving a note. It simply said, 'Your master lies dead in the large salon. He died resisting arrest. If any need to speak to me on this matter I shall be at The Onslow Arms for the next few days.'

"There, that's done," he said, and marched out of the front door.

Never before, thought John, had he seen him in such a ruthless mood, nor quite so hard of purpose. Lost in wonderment, he followed on, almost blindly, to where the horses were tethered.

"Joe?" he said, as Jago began to unloop the reins.

"Yes?"

"Are you really going to leave it like that?"

"What?"

"Greville. After all, the man is dead."

"Mr. Rawlings," said Joe, suddenly earnest, "if he had not have died, we would. It was a case of him or us. I had spoken the words of arrest but he did not come quietly. Now, truly, that is all I have to say on the matter."

And with that the Apothecary was forced to be satisfied.

The only sign of weakness that Joe Jago exhibited was to drink two big draughts with his breakfast. Then, whilst still consuming the third, he turned to John.

"Well, Sir, do we head for Foxfire Hall?"

"It's still only nine o'clock, we'll be there by mid morning. I think we should get it over, don't you?"

"Yes, I do."

"In fact the sooner we draw this wretched business to its conclusion the better it will be for all of us."

So, almost on the dot of half-past nine, the two riders set out in the direction of Stoke d'Abernon and the great house of shadows, as John now thought of it, that lay beyond. He shivered, remembering the first time he had driven there with Irish Tom on the box and how they had followed the River Wey's meanderings until finally they had come to a track. Now he and Jago took the same route, passing through dense woodland as they did so.

"How much longer?" asked Joe.

"About another thirty minutes or so."

They rode on a mile or two and then the rain, which had been threatening since daybreak, arrived, drenching them.

"I don't care for this at all," said Joe, pulling up in the shelter of some trees, and at that precise moment his mount cast a shoe. "Damnation!" he exclaimed, and slid from the saddle to have a look at Finn's hoof. The shoe was almost completely off, sticking out at an angle and secured by only one nail. "I'll have to get to a smithy," he said. And at that proceeded to yank out the one remaining nail with the aid of a knife retrieved from his coat pocket.

"There's bound to be one in Stoke d'Abernon."

"Yes. I'll get there as best I can."

They proceeded on slowly, scarcely able to see because of the driving rain. Then, at last, the spire of St. Mary's appeared in the distance, recognisable because of its openwork wood beneath.

"I'll see you to the forge, then I'll go on to the house," said John.

334

"Is that wise?"

"Our poisoner won't suspect me. I promise I'll behave in a perfectly normal manner until you come."

"Very well, but take care. I'll be as quick as I can."

The forge was easy to find in that small, insular community. And there Joe Jago, still warning the Apothecary to take no risks, parted from him. Water streaming from his hat and running down his nose, John noticed fondly, in a farewell look over his shoulder. With a feeling of portent, he trotted through the downpour towards Foxfire Hall.

The lodge gates stood open, though the keeper was around in his garden, protected by a burly oilskin. In reply to a shouted question, he yelled back that the family were in residence and had visitors.

"But you'll be welcome, Sir."

I wonder, thought John. But he showed none of his fears and gave a salute as he passed up the drive.

The house which in summer would be heavy with the scent of roses, looked dismal in the rain. Yet even despite the inclement weather nothing could take from its grandeur, nor from the mellowness of its brickwork. John paused a moment on the steps and sighed before he rang the bell. It was a loathsome task he had come to do, to drag out of the bosom of the family a well-loved member, accusing them of hideous crimes. Yet he knew that there was nothing he could do except this. That he must put a stop to the poisoner's hand before it struck again. For the fact that the poisoner was totally insane he did not doubt for one moment.

A footman admitted him to the Great Hall. "The family are showing the visitors the Valley of Shadows, Sir. A foolish caprice but one which they are fond of on wet days." The man smiled benignly.

"Quite so," said John. "I shall wait in the parlour."

But no sooner was the servant out of view than the Apothecary, drawn against his will but for all that acting under a compulsion that refused to leave him, mounted the Grand Staircase and made his way to the Long Gallery. As ever, his eyes turned instantly to the portrait of Lady Tewkesbury which hung, dominating all, at the end. John found his feet turning in that direction, even though every instinct warned him not to do so.

Once again he gazed into that secretive Tudor face, trying desperately to read its hidden message. But, as ever, she looked back at him inscrutably, refusing to be drawn. John's eyes dropped to the monkey which stood, pathetically, in the background, forever captured in paint, as much a victim as the sitter herself. Then, before he could stop himself, his hand had reached out to the panelling below the portrait and had started to press. And this time, almost as if it were expecting him, the panel whirred back. John stared into the darkness beyond and then, quite slowly and deliberately, stepped into it.

CHAPTER
TWENTY-FOUR

It was a terrible sensation, stepping into the blackness. Yet he was aware that a room lay beyond, a room which would become familiar to him as soon as his eyes adjusted to the light. The Apothecary stayed absolutely still and a familiar whirring sound behind him told him that the panel had closed again. But then he realised that a candle was burning, admittedly very low but for all that casting a faint illumination. Mustering his wits as best he could, the Apothecary headed for it.

It stood on the mantelpiece above the great fireplace, guttering in the airless room. Yet somebody had placed it there and not long ago at that, judging by the amount still left to burn. The Apothecary spoke.

"Is there anybody there?"

There was no answer, other than for a faint rustling which could have been a rat or mouse.

"Who's there?" he called.

Again no answer but this time he distinctly heard a very faint giggle.

"Look, I know you think this is funny, but I don't. Show yourself, damn you."

The candle blew out suddenly and shockingly, leaving John peering into the shadows.

"Where are you?" he said, and there, in the gloom, he felt his pistol in his pocket and drew it out silently.

Again there came that unearthly giggle; an eerie, frightening sound which had every hackle on his body on end.

"Come and find me," whispered a voice that seemed neither of this world nor the next.

"Where are you?" John answered tersely.

But once more there was that disembodied laugh, followed by a very slight movement. John lunged in the direction from which he thought it came but there was nothing there.

"Catch me," said the murmuring voice and this time there was a stirring at the door leading to the corridor.

So this was to be it. John was going to have to trap his victim. Holding his gun firmly, the Apothecary made for the passageway which lay beyond the room.

But here he was forced to stop and take stock. As he knew from his earlier experience in this dread place, the corridor ran both right and left. But which way his quarry had gone was not at all clear. To his left lay the staircase and eventual freedom, to his right, dark and frightening, lay the other part of the corridor — and the unknown. Still the Apothecary hesitated and then, quite distinctly, he heard a noise. Without hesitation he plunged into the mysterious path on the right.

He was ill-prepared for this venture, having no candle on him. Then he remembered his tinderbox and struck a tinder. He was given a momentary glance of a

338

winding passageway before it went out and he was thrust once more into blackness. Then as he stood still, blinking, a faint glow ahead of him told him everything. He was not only going in the right direction but he was gaining on his quarry — his giggling, faceless prey — and would soon catch up.

A sense of elation mixed with his fear and took him forward towards the candlelight, creeping silently, his pistol still in his hand. Nearer and nearer he drew, the illumination getting ever brighter, till at last he made out that it came from a room leading off the corridor. Quietly, John drew level with the entrance and peered inside.

He was reminded, instantly and vividly, of the den of a wizard of storybook fame. For there were retorts and alembics and copper pans, a pestle and mortar and knives. This room, which was a natural one formed by the rock, had many candles, either sticking onto the rock where natural shelves occurred, or also in elegant holders, quite at odds with the rest of their surroundings. Almost against his will, the Apothecary took a couple of steps inside.

A voice spoke from the doorway. "Hello, Mr. Rawlings," and he heard a pistol cock.

What instinct made him throw himself flat he never afterwards could tell. But flat he went and the shot passed clean over his head. Turning, from where he lay, John aimed at the arm of the person in the doorway and fired. There was a scream and then the sound of someone falling to the floor. Scrambling to his feet, John hurried to the person, lifting them up in his arms. She was wounded but not badly.

"Pass me that drink on the table, I beg you," she gasped. "It will revive me."

"More likely kill you," John answered tersely. "You've poisoned everyone. I can just see you, sidling in and out of society. Poor Miss Prim, the impoverished relation. And all the time you had murder in your heart. But why, in God's name? Why?"

She looked at him and gave the most wicked smile he had ever seen in his entire life. "Because I loved the three sisters. I wanted it just as it used to be. Just the four of us. That's why I killed Horatio Rayner. He led my girl a merry dance with his philandering. Jocasta was always my favourite, you know. Oh, Mr. Rawlings, please pass me that drink."

He shook his head. "Go on."

"Then those wicked youths killed Aidan. So I poisoned Ariadne's glass at the wake, then I invited Montague to tea and served him poisoned cake."

John shook his head in wonderment. "You are an expert, aren't you? A mistress of venoms."

She giggled, high and slightly frantic. "I know a great deal, yes."

He lowered her gently to the floor. "Listen, I'll tie up your wound then I'll go and get help. I don't think I can carry you out, even though you are no more than a featherweight. It's very rough underfoot."

"Oh leave me be, Mr. Rawlings. You won't be long, I'm certain of it."

He picked up a candle tree. "No, I won't, I promise," he said grimly.

Then, having dressed her wound as best he could, John hurried down the corridor to the left and out into the open countryside, where he ran as fast as he could back towards Foxfire Hall.

The same footman, looking frankly astonished to see him back at the front door, let him in and he was shown immediately into the Great Hall. But this time Jocasta was there in advance of him, surrounded by a jolly group of people. John saw Louisa, Lieutenant Mendoza, even Mrs. Trewellan and Sperling were among the merrymakers. Jocasta's thin face turned towards him, then transformed itself with a wonderful smile.

What a contrast, John thought, with the smile the poisoner had given him a mere thirty minutes ago.

"Mr. Rawlings . . . John . . ." she began. "How lovely to see you."

He cut across her, hating himself for doing so. "I'm afraid there has been an accident," he said. "One of your party has been shot."

Everyone, who had been buzzing with some strange excitement, suddenly went quiet.

"An accident?" repeated Jocasta. "Shot, you say?"

"Yes. I suppose you know who it is?"

"No, I really can't think."

Was it John's imagination or had all their faces assumed a mask-like expression, as if they had closed ranks against him? In his mind's eye they took a step towards him.

And then, from the Grand Stairs came a trilling voice.

"Cooee. Are you there?"

Everyone turned, including John, and slowly, agonisingly slowly, Cousin Millicent came into view. She was covered in blood, which dripped from the wound in her arm, and she shambled rather than walked. Yet her face was smiling, quite radiantly.

"Ah, there you all are," she called, and tripped on the first stair, righting herself before anyone could make a move.

John stood frozen, aware that Millicent had not only raised herself from the floor but that she had come back, presumably through the picture in the Gallery, and had made her way to the Grand Staircase. She was in a pitiable state, the skirt and bodice of her gown dyed red, but when she stumbled once more on the next step, he narrowed his eyes. Surely the wound alone would not make her that weak; surely some additional substance was causing her to be so unsteady. And then it came to him.

In a flash John elbowed everyone else out of the way and raced up the stairs to where Millicent was struggling at the top of the third step.

"What have you taken?" he said urgently. "Tell me, just tell me."

She collapsed downwards, falling awkwardly into his arms. Then gave him another look, but this one not evil, merely peaceful.

"Wouldn't you like to know," she said, then she contorted, twisting sideways, and died.

Why he wept, John had no idea. But cry he did, as he sat in the small parlour, comforted by everyone, which somehow made things worse.

The entire story was relayed, in all its horror, even to the poisoning of Horatio Rayner.

Jocasta went very white. "So she was responsible. My God! And to think the mushrooms were blamed. They, and the poor wretched cook."

John got a grip on himself. "She was quite insane, you know."

Jocasta nodded slowly. "Oh yes, it was all to do with obsession. She was utterly in love with my father. And I suppose she was happy just to be under the same roof as he was. But when Justin and Greville did for him, then they unleashed her in all her cruelty."

"Was it her you meant when you wrote 'There is a Poisoner in our Midst'?"

Jocasta flushed. "Yes. You see, I witnessed something at Father's wake though at the time I thought nothing of it. I had seen Millicent — or rather, I thought I had — tip something into Mrs. Bussell's glass. I don't know why I told you, trying to help you I suppose. But when you faced me with it, I said Montague Bussell. I just couldn't bring myself to name her. You see, despite all, I loved her."

It was a simple statement, yet said with great sincerity. So much so that John felt the spring in his eyes once more but deliberately forced them away. He cleared his throat.

"Something kept nagging in my brain, something I knew I should connect. But it wasn't until I thought of Horatio and the mushrooms and who was present at the time, that the veils finally fell."

Jocasta lowered her voice and looked the Apothecary straight in the eye. "Poor Horatio, he considered himself quite the ladies' man, you know. Yet, in fact, he was treated by them as a figure of fun. Everyone felt so sorry for me but there was truly no need."

"Did you love him?" John asked.

"No, I was fond of him," she answered in the same even tones. She stood up from where she had been kneeling beside John. "May I get you another brandy?" she asked, speaking quite normally.

"If you would be so good." He held out his glass.

"I have some news for you," she said, her back turned, busy with the decanter.

"What is that?" John asked, suddenly weary from all the day's activities.

"I am going to marry Mr. Swann."

And she turned to look at him. In her smile John saw immense future happiness for his old friend and also for Jocasta herself. He got to his feet.

"My very dear girl," he said, and grubby and smelly that he was, he took her in his arms and kissed her tenderly on the cheek.

CHAPTER
TWENTY-FIVE

June came, that gentle month, and in the middle there was a sweet little wedding in St. Mary's, Stoke d'Abernon. It was very quiet, only family and friends attending. John, who had started to think that the day would never come, willingly stood as bridegroom's witness to his old and dear friend Samuel Swann. Old Mr. Swann, well in his seventies, attended, as did Sir Gabriel Kent, very fine in a suit of silver and black.

The bride, clad in crimson velvet, came up the aisle on the arm of Lieutenant Philip Mendoza and there, at the altar, the former Jocasta Rayner became Jocasta Swann. John, dashing a tear away, signed the register and then everyone repaired back to the great mansion, Foxfire Hall, to celebrate.

The first roses were out and the house looked at its best as the carriages rolled up outside and the guests disembarked. Within, the shadows were gone and all was jolly. And John and Emilia, with their baby Rose, who slept most of the time and made no trouble, drank toasts and then danced well into the night. Eventually, though, it was time for the ancient ceremony of preparing the bride and groom for the bedchamber. So, at last John got a few moments for talk with his great friend.

"My dear," he said, "so you've done it at last."

"Samuel nodded. I was thirty-one last month. I am sure you looked on me as a confirmed old bachelor."

This he said with a great deal of joviality, expecting his friend to disagree. Which, politely, John did. But, in truth, he had begun to worry that all Samuel's romances seemed doomed to failure and had half expected him to end on the shelf.

"So you took my advice and married someone a little more mature," he said.

"Yes, I did. Jocasta is but a few months younger than I am. Yet she has the resolution of someone much older and the delightful side — not fully realised at present — of a girl."

"Tell me, Samuel, in the minutes left to us before Philip and Sperling come, how has she reacted to all the death surrounding her?"

Instead of giving a bluff reply, Samuel sat silently for a moment, and the Apothecary secretly rejoiced that his friend was showing signs of maturity at long last.

"She has drawn a great deal of comfort from Louisa," he said eventually. "Of course, the truth is out now. About Mrs. Trewellan being her sister's mother-in-law and so on. And, strangely, Jocasta seemed to like the fact that there was additional family rather than less. They . . . we . . . have decided to share Foxfire Hall with them, strictly as a summer place. In the winter we are going to live in Curzon Street."

John's jaw dropped. "My, you've married well, Samuel."

"I married for love," said his old friend, so honestly that John could do nothing but clutch him to his heart in an embrace that seemed to sum up all their years together.

The door opened and the Lieutenant and his half-brother came in, slightly drunk but none the worse for it.

"Why, he's not even undressed," said Sperling, whose pimples had very nearly cleared up.

"Let's to it," answered Mendoza, and there was a lot of high-spirited horseplay in which John took some part.

Then the bride, demure in a white nightgown, was led in by the female guests and the couple were put to bed, amongst great merriment and further hilarity. Afterwards everyone went downstairs to drink their health, and there they continued to dance until the candles burned low.

At last the old house began to make the noises of a great place settling down. Wood creaked, fires gave a last crackle and burned out, the candle trees disappeared with the guests making their way to the bedchambers which had been prepared for them.

Emilia turned on the stairs. "You won't be long, will you?"

"No, I'll just finish my drink, then I'll come."

"Promise. This old place is full of shadows by night."

"I promise."

He stood for a while, gazing into the dying flames of the huge fire, then picked up his candle tree. But when he reached the top of the Grand Staircase his feet, almost as if they had a will of their own, turned towards the Long Gallery.

She was there, waiting for him, at the end. Lady Tewkesbury, her Tudor face shuttered and secretive as ever, watched every step he took as he approached her portrait.

"Well," John said aloud, "you've seen a few things in your time, Madam."

There was no reply but the dark eyes burned into his. Without really meaning to, John leant forward and tried to find the mechanism that led to the room beyond. But strive as he might, his fingers searched in vain and in the end he gave up and stepped back.

Emilia, sleepy and cosy, was in his bed, waiting for him, but still he lingered a second more.

"A penny for your thoughts," he whispered to the portrait.

And was it a trick of the candlelight that her mouth momentarily curved into a smile?

Also available in ISIS Large Print:

Jam and Jeopardy

Doris Davidson

Was it the raspberry jam that finally killed her?

Revenge, lust, hatred and murder envelop a small Aberdeenshire village in Doris Davidson's latest novel

Wealthy 87-year-old spinster Janet Souter takes pleasure in raking up scandal, old and new, about her neighbours. She also relishes refusing her two nephews the money they desperately need to bolster their struggling businesses. So when she acquires some arsenic to deal with rats in her garden, she decides to test them: whichever attempts to kill her will be her sole beneficiary; if both do, they will each get a half share of her substantial savings. Naturally she takes precautions to ensure that her life will be in no real danger, but news of her newly acquired poison spreads round the village, sowing the seeds of murderous intent in several people. And one of them will succeed in silencing her vicious tongue forever . . .

ISBN 978-0-7531-7848-5 (hb)
ISBN 978-0-7531-7849-2 (pb)

The Governor's Ladies

Deryn Lake

For many years, Thomas Gage believed he did not
have the time or the inclination for romance, but
everything changed when he fell in love with the
vivacious Margaret Kemble. Years of happiness ensued
in which he rose to become the British Governor of
Massachusetts. But in 1775 the ever-building tensions
in the troubled state suddenly erupt into violence.

Having risen through the army ranks before meeting
Margaret, Thomas has known many battles in his time.
But this one — the War of Independence — is different;
there are personal passions and beliefs involved. Being
a British Governor living in America means that
Thomas's allegiances, and those of his American wife,
are sharply divided. Thomas seeks solace through
teaching his pretty black slave, Sara, the simple
pleasures of reading and writing. But with conflict,
heartbreak and death close at hand, can true love and
happiness ever prevail for the Governor and his lady?

ISBN 978-0-7531-7782-2 (hb)
ISBN 978-0-7531-7783-9 (pb)

The Endings Man

Frederic Lindsay

"Why is it," Barclay Curle grumbles to his agent Jonah, "that all the regional Edinburgh detectives have monosyllabic first names like Jack and Bob?"

Then Curle publishes his newest book — about an Edinburgh detective called Doug — which incites a letter from an anonymous admirer accusing him of stealing the murders she has committed.

Fact and fiction become increasingly inseparable when a woman discovered dead in a Newtown flat is found to have been murdered by the method favoured by the serial killer in Curle's novel. For Detective Inspector Meldrum — first name Jim — Curle seems the most obvious suspect.

Faced with a second murder and a darkening cloud of suspicion, Curle decides the time has come to take action. After all, he asks himself, who has more experience of solving murder mysteries than a crime novelist?

ISBN 978-0-7531-7800-3 (hb)
ISBN 978-0-7531-7801-0 (pb)

Death and the Cornish Fiddler

Deryn Lake

The spring of 1765 brings a sense of recovery to the recently widowed Apothecary John Rawlings, but this does not last for long: a young child disappears in strange circumstances at the Helstone Floral (Furry) Dance and a blind musician is never far away. Whilst this mysterious figure intrigues Rawlings, the case of the missing child alarms him: he feels he must do all in his power to attempt to rescue the young life.

Rawlings is just about to give up the child for lost when a courtesan dies one night. An examination reveals that she was smothered and the hunt is on to find which of her lovers was responsible. Accompanied by one of them, John travels to Redruth and stumbles across a coven who practise the black arts. Recognising some of its members from the Furry Dance, he returns to Helstone, this time to find his own daughter in deadly peril . . .

ISBN 978-0-7531-7700-6 (hb)
ISBN 978-0-7531-7701-3 (pb)